"I'll be in touch, Ben."

He nodded and handed Abby his card. "You do that," he said, then slammed the car door.

She watched him saunter away, strides long and easy, his broad shoulders formidable, his butt— For Pete's sake, they were working together, not getting involved.

You can admire, a little voice in her head whispered.

"No," Abby told herself, "I can't."

Dating was fun. Right up there with the perfect ski run, and no more serious. Ben Shea didn't smile. He didn't flirt, and he took her seriously. All of which made him a dangerous man. Abby didn't do dangerous men. After years as a firefighter, she knew what it meant to get burned.

Anyway, thanks to the shining example of manhood set by Daddy dear, revered police chief, Abby had no desire to bring home a man for good. Sometimes her two brothers-in-law gave her pause, but not for long.

Abby put her car in gear and pulled out onto the road, hoping the big dark cop would recede in her thoughts as surely as he did in the rearview mirror.

Dear Reader,

Two of the most interesting characters I've ever written about happen to be in the PATTON'S DAUGHTERS trilogy: Abby Patton and Jack Murray. Both challenged me in unanticipated ways. They're more complex, more flawed, less obviously "hero" or "heroine" material than usual. Abby, I came to realize as I wrote, had to be deeply troubled. How could she not be, given her abusive father and desertion by her mother and older sister, her mother-surrogate? In defense she had learned not to care, and to manipulate men because she felt that they must all, on some level, be like her father. I found that I cared about her. I wanted to heal her, but in a believable way.

Jack, of course, wasn't the answer. His entire life has been shaped by one painful, humiliating moment when he wasn't strong enough to stand up for the girl he loved. One of these days, Jack Murray must be a hero, because that's the only way he can redeem himself.

As you're reading *A Message for Abby,* I'm writing about Jack and finding that I love the challenge of writing about people who aren't any simpler in their motivations and reactions than you or I are. I'm crossing my fingers that some of you choose to let me know what you think about PATTON'S DAUGHTERS and especially about the brittle, intelligent woman in *A Message for Abby.*

Thanks for reading my stories. (I invite you to visit my website at http://www.superauthors.com/)

Janice Kay Johnson

A MESSAGE
FOR
ABBY
Janice
Kay
Johnson

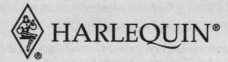

HARLEQUIN®

TORONTO • NEW YORK • LONDON
AMSTERDAM • PARIS • SYDNEY • HAMBURG
STOCKHOLM • ATHENS • TOKYO • MILAN • MADRID
PRAGUE • WARSAW • BUDAPEST • AUCKLAND

ISBN 0-373-70866-1

A MESSAGE FOR ABBY

Copyright © 1999 by Janice Kay Johnson.

This edition published by arrangement with Harlequin Books S.A.

® and TM are trademarks of the publisher. Trademarks indicated with ® are registered in the United States Patent and Trademark Office, the Canadian Trade Marks Office and in other countries.

Visit us at www.romance.net

Printed in U.S.A.

A MESSAGE
FOR
ABBY

CHAPTER ONE

HER DEAD DADDY'S PICKUP sitting beside the road, smoldering from an arson fire.

That was Abby Patton's first thought on seeing the truck—that it was Daddy's—and now she couldn't get rid of the willies.

The pickup wasn't really his, of course; it couldn't be. Ed Patton had been dead for three years, his Chevy sold only months after he went in the ground. This one was just the same color, the same vintage.

Coincidence, is all.

Abby prowled around the pickup. For sure these plates weren't the ones that had been on Daddy's truck—but then, she'd bet ten to one this pair had been stolen from another vehicle anyway. Shiny, tabs new, they didn't go with the red dust coating the dented, fading green paint of the pickup.

Firefighters had smashed the passenger side window and pumped foam on the seat, just to be sure a blaze didn't leap to life later. Wearing their gear and sweating in the hundred-degree heat, they had made a few choice remarks about the dumb ass who'd gone to all the trouble to rip the stuffing out of the seat, soak it with gasoline and set it on fire, only to roll up the windows and lock the doors.

"Doesn't every schoolkid know fire needs oxygen?'' one of them had asked, shaking his head. A minute later they'd tooted a fare-thee-well and were gone.

Now, left beside the road with nobody but jackrabbits and the wind to keep her company, Abby said aloud, "And why bother?" Why not junk the truck if it wouldn't run, sell it on a lot if it would?

Because setting fires was fun? Because the pickup was stolen and some teenage perp thought he could get rid of fingerprints this way? Or because the arsonist needed to destroy the vehicle for some other reason? There sure wasn't anything in the rusting bed of the pickup.

Before taking a closer look, Abby got on the radio to run the plates. While she waited, she leaned against her car door and looked around.

Barton Road was paved, even had a yellow stripe down the middle, but at the bottom of the gravel banks to each side, gray desert scrub stretched away, bordered by ancient barbed wire attached to rotting fence posts. Cattle must have grazed out here once upon a time, or why bother fencing, but this now looked like the pronghorn country it had once been.

She guessed she was five miles outside the Elk Springs city limits, east of town where the land got bleak and flat mighty quick. Just a few miles west, ranches started studding the landscape, including her brother-in-law's, the Triple B. But here no houses were visible, and only three vehicles had gone by in the past twenty minutes. Plus, the arsonist could have seen anyone coming far enough away to disappear in a cloud of dust before the passerby arrived.

Some teenage boys out here target shooting had

used a cell phone to report the fire. Interesting they'd seen flames. Either the fire setter had just left, or they'd lit this baby themselves.

A voice crackled from the receiver. "Marshal Patton, the plates belong to a blue 1997 Chevrolet Lumina, registered to—"

"Whoa," Abby interrupted. She repeated the plate number. "You're sure about the vehicle?"

"Yes, ma'am. The registered owner is Shirley Barnard, address 22301 Butte Road, Elk Springs."

Shock silenced Abby long enough for the dispatcher to say, "Do you need a repeat?"

"No! I..." She shook her head. "No. Thank you."

The prickle of some kind of primitive fear crept up her spine.

A fire set in a pickup that could have been Daddy's decorated with stolen plates belonging to her sister Renee's mother-in-law. And one of Daddy's daughters was an arson investigator.

Coincidence, Abby tried to tell herself again, but disquiet stirred the hair at her nape. She suddenly felt as if somebody was watching her.

She gazed around one more time, but the sagebrush wasn't dense enough to hide a man and the road stretched bare and shimmery in the noonday sun.

Abby shivered despite the heat. Pulling on latex gloves, she walked back to the pickup. Reaching through the broken window, she gingerly lifted the latch and shouldered open the door.

The interior was filthy and dripping with gasoline and retardant. The upholstery appeared to have been slit with a knife and then ripped open; most of the fabric was on the floor. Blackened from the fire, stuffing cascaded after the seat covering, exposing springs.

The smell was bad. Really bad. Instinctively Abby began breathing through her mouth. Gasoline, charred plastic and fabric and some sharp overtone that made her think of burning urine. What *was* that stench?

Oh, no.

She lifted the guts of the upholstery and turned it. Burned bits crumbled. She didn't notice, was too absorbed in the dark stain on the woven material. When she let it go, the latex fingers of her gloves were pink.

Blood, and plenty of it. Could have been dried before the gasoline and then the foam used to put out the fire had liquefied it again.

Abby stepped back, scanning the road and the dry landscape again, reassured by the emptiness and by the weight of the revolver at her hip.

She proceeded methodically then, examining every inch of the cab. Glove compartment was empty but for dirt, an old paperclip, a 1985 penny. More of the same—and nothing else—under the seats; the floors looked as if they hadn't been vacuumed since the year the penny had been minted. No stickers on the door or windshield showing when oil changes or tune-ups had been done. She bagged and tagged what little she found, in case it became evidence in a homicide, but she was betting whoever had set the fire hadn't touched any of this. He'd been damned sure nothing incriminating was left, however.

She looked beneath the hood, even scooted on her

back under the chassis just to check for the unexpected.

Then she returned to her car and called the Butte County Sheriff's Department, Investigations Unit. Too bad Meg was on maternity leave, Abby thought as she waited to be connected. Married two years now, Meg and Scott had decided to give Will and little Emily a brother or sister. Not that Will would care—he'd be off to college soon.

Abby's call was eventually relayed to Detective Ben Shea. Abby knew her sister had worked with Shea and thought highly of him.

"Patton?" he said in a deep, easy voice. "This Abby?"

"Yes." She watched in the rearview mirror as a dust cloud materialized into a camper coming down the road toward her. "Meg's told you I'm with the arson investigation squad, right?" If two investigators could be called a 'squad'—Butte County wasn't New York City yet, thank God. They were kept busy enough, but in these parts most arson fires could be nailed on teenagers or business owners.

"Sure. What's up?"

The camper passed, several people—kids among them—craning their necks to see why an official vehicle sat beside the road. She relaxed again.

"I'm on Barton Road, approximately five miles east of the city limits. I have a pickup truck with stolen plates. The seat was ripped up, soaked with gasoline and set on fire. The perp forgot to roll down the windows, so the fire didn't go far. Appears the seat is soaked with blood. I thought you folks might be interested."

"Yes, indeedy," he said. "Do you mind sitting tight? If you want, I'll call for a tow, but I'd like to see the vehicle before we take it into the yard. Just in case," he echoed her earlier thought, "this amounts to anything."

"No problem," she assured him. "I'll wander around here a little, see if maybe he got careless and tossed a cigarette butt or something."

While she waited she wondered why she hadn't told him the pickup was a ringer for her father's, or that the plates belonged to Renee's mother-in-law. That part she'd have to tell him, of course, but would he think she was shying at shadows if she admitted to wondering that there might be some message for her in this whole business?

Maybe. She'd see what she thought after meeting him. Despite the fact that he worked off and on with Meg, somehow Abby never had come face-to-face with Shea. She supposed it was natural that he and Meg hadn't socialized. From what her sister had said, he was closer to Abby's age than Meg's. And unmarried without children. Outside of work, they probably didn't have much in common.

She walked a hundred yards up the road, then back on the other side, doing the same thing going west. The dry gravel and dirt didn't hold tracks well. She'd parked on the opposite side of the road from the pickup, but the fire truck had pulled in ahead of it and could have obliterated other tracks.

Abby slid down the bank and climbed over the fence, snagging her trouser leg on the barbed wire and swearing. She wanted to go back up to the road and sit in her air-conditioned car. She could feel wet patches under her arms, trickles of sweat making their way down her spine to her panties. She could hardly wait to plunge into the YMCA pool after work and swim her laps.

Scouring the ground for footprints or anything that didn't belong, she searched in steadily widening semicircles from the pickup. Nothing but reddish dirt, rabbit holes, largish round droppings—maybe deer?—and gray-green sagebrush.

One other car passed, slowing briefly. She was too far away to see faces. The next vehicle, a Bronco with the sheriff's department emblem on the door, pulled to a stop on the shoulder behind her car. Abby trudged back, stepped carefully over the barbed wire and scrambled up the bank, feet slipping in the loose gravel until she had to put her hands down. Sweat fogged her vision as she topped the bank, shoved sticky hair off her forehead, and straightened to face Detective Ben Shea.

She blinked and stared in horror. She was going to kill Meg. Why *hadn't* she thought of some excuse to introduce him to her younger, single sister? At the very least, how could she have failed to mention, if only in passing, that Detective Shea was a spectacular man? Mr. January. No, Mr. Calendar Cover himself. Six-two or three, straight dark hair, cool gray eyes and a strong, impassive face.

And *she* was both sweaty and filthy. Her hair must be lank, her mascara dripping down her cheeks; she could taste grit.

Oh, yeah. Meg was going to pay.

If he'd smirked, Abby would have killed him, too. His gaze flicked over her in a lightning-quick assessment, but his mouth formed no smile. "Marshal Patton?"

"That's right." Her voice *sounded* gritty. She cleared her throat. "Detective Shea?"

"Ben." He held out a hand, which she took; his enveloped hers.

Abby would have given anything to be...well, *herself.* Made up, hair smooth, smile saucy. To be *together.* She liked his big warm hand, his strong clasp. She wanted to see interest spark in those cool eyes.

"Abby," she said with a wry smile.

He dropped her hand with unflattering speed. "Let's take a look," he said, and he wasn't talking about her. Unfortunately.

She trailed behind as he strolled to the pickup, pulled on a latex glove and fingered the upholstery fabric as she'd done.

"Run the plates?" he asked without looking over his shoulder.

"Yes. Do you know my sister, Renee?"

That earned her a startled glance. "Yeah."

"These plates should be on her mother-in-law's car. I know Shirley is over in Portland visiting her daughter and grandson. Which means her car is most likely garaged at the Triple B."

Shea swore softly and moved away from the pickup. "Funny coincidence. I mean, you being the one finding out."

"There are only two arson investigators in Elk Springs." Facts were facts. Today, she didn't like this one. It fed that uneasy feeling this pickup had been waiting for her. "Even if you didn't know our schedules, chances would be fifty-fifty I'd be the one to check out this fire. Actually, John is always off on Mondays.''

Ben Shea's gray eyes narrowed for a moment. ''You don't think it *is* coincidence.''

''No.'' Okay, there it was, right out in the open. ''The thing is, this pickup is the exact model and color of my father's. We sold it after he died three years ago.''

The detective muttered an obscenity. ''Vehicle ID number?''

''Haven't checked yet.''

He turned and stared at the pickup. ''Goddamn.''

''You're supposed to tell me I'm being paranoid. That coincidences happen.''

''Coincidences happen,'' Shea said automatically. He didn't have to add that he didn't mean it. ''Better make sure, first of all, that Renee's mother-in-law made it to Portland.''

''Oh, my God,'' Abby said, already backing away. Fear had leaped into her throat, nearly gagging her. She liked Shirley Barnard. ''I didn't think of that. I should have. All that blood…''

At her car, she grabbed her cell phone rather than her radio.

''Triple B.'' A male voice picked up.

''Daniel Barnard,'' Abby said peremptorily.

''He's riding, I think. No.'' She heard laughter in the background. ''You're in luck. Who's calling?''

She told him; a moment later she was talking to her brother-in-law with the blue eyes to-die-for.

Poor choice of words, Abby thought with a lurch.

"Daniel, we just found a pickup with stolen plates. They belong on Shirley's Lumina."

"What the hell?"

"It gets worse," she warned. "The seat of the pickup is drenched in blood." Into the silence, she asked quietly, "Daniel, have you talked to your mother? You're sure she got to Portland okay?"

He swore, which he seldom did. Then, "Yeah. Yeah, she called last night. But I'll phone right now. And go check her car. Where are you?"

She gave him her cell phone number so he didn't have to hunt for it. "You'll get right back to me?"

"Count on it." He sounded grim.

She flipped her telephone closed and, still sitting in her car with the door open, looked up to find Ben Shea leaning against the left fender of her car, arms crossed. Even through her haze of anxiety, Abby had a fleeting twinge of awareness. His strong body filled out his uniform very nicely.

"Daniel talked to his mother last night," she said.

Glance razor-sharp, Shea remarked, "Blood's fresh."

"But she was in Portland. Do you really think somebody went over there and kidnapped her, murdered her and abandoned the pickup here?"

He frowned at her. "No. But it seems as if you were meant to think that."

"You really don't believe I'm imagining things," Abby said hollowly.

"Nah." His mouth twisted. "This looks real personal to me."

"Aimed at me? Or Shirley?"

"There's a question." With a sigh he straightened. "You take your own pictures?"

"Usually. But if this might be a murder scene…"

"I'll call for the techs," he agreed.

While he was doing that, her phone rang.

"Shirley's fine," Daniel said without preamble. "The garage was still locked, but damned if the license plates on her car aren't missing."

"I'll send someone out to fingerprint, just in case this guy got sloppy."

"What the hell is going on?" Daniel asked, tone baffled.

"I don't know." She couldn't lie and tell him it had nothing to do with his family, because it did. Somebody had gone to a lot of trouble to steal those plates from Shirley Barnard's garaged Chevy. The Triple B, where she lived in the original farmhouse, was isolated. A cutting horse operation, the ranch employed a dozen or more stable hands and trainers. You didn't just drive up, hop out, break into the garage, unscrew the plates, then depart without somebody noticing.

"Keep me informed," he said.

"Will do." She pushed End and looked up at the detective. "Evidence crew on the way?"

"Yup." He was frowning at her.

Abby sneaked a glance at herself in her rearview mirror and almost groaned at the dirty gamine face reflected there. No wonder he was frowning.

"Hot out here," he said, seemingly at random.

Or was he acknowledging that he understood why she looked like hell?

Maybe. But why didn't *he?* she wondered resentfully. The sheen on his brow added to his masculine appeal. Even the smell of sweaty man was pleasing to a woman's nostrils. Life wasn't fair.

"So," he asked in an idle, musing way, "have you ticked anybody off recently?"

"Not in the past couple of days," Abby snapped.

He lifted a dark brow. "Try the past ten years."

"I was a firefighter until last fall. I don't make people mad as often as you do."

He stayed leaning against the fender, relaxed, his stillness annoying her as much as his questions. She felt wound tight. If it weren't so hot, she'd have been out of the car pacing. As it was…

"You want to get in, so I can turn on the air-conditioning?" she asked.

He looked surprised, which also irked her. Man, impervious to climactic conditions, was reminded of the frailty of mere Woman.

Detective Shea shrugged, as if to humor her. "Why not?"

"I hate heat," she muttered when he got in.

"Move to the coast," he suggested.

Cannon Beach with its rearing sea stack, rocky beach and cool afternoon fog sounded blissful to her right now.

"Winters there are dreary." She turned on the ignition and cranked up the air-conditioning. "I like to ski. Besides, my family is here."

"Speaking of which…"

"Yeah, yeah." Abby gazed out the windshield at the straight empty road. Not a car had passed since he arrived. "I just can't imagine Shirley having made anybody mad. Have you met her?"

"Yeah, she works part-time at the library. Nice lady."

"You read?" she asked in mock astonishment before thinking better of it.

"Learned in first grade."

Unaccustomed to feeling graceless, Abby said, "I was kidding."

"Uh-huh."

Chagrined, she decided it was best get back to the subject at hand. "Unless Shirley made somebody mad when she phoned about their overdues, it's hard to imagine how she can be the target of this."

"I agree. Although appearances can be deceptive."

"I know her."

The narrow-eyed glance he flicked Abby's way was impatient. "What, the Patton clan is without sin?"

Abby wrapped her fingers around the steering wheel, feeling the need to steady herself. "No," she said slowly. "My father was…not universally liked."

"So Meg says."

"But he's dead," she argued, making the point to herself more than him.

"Yup."

Abby let out a huff of air. "This is pointless."

"You're right," he said agreeably. "All we can do is our jobs, and then wait and see."

"Right."

Detective Shea cleared his throat. "Abby? I'm freezing."

"Really?" She turned to look at him in surprise.

As far as she was concerned, the temperature had just gotten pleasant.

He'd tucked his hands in his armpits. "You had your metabolism checked lately?"

"Maybe your blood's too thin," she suggested. "You ever thought of moving to Arizona?"

"I don't mind seasons." He reached for the door handle. "My body just doesn't much like changes that are too abrupt. An icy oasis of winter in the middle of a July day is a shock to the system."

"No, it's a blessed relief."

"Uh-huh." He seemed to like saying that, in a tone that indicated anything *but* agreement. Relief infused his voice when he added, "Ah. Here comes the cavalry."

Abby suddenly had an itch to leave. Just drive away. She'd done her part. If murder had been committed, the arson had been no more than a failed effort to cover it up. She liked solving puzzles, but this one wasn't her kind. As Ben Shea had said, it was personal. It seemed to be tapping at the door to her subconscious, saying, *Want to think about long ago? Remember nights of terror and tears?*

Well, no thanks, she didn't. The past wasn't something she thought about much. She left worrying to her sisters. She didn't like to get too emotional about anything.

And no creep with a grudge was going to shake her foundations.

"Do you need me to stick around?" Abby asked, giving in to her restlessness.

Looking briefly surprised, then thoughtful, Shea

stopped with the passenger side door open. Hot air shoved in. "Nah. I can stay. You have another job?"

"Fifteen." She lifted her contractor-style clipboard. "That's assuming nobody torches any other cars or buildings today."

"Thunderstorm's building up over the mountains." He nodded toward Juanita Butte and the Sisters. "Nature's going to do some torching of her own this evening."

She glanced uneasily over her shoulder toward town and the mountains beyond. Dark clouds climbed above them. She was just as glad she wouldn't be called out tonight when a spear of lightning set the dry woods aflame.

"I'll be in touch." She handed him her card.

He nodded, taking it and producing one of his own. Then he climbed out and hesitated with his hand on the car door. She felt his gaze, turned to meet it. For just a second something as intense as those white bolts of lightning crackled between them.

The next instant he'd shuttered the sheer force of that look and Abby wondered if she'd imagined it.

"You do that," he agreed, and slammed the door.

Shaken, she watched him saunter away, strides long and easy, his broad shoulders formidable, his butt— Abby exclaimed aloud. For Pete's sake, they were working together, not getting involved!

You can admire, a little voice in her head whispered.

"No," Abby told herself, "I can't."

Dating was fun. Right up there with a perfect ski run, and no more serious.

Ben Shea didn't smile, he didn't flirt, and he took

her seriously. All of which made him a dangerous man.

Abby didn't "do" dangerous men. After years as a firefighter, she knew what it meant to get burned. Besides, she'd made that particular mistake once, and she was a quick learner.

Anyway, thanks to the shining example of manhood set by Daddy dear, revered police chief, Abby had no desire to bring home a man for good. Sometimes her two brothers-in-law gave her pause, but not for long. You never did know what went on behind closed doors, did you?

Still, she could let herself be comforted by Detective Shea's competence and by the fact that he *had* listened to her. She knew cops, and plenty of them would have sneered at her fear.

But it was real, sitting in the pit of her stomach like potato salad gone bad. Because, damn, that did look like Daddy's pickup truck, and she hadn't seen one that color since they'd sold his. Somebody had spilled a hell of a lot of blood in it and then set it on fire.

Sort of like sending her an obscene note.

She just wished she could read this one.

Abby put her car in gear and pulled out onto the road, hoping the big dark cop would recede in her thoughts as surely as he did in the rearview mirror.

CHAPTER TWO

BEN SLOUCHED IN HIS CHAIR and propped his feet on his desk, crossing them at the ankles. A swallow of coffee woke him up, the acid burning another millimeter of tissue on the ulcer he felt forming. His imagination, the doctor said. The doctor golfed on Sundays. He didn't look at dead bodies.

Holding up Abby Patton's business card, Ben dialed. Though her voice mail wasn't what he had in mind, he left a message. Her card included a cell phone number, so he tried that.

She answered brusquely on the second ring. "Patton here."

"Detective Ben Shea."

"Shea." She sounded…something. He couldn't put his finger on what. Not neutral. Not surprised. But a quiver of some emotion had briefly changed the timbre of her voice.

He was hoping it meant that she was pleased to hear from him. Unfortunately, there was another possibility, which was that she'd disliked him from the get-go.

Ben chose to be an optimist.

"News?" she asked.

A direct man, he got right to it. Business first. "That blood came from a deer."

"What?" she exclaimed.

"The kind with horns and a hide," Ben elaborated helpfully.

After a long silence Abby Patton said, "I wish I could look on that as good news."

He turned his head to gaze, unseeing, through the slanted blinds at the parking lot. "You want my opinion?"

"Yeah."

"It is good in that I don't have another murder to investigate. But for you personally…" He rubbed the back of his neck. "Well, I'd say this makes it even more likely that coincidence didn't play a part in your discovery yesterday."

"He had those windows rolled up on purpose. So the fire *wouldn't* get very far. So I'd be sure to see the blood."

"That's my guess."

Again she was silent.

"No fingerprints on the door handles, steering wheel, emergency brake… The ones we found were in spots he didn't wipe clean. My bet is, they're old."

"Did you run the VIN?"

"Yup. It isn't your father's pickup. This one was sold by a rancher up in the Dalles a year ago to a—" he glanced down at his notes "—Julia Carvenas. She reported it stolen a week ago."

"Did you check her out?"

"I can't see any connection to Elk Springs."

"Horses? You know my brother-in-law—"

"No horses," Ben interrupted. "I asked. She runs a landscape business."

"Then this is a dead end." Dismay sounded, clear as the cry of a hunted animal.

Abby Patton had struck him as a supremely poised woman. She'd been a firefighter; now she'd added the training to make her a cop. He wondered when was the last time she'd felt any emotion approaching fear.

He kept his gruff voice low and soothing. "I'll be talking to the teenagers who discovered the fire. I'll go door-to-door at the houses on the outskirts. See if anybody noticed the pickup passing. I'd like to know how the perp got back to town."

"Motorcycle?" she suggested. "He could have carried it in the bed of the truck."

Okay, so she was sharp. Ben didn't know why that surprised him, even faintly. Yeah, she was a leggy blond beauty with sky-blue eyes, Hollywood's stereotype of a bimbo, but so was her sister. And he'd long ago learned that Meg Patton was smart and tough, a cop first and a woman second. Hell, their sister Renee, just as pretty and blond, was about to be sworn in as the new Elk Springs police chief.

"Motorcycle's my guess, too," Ben said. "Usually loners are the ones who do something so…" Not wanting to alarm her, he hesitated.

"Warped?"

He cleared his throat. "Well, I wouldn't go that far."

"I would," she said, blunt enough to satisfy him, before she added dismissively, "Thanks, Shea. Let me know if you learn anything further."

"Wait." Okay, where had that little spurt of panic

come from? So what if she hung up—he could call her back. He knew where to find her.

"You have something else?" she asked, her surprise edged with curiosity.

This should be easy. He'd thought about it all day. She was a foxy woman; he knew from Meg that Abby wasn't dating anybody seriously.

So why did he put his feet on the floor and sit up straight as if for inspection before he could spit out his question?

"Any chance you'd like to have dinner?"

"Dinner?"

She didn't have to sound as if he'd suggested bungee jumping naked, thought Ben, stung.

Nonetheless he said doggedly, "Yeah. We could maybe talk this over. Uh... Get to know each other." Smooth. Real smooth.

"As in a date."

Goddamn it. There she went again, making him feel small.

"That such an outlandish idea?" he asked, his voice edgy.

He could feel her thinking in the moment of silence that followed.

"No," she said finally. "I don't usually date cops, is all."

"There some reason?"

"We're just...too much alike. We have too much on our minds. I like to have fun. Lighten up. You know?"

"I can have fun," he said defensively, knowing it was a lie. Yeah, okay; sure he enjoyed himself sometimes. But fun? The way she meant? Probably not.

He didn't drink, hated loud music and detested parties. "We don't have to talk about work," he added.

"Dinner." She sounded cautious. Wheels were turning in her head; he could damn near hear the clatter.

"How about tonight?" Ben asked.

"I'm going to Renee's tonight. We're having a war council. So to speak." She paused. "If you want to come…"

What did this mean? She went from telling him he might not be fun enough to taking him home to meet her family?

"I don't want to intrude…"

"No, you might have something useful to offer. Daniel's the one who wants to talk this out." She sounded mildly impatient. "He'd be glad to have you."

"What about you?" Ben asked. "Would you be glad to have me?"

"To dinner?" She paused just long enough to be sure he got the point—no innuendos allowed. "Why not?"

He knew where the Triple B was. She suggested they meet there, which he accepted without argument. Most women liked to drive themselves on first dates. She wouldn't be stuck with fending him off on the doorstep if she came to the conclusion that this had been a mistake.

Hanging up the phone, Ben wasn't sure how to feel about this evening. Hell, he didn't know whether it was a working dinner or a date.

He did know he wasn't used to being rejected. *I*

don't usually date cops, she'd said, as if he'd crawled out from under a rock.

He wouldn't take it personally, Ben decided. Maybe she got hit on all the time down at the station. Given her looks, she probably did.

Funny, when he thought about it, because it wasn't her glorious legs or lush mouth or tangle of honey-blond hair that had gotten to him—although he'd noticed them, he couldn't deny it. But he didn't ask out every beautiful woman he met, either. And normally her princess act would have turned him off. A man couldn't warm his hands on a chilly woman.

But he'd seen something in Abby Patton's eyes. Something defensive, even scared. Her defiance was a cover-up, he thought, for a woman who didn't want to admit she was lonely.

And if he was wrong—well, maybe he, too, would be glad they were going their separate ways tonight.

TIRES CRUNCHING on the red cinder lane, Ben drove past the turnoff to the handsome new home that crowned the ridge above the Triple B barns and the pastures, improbably green from irrigation in the midst of brown, high mountain desert country at mid-summer. Fences enclosing pastures, paddocks and two outdoor arenas sparkled with fresh white paint. The place was prosperous, the horses and cattle he could see at a distance glossy.

Someone was working a cutting horse in the nearer arena. More like going along for the ride. The horse seemed to be doing the thinking. He was separating one steer from a clump of six or eight, anticipating the poor dumb cow's every dodge, moving so surely, so quickly and fluidly, it was pure poetry.

Ben had never been out here, but he'd heard stories about the ranch: the senile old man—Daniel's grandfather—wandering out into the wintry night, his body never found; Daniel's father dying when he got thrown into a fence post; and finally the human skull brought home by a dog.

Now this.

On the way to the Patton family war council, Ben had decided on a minor detour. He wanted to see for himself how hard it would have been for a thief to slip into Shirley Barnard's garage to steal the license plates from her car.

The guy sure as hell couldn't have driven right by in broad daylight. Before Ben reached the first barn, two men stepped out, looking toward him.

He pulled to a stop, set the brake and turned off the engine. Between barns, he saw a young cowboy walking a horse with sweat-soaked flanks. In the aisle of the barn, another horse—this one a fiery red—was cross-tied and being shod, from the sound of metal ringing out.

Ben got out of his car and nodded at the two men waiting. "Good day."

"Can we help you?" one asked.

"I'm with the sheriff's department. Detective Ben Shea." Ben showed his badge. "And you are?"

"Lee LaRoche." The taller and older of the two tipped back his Stetson. "I'm a trainer."

"Jim Cronin." The younger guy couldn't be much over twenty-five. Stocky and strong, he wore the ranch uniform: dusty denim, worn cowboy boots, white T-shirt and buff-brown Stetson. "I just work here."

Ben nodded. "You two fellows know about the break-in at Mrs. Barnard's?"

"You mean, her garage?"

"Yes, sir."

"Hell of a thing." The trainer shook his head. "Shirley wouldn't hurt a fly. Why would someone go picking on her like that?"

"Maybe just to show he could." Ben watched the two carefully; saw nothing but perplexity and mild curiosity about why a Butte County detective was out here questioning them about such a minor crime. "I just thought I'd find out whether someone could go right on down there without being noticed."

"Not in a car." LaRoche sounded sure. "We don't get much traffic out here. Someone's coming right now." He nodded past Ben toward the main road leading from Butte Road and the Triple B gates onto the ranch.

Ben turned. A plume of lava red dust rose like the spray behind a hydroplane. That nice shiny 4x4 was going to need a bath.

Like his own car, he realized ruefully.

LaRoche continued. "Especially at this time of year, we have plenty of warning. Somebody always pokes a head out to see who's come calling."

"What about at night? With Mrs. Barnard away?"

"I live there." The lanky older man pointed to a small white-painted cottage in the cottonwoods beside the creek. "Some of the hands have places in town, but a couple room in the bunkhouse. Cronin here's one of 'em."

The young ranch hand scratched his chin. "Well, I won't say if we'd heard a car we would have fallen over our feet rushing out to see who was here. But we'd have most likely glanced out. Mrs. Barnard don't get that many folks coming by, and Lee's place is the only other one on down the road."

"But he could have parked a ways back and walked."

Lee LaRoche slowly took off his hat and ran a hand through sweat-streaked hair. "Well, now. Sure. I suppose so. 'Course, if someone had come along he wouldn't have had anyplace to hide. With no trees till you get down to the creek. And his car would've stuck out like a palomino in a herd of bays. Say, if Daniel or Renee had come or gone. But at, oh, three, four in the morning... Sure."

He sent Cronin with Ben to check out the garage itself. The structure was detached from the original farmhouse where Daniel Barnard's mother still lived. Through a small dusty window, Ben could see the blue sedan. The lock on the side door was one of those push-button models, not a dead bolt. Anyone good with a paperclip could have gotten in. The main door, the cowboy told him, had an automatic opener.

"So Mrs. Barnard can drive straight on in, like in the winter. Daniel installed it himself."

"How long have you worked here?" Ben asked idly.

"Only about a year." Jim Cronin's face was boyish, despite the beginnings of lines at the corners of his hazel eyes. "I like to move around. See the country."

Not so different from the ski bums who operated

lifts up at Juanita Butte, or the temporary crews that fought fires in the dry woods every summer.

"Barnard good to work for?" Ben asked.

"The best," the man said simply. "Cutting horses bred and taught their tricks here are in the top ten every year. I'd like to train horses, not just ride 'em and muck up after 'em. This is the place to learn."

The two men walked back to the barn where Ben had left his car. Ben thanked Jim Cronin for his time and watched him disappear into the barn. Well down the aisle, Lee LaRoche appeared briefly, looking Ben's way. When his gaze met Ben's, he tipped his hat and faded back into the shadowy interior of the huge barn. Had he been watching for Ben? Making sure Cronin went right back to work?

Ben paused before getting behind the wheel of his car. He liked to take in his surroundings, soak them up as he did the sun's midday warmth in winter. It never paid to be hasty, he'd found; he learned things on a subliminal level if he allowed time.

Giving him curious glances and civil nods, a man and a woman rode by. The horses ambled, heads down, sweat darkening shoulders and flanks. Tiny puffs of dust bloomed beneath their hooves. Reins lay slack against the dark shiny necks.

Car door open, Ben watched them go, the horses both possessing the powerful, chunky hindquarters of the quarter horse breed, the two riders swaying easily in the Western saddles. Two barns away, a mare and foal were being loaded into a fancy-looking trailer. The foal didn't want to go, and kept shying away at the last minute, skinny legs flying. The men doing the loading were patient, giving the skittish colt time to settle down. In the arena, a different horse was being worked now. A gray-haired man with a skinny butt sat on the fence watching, heels hooked over a rail.

Busy place, this. An unlikely choice to burglarize. No, someone had wanted to send a message: *I can get at you anywhere.*

More than the blood or the stolen pickup truck, the license plates lifted from Shirley Barnard's car were what worried Ben. The message was not a comforting one.

And he had to believe, it wouldn't be the last.

Ben slid in behind the wheel and slammed his car door. Time to be getting up to Daniel Barnard's place, before Abby started to worry about his absence.

In your dreams, he jeered, and started the car.

THE LAST TO SIT DOWN, Abby scooted her chair forward and braced herself for an in-depth analysis of the arson fire set in the pickup truck.

In his paternalistic mode, Daniel Barnard looked around the table with an air of quiet satisfaction. The troops were gathered. Even Will, Meg's sixteen-year-old son, had been allowed to stay. Only Emily, Meg's three-year-old adopted daughter wasn't at the table; Meg had settled her in the living room where she was out of earshot but in sight, happily occupied with a pile of blocks and half a dozen puzzles.

Meg had even wanted to invite Jack Murray, her former lover and Will's father. "This concerns Will," she'd said. "Which means it concerns Jack."

Abby had gently discouraged her sister. There

were things Meg didn't know. Jack was just as uncomfortable with Abby as she was around him.

Both did their best to encounter each other as seldom as possible.

Now, Daniel's survey of the family complete,
Abby's brother-in-law nodded toward Shea. "Good
of you to come, Ben."

The detective inclined his head. "Abby suggested
it."

Beside him, Abby said nothing. She wasn't about
to admit that she hadn't invited him as the investigating officer, that in fact this was a trial run for a
real date. That she was trying to decide whether her
original assessment of Ben Shea was accurate.

Could she have a good time with the guy? Or
would he be getting serious before he broke off the
first kiss?

Really, it would be too bad if she had to tell him
to get lost before that kiss. Darned if he didn't look
even better out of uniform than he did in. Faded jeans
hugged long, powerful muscles in his thighs. A sage-
green T-shirt got just as familiar with the planes of
his chest and solid biceps. Nice neck, too, Abby
thought, sneaking a glance. Tanned, smooth, strong
without being bullish. Assertive jaw, sexy mouth, icy
clear eyes, and cheekbones prominent enough to cast
shadows on his clean-shaven cheeks.

Kissing him would be fine. Better than fine, she
suspected. Maybe *too* fine, which was her biggest
fear. Only once had she come close to falling in love,
and what a mistake that had been! Jack Murray had
been using her. She'd been barely out of high school,

but she had spent years seething at the knowledge that she'd been a Meg substitute.

No, once was enough. Giving a man the upper hand—that was scary stuff. She didn't need it.

"Abby?"

She started, to find that her entire family—and Ben—were staring at her.

"What?" she said.

Daniel lifted his brows in that way he had. "Why don't you get this rolling? Tell us what you found."

"And make it snappy," Renee chimed in. "The turkey breast is coming out of the oven in fifteen minutes, whether we're done talking or not."

"Well, I don't know what you think this will accomplish, but here goes." Succinctly, Abby described the pickup, the lack of fingerprints, the blood and the short-lived fire.

"Maybe this guy was just dumb," suggested Scott McNeil, Meg's big auburn-haired husband. General manager of the ski area, he knew the great American public. "Believe me, dumb is not uncommon."

"But why would he set a fire to burn up upholstery soaked with deer blood?" Meg asked, lines of worry puckering her forehead. She sat with her hands splayed on her belly, swollen with a baby due in a few weeks.

Daniel leaned forward. "Maybe because he took it out of season. He was afraid somebody would see the deer if he slung it in the bed of the pickup."

"He could have just put a tarp over it," Renee said. "Plastic garbage sacks. Anyway, the truck was stolen. He was abandoning it. Why bother with the fire?"

Forestalling Abby, Ben raised his voice. "You're missing the point. None of this was casual. Whoever this guy is, he worked hard to get his hands on those license plates. There had to be a reason for that. A message. He's saying, 'See how easy I can get to you?' And when part of that message is a whole hell of a lot of blood, I'd have to take that as a threat. Unless anybody has a better idea."

No one did. He'd silenced them. They'd *wanted* to believe there might be logical explanations for what Abby had found yesterday—explanations that had nothing to do with the Barnard or Patton families. But Abby agreed with Ben: why waste time and hope?

A muscle jumping in his cheek, Daniel spoke up. "I talked to my mother again. With one exception, she's never had an enemy. Some of you know she was raped years ago by a ranch hand."

Will jerked. Obviously he hadn't known. "Aunt Shirley was *raped?*"

His mother touched his arm. "Pretty crummy, huh?"

Looking disconcertingly like Jack, Will frowned. "But why didn't I know?"

"Because it was her right to tell people or not," Meg said gently.

"Oh." The tangled emotions of a teenager flitted across his face, but at last he nodded.

Daniel continued. "Dad beat the crap out of the guy and threw him off the place. Mom didn't want to testify. When this came out three years ago, we found out the bastard is in the Washington State penitentiary at Walla Walla for another rape. After you called yesterday—" he looked at Abby "—I had Renee check on him. Harris. Theon Josiah Harris. He's out. They released him a year ago."

"But what's the connection? It doesn't make sense," Renee said persuasively. "Shirley didn't prosecute. Why would he come back? He has nothing to get revenge *for.*"

Ben propped his elbows on the table. "Unless this guy has some reason to think she tried to get him. Maybe influenced a judge to give him the top end of the sentencing range."

Will, with the gruff voice of a man, said, "But if Aunt Shirley never told anyone…"

No wonder he didn't sound like a kid! Abby thought. Will Patton was used to cop talk. Murder and rape weren't big-screen fun and games to this kid.

His mother shook her head. "Let's face it, none of this is exactly sane. Going to all the trouble to steal those license plates out of a locked garage here on the ranch, then killing a deer just for the blood… Things fester, when someone is in prison long enough."

"I don't believe this has anything to do with Shirley." Abby hated to be the one to remind them, but somebody had to. "This guy may have gone to a lot of trouble to steal the plates off her car, but that was nothing compared to finding a pickup that looked exactly like Daddy's and stealing it."

"That could be coincidence," Renee said, but her voice held no conviction.

Abby shook her head, but said no more. What was the point?

Emily abandoned her puzzles, pieces scattered all

over the floor, and trotted into the dining room. "Mama! I wanna sit on *your* lap."

Meg gave her a distracted smile. "Sure, punkin, but I don't have very much lap right now."

"Why don't you come and sit on Daddy's?" Scott pushed back from the table and lifted the little girl into the air. Over her happy squeal, he said, "Seems to me we can't do anything just yet except be extra careful."

"Maybe nothing will come of this." Meg almost sounded convinced.

Abby could hardly believe big sister Meg, the cop, could sound so foolishly optimistic. The bad guys would all go away. Why worry?

Was it marriage or pregnancy that had blunted her wary intelligence?

"Ben's still hoping to find an eyewitness," Abby said.

"Nobody is invisible," Shea commented. "I might get lucky."

A few nods all around, and Renee said, "If you'll all excuse me, I'd better work on dinner."

Abby stood, too, shaking her head at her older sister who was making "getting up" motions. "No, you stay put, Meg. Watching you on your feet makes me tired. I'll help Renee."

In the kitchen, Renee turned on the burner under a pan of green beans. "What's the point of a threat if someone doesn't understand it?" she asked.

"I don't know," Abby said with a sigh. "These rolls go in the oven?" At her sister's nod, she ran cold water over the paper bag. "Maybe one of us is supposed to understand the threat. You ever arrested anyone for something having to do with blood on the seat or…'' Knowing even that much sounded weak, she ran out of ideas. ''Heck, maybe he's a poacher who's just trying to tell us he can kill a deer anytime he wants.''

''With my mother-in-law's license plates on the pickup he stole up in the Dalles just so he could abandon it here?''

''Maybe it broke down.'' Now she was the one trying to find an out, Abby thought ruefully.

''Oh, jeez.'' Oven mitt dangling from her hand, Renee looked at her sister. ''It's all too tangled, isn't it? Too…purposeful.''

''Yeah.'' Abby stirred the green beans unnecessarily. ''But what's the purpose?''

Her sister actually shivered. ''I don't know. I don't think I want to know.''

Abby rubbed the goose bumps on her own forearms. ''Worse yet is the fact that we're going to have to find out. One way or the other.''

Renee didn't answer. She removed the turkey breast from the oven, popped the bag of rolls in, and took up the carving knife.

''I don't see how Meg can have three weeks to go,'' she said as if they'd been discussing their older sister all along. ''I wish the doctor had done an ultrasound.''

''You're not thinking twins?'' Abby asked, shocked out of her absorption in the case.

''She's awfully big.''

''Wouldn't the doctor have noticed two heartbeats?''

"I don't know." Renee fretted. "But take a look at her."

"Maybe they got the due date wrong." There she went again; little Miss Pollyanna, smoothing away any difficulty.

"The doctor should *know*," Renee said fiercely. "I just worry Meg's not getting the care she should be."

"Have you heard anything bad about Dr. Kennedy?"

"No-o."

Then it came to Abby; she looked closely at her sister. "You're just scared, aren't you? It's not as if having twins would be the end of the world for Meg. I mean, maybe she couldn't go back to work, but she's pretty much into this motherhood thing right now, anyway." What the mysterious attraction was, Abby didn't get. Emily was cute, sure, but her squall when she was tired made Abby think of fingernails maliciously drawn down a blackboard. But they weren't talking about her, thank God. Dragging herself back to the point, Abby accused, "You're afraid of losing her again."

To her astonishment, Renee burst into tears. "Meg's just so tired!" she wailed.

Abby gently took the carving knife from her sister's hand, set it on the countertop and wrapped her in a hug. "Hey, what's the deal?"

"I always said I'd make chief, and now I have, but I'd rather be pregnant!" Renee pulled back to show a pathetic, blotched face. "I want it so bad, but then sometimes I look at Meg and wonder if I really do, and if something happens to her I'll be too scared ever to have a baby of my own! So really I'm self-ish!"

*O*kay.

"Renee," Abby said carefully, "you're acting really weird. You know that, don't you?"

A sniff and a nod were her answer; Renee had buried her face in a dishtowel, using it as a giant hankie.

"PMS?" Out of nowhere, a thought zapped Abby. "Are you sure you *aren't* pregnant?"

"What?" Renee whipped the dishtowel from her face.

"You heard me."

"I…" She blinked. Blinked again. "It must be PMS. You know I get cranky."

"But not deranged," Abby gently suggested. "When are you due?"

"Due? Meg's the one… Oh. You mean…" Her brow furrowed. "I don't keep track. It just… comes."

"Uh-huh."

"I guess it's been a while." Renee's green-gold eyes widened. "Ohmygod. What if I'm pregnant?"

"You celebrate?"

"I'm being sworn in two weeks from tomorrow!"

"Surely you wouldn't be the first police chief in America who was pregnant."

"Most of them are still men." That dry comment sounded more like Abby's big—well, middle sister.

"Buy one of those home pregnancy tests," Abby advised. "In the meantime, *I'll* carve the turkey. You go do something to your face."

Renee squeaked at the sight of herself reflected in

the door of the top oven. "I promise. I'll be right back!"

Shaking her head, Abby picked up the knife.

"Want me to do that?"

The deep voice came from so close behind her, she was the one to squeak and jump this time. Wheeling around, she pressed a hand to her chest. "You scared the daylights out of me!"

"Sorry." Ben Shea lifted one dark brow as smoothly as Daniel did. It gave Ben's face a saturnine look. "Just thought I'd offer to help."

Crowd me, you mean, she thought unkindly. But this was her fault; she'd encouraged him by inviting him tonight. No surprise he didn't want to be abandoned to her family.

"Here. You carve the turkey." She set down the knife instead of handing it to him. "Renee didn't feel good for a minute. I'll see if the rolls are hot, figure out what else she was going to feed us."

"All right," Ben said agreeably.

A potato salad and a fruit salad were ready in the refrigerator. All Abby had to do was peel back the plastic wrap and stick in serving spoons.

She carried them out to the dining room, tickled Emily who giggled gratifyingly, and went back to the kitchen. Intent on his job, Ben barely glanced up.

"That wasn't you crying, was it?"

"You heard…" She stopped. "I don't cry."

"You don't cry."

"That's what I said."

He looked her over with the same curiosity and lack of emotion he'd shown toward the bloody cab of the pickup. "You figure men don't cry, so you shouldn't, either?"

"I don't care what men do," Abby said shortly.

"As long as they're fun."

She lifted her chin a notch. "And it's fun I can live without if I have to."

He shook his head and went back to carving. "You got a real healthy attitude."

Oh, yeah, he's going to kiss you good-night now.

"You want a healthy attitude, don't ask out another cop. Try the clerk at the health food store."

"Very funny."

What on earth was wrong with her? Ben Shea was nice; he was gorgeous; he was unmarried. Vouched for by her sister. She should be batting her eyelashes, not being as disagreeable as a streetwalker about to be booked.

Oh, good analogy, she told herself.

He studied her with those penetrating eyes. "When's the last time you cried?"

"I don't know. Years."

He muttered a profanity. "Are you armor-plated? How can you help but cry sometimes?"

She froze in the act of taking the hot bag of rolls from the oven. "*You* cry?"

He wanted his shrug to look careless, she could tell. "Sometimes. Like just a couple of weeks ago. This guy killed his wife and two-year-old daughter, then swallowed the gun himself. It was seeing that kid…" His body jerked, and then his eyes shuttered and he went back to carving turkey. "I did my job, but when I got home, I cried. I'm not afraid to admit it."

Her back to him, Abby dropped the crisp, hot paper bag on the counter. Cops and firefighters didn't often confess to that kind of weakness—for so it would be considered in the station house. Maybe he'd done it to test her—to see how deep she went. Maybe he was a sensitive kind of guy who liked talking about feelings.

Or maybe the sight of the dead child had eaten at his soul until he had to tell someone the horror, and she was just the lucky nominee. Whatever his reason for talking so frankly, she knew she couldn't blow him off.

Past a sudden lump in her throat, she said abruptly, "It was two years ago. The last time I cried." She wouldn't look at him. "House fire. We found these kids, all under the bed. Like they were hiding from an intruder. But you can't hide from fire, or smoke. They looked…like dolls. Waxy and stiff. The fire had been set. Mama had dumped her boyfriend, and he was pissed. Didn't even get Mama. She'd left her three children, all under five, alone while she worked a graveyard shift cleaning an office building. After that night I decided to become an investigator. Putting out the fire isn't enough anymore."

Whether the tears had been cause or effect, she didn't know. Maybe she'd become an investigator because she didn't want to cry anymore, not to right wrongs. How could anyone judge her own motives?

All Abby knew was, she'd hidden under the bed more than once, small and scared.

And crying made her feel weak. A big girl now, she allowed no weakness.

"Shedding some tears helped," Ben said. "I felt better."

Abby dumped the rolls into a basket. "I didn't."

His hand shot out to stop her as she passed to return to the dining room. "Are you as tough as you sound, Abby Patton?"

Tough was her private ideal, not her public image. *Tough* was the shield she wore like a bulletproof vest—it would keep you alive only if no one noticed you were wearing it. Because if they did, they might shoot you in the head.

Letting someone—this man—see that tough outer shield might put her in danger.

So she batted her eyes, smiled slow and mysterious, and said, light and flirty, "Oh, I don't know if tough's the first word I associate with myself. What do you think, Detective Shea?"

Eyes narrowed, he let her go. "What I think is, finding out might be fun. And that's important, right? Having fun?"

She had to work at making her smile saucy. "Oh, number one. Absolutely." She could sound blithe, unconcerned. "Why don't we go dancing after this?" *Somewhere,* she thought, *with really loud music. Somewhere they couldn't talk.*

"Why don't we," he said. "Something tells me you'll know just the place."

CHAPTER THREE

ABBY HAD KNOWN A PLACE, all right. Ben's ears were still ringing the next day when he drove toward the outskirts of Elk Springs to begin knocking on doors in hopes of hitting on someone who'd seen either the green pickup or a lone motorcyclist pass down Barton Road at the right time.

After leaving her brother-in-law's last night, Abby had taken Ben to Paganucci's, a club aimed at the twenty-something crowd. With a population of twenty thousand and climbing, Elk Springs had gone from hick town to resort town in a few short years, although the process had been well advanced by the time Ben had taken the job here. But even since he came, the downtown hardware store had moved off Main Street to make way for an art gallery and café combo. Downtown was no longer for locals. Now antique stores, boutiques and espresso joints jostled trendy restaurants and nightclubs that appealed to skiers.

Paganucci's was one of them. Sleek decor, dim lighting jolted by flashes of brilliant white strobes, music that vibrated through the floor and penetrated the very air the way an electric shock did. The drinks had names he didn't recognize. The other men looked as self-consciously stylish as Don Johnson had on "Miami Vice."

In this crowd, Ben might as well have been a cow horse among the parade at Churchill Downs.

But he'd tried real hard to have fun. Or at least to *look* like he was having fun, which was what counted. He felt like a goddamn idiot out on the dance floor. But every time Abby leaped to her feet with that manic glitter in her eyes and said, "Let's dance," he said, "Sure."

She was in restless motion the whole evening. Dancing, tapping her fingers, swaying to the music. Never really looking at him, her gaze always elsewhere, watching other couples dance, laugh, flirt. When she talked, it was with stagey animation. Oh, yeah, she was playing for the crowd.

Or for him, Ben wasn't sure which.

He'd be ready to write off Abby Patton and any possibility of a future with her, except for one thing: he'd have sworn that she wasn't having fun, either. She was making a point, hammering it home.

I'm not your type, she was saying. *This is fun. This is me.*

Ben didn't buy it. She fidgeted too much; her gaiety was too forced. The only real moment they'd had all evening was during the one slow dance she'd allowed him. They'd gone toe to toe; he'd eased her up against him, felt the tension and the resistance shimmering through her. Picturing a coil of wire that kept springing free of his fingers, he had nonetheless played with the fantasy of what making love with her would be like. Abby Patton would be the farthest thing from passive. He pictured her determined to be on top, willing to wrestle him for the privilege.

Now *that* would be fun.

The music whispered of love and the soft light of the moon, of night breezes and the tangle of sheets. Even for him, the lilting notes were suddenly evocative, sensual. He bent his head, breathed in the tangy scent of her hair, gently rubbed the taut muscles of her lower back.

And, wonder of wonders, she began to relax. She let out a sigh, laid her cheek against his neck, matched the sway of her hips to his easy movements. For one brief shining moment, they meshed.

But the music died, to throb forth a frenzied beat. The strobelight blinded Ben. Abby shot away as if he were trying to cuff her. He'd swear she didn't meet his eyes again all night.

And out in the parking lot, she had made a breezy escape. A good-night kiss was not on the books.

Caught up in remembering—regretting the lack of a kiss—Ben took a minute to snap back to the present.

"Damn," he muttered.

He'd already driven past the last ranch before Barton Road stretched into empty country. He'd have to go a mile back. Hell, and that ranch house had been a hundred and fifty yards off the road. What were the chances anyone had noticed the traffic two days ago?

He didn't think about not trying. He'd have gone through the motions no matter what, but under different circumstances that's what he'd have been do-

ing. Every question he asked would have been per-
functory.

Today his questions would be deadly serious. The
Patton sisters were all cops. A threat against them
was a threat against him and every other cop.

The shoulder of the road briefly widened and he
made a U-turn.

He'd wanted to kiss one of the Patton sisters last
night.

Abby Patton reminded Ben of the stray cat he'd
been feeding for a couple of years now. Cinderella,
he called her; Cindy for short. A dainty calico with
the soft hues and electric-blue eyes of a Siamese mix,
Cindy had been so wild at first, he had caught only
glimpses of her. She'd gobbled the food he put out,
always poised for flight, her head lifting constantly.
She'd gotten wilder yet when he trapped her and had
her spayed and vaccinated.

It had taken six months before she would come to
his call, hovering a safe distance away while he
opened a can. More months before she would allow
him within an arm's reach. This spring, he had
touched her. She'd erupted into the air and fled, but
come warily back. Now she let him stroke her back.
Someday, he was going to cuddle that cat. Take her
in the house, feel her curl trustingly at his feet during
the night.

Cindy had never known loving care from a human
being until Ben set out that first bowl of food. She'd
probably had rocks thrown at her. Loud voices had
run her off.

Ben wanted to know what Abby's excuse was.

He had a feeling he might never find out, though.

She hadn't wanted to date him from the beginning, and her minor enthusiasm had clearly waned. He was betting that if he called her today and suggested they do it again, she'd have an excuse.

No, he thought, putting on his turn signal, excuses weren't her style. She'd be blunt. *I could tell you weren't having fun,* she'd say. Or, *I didn't have fun with you.* Or, *You're not my type.*

He wasn't her type. She wasn't his.

He wanted her anyway.

The tires crunched onto the long gravel driveway that led to a rundown ranch house. He took note of the dogs racing to meet him, the sagging barbed-wire fence, the gaping hole in the old barn roof, but he kept thinking about Abby Patton.

Maybe the challenge was what appealed to him. Maybe it was more complicated; could be he had some deep-seated need to erase fear where he found it, to coax trust from the smallest seed.

But Ben didn't know why that would be. He was usually attracted to confident, smart women. He liked honesty, serenity, a witty tongue. Timid women in need of protection weren't his thing.

He snorted at the idea of Abby Patton, arson investigator, needing a protector. At five foot ten inches or so, she wasn't small.

But honest, serene… He didn't think so. She might find serenity in her old age, but that was fifty years away, give or take a few. And blunt didn't equate to honest. Ben doubted that Abby was honest even with herself about what she felt or why.

He shouldn't want her any more than he should indulge the hope that the small feral cat living like a ghost around his house might someday become a real pet, the kind other people had.

Rolling to a stop, Ben shifted into park, set the hand brake and turned off the engine, giving the dust and the dogs a minute to settle.

Yeah, he thought, but just the other day Cindy had hopped onto the porch railing so close to his hand she was clearly asking to be petted. So you never knew, did you?

He opened his door just as a man came out of the barn.

"Goddamn it, shut your mouths up!"

A few yaps later the two shepherd mixes sniffed Ben's hand and decided he wasn't the enemy.

The rancher, tall and skeletal, must have been working on some piece of machinery. His hands were black with grease, some of which he'd smeared onto his face, weathered to the texture of the desert.

"Won't offer to shake hands." He cast a dubious eye at the shield Ben extended. "You fellas don't get out this way much."

"Not much reason," Ben said. "Day before yesterday, a pickup was abandoned and set on fire up the road a piece. I'm wondering if you ever notice passing traffic."

"If the dogs don't bark, I don't come out."

"Kind of figured that." Ben nodded ruefully. "Hope you don't mind my asking."

"Anybody can ask me anything." The rancher shrugged. "You need a little old lady, hasn't got much better to do than peep out from behind her blinds."

Ben nodded toward the house. "You wouldn't have a wife or mother in there?"

"Wife never looks away from her soaps."

Ben extended a card. "Well, if you wouldn't mind asking her tonight," he said just as laconically. "I'd appreciate it."

"I'll ask."

He had already disappeared into the barn before Ben got back in behind the wheel. Tongues lolling, the dogs gave halfhearted chase. They'd given up long before he turned onto paved road.

This was going to be a waste of time. He'd known it would be. But hell, now and again you got a surprise. At least, you did if you looked for it.

Seemed to him, Abby Patton might be one of those surprises.

BURNED WOOD had the texture of alligator hide. Abby crunched across the blackened floor of the corner grocery store in her steel-reinforced boots, not worrying too much about where she stepped.

Char licked up the walls. This baby had definitely started at floor level.

It was a no-brainer, but she did a meticulous search anyway, clicking photographs as she went. They were essential to document what she saw. Good pictures sold the prosecutor's case to the jury like no testimony ever could.

The wooden subfloor was deeply scorched in half a dozen places, always a dead giveaway. The samples she took would show the presence of a flammable liquid, sure as shootin'. Fuse box indicated no electrical troubles; the point of origin wasn't near wiring, anyway.

What interested Abby was the lack of ash and bits of debris on the crumpled, seared metal shelving.

Earlier the owner had come out of his hysteria long enough to claim the store was fully stocked.

"What the hell do you think?" he demanded, face flushed with fury and—she suspected—guilt. "People keep coming back if they don't find what they want the first time? This is a grocery store. We have regular deliveries."

Yeah, but about six months ago Price-Right had built a big store three blocks away. A little mom-and-pop place like this might have been a going concern until then; people liked convenience. They wouldn't do their week's shopping here, they'd go to Safeway a mile away, but they'd stop by here for a six-pack or some forgotten item. But the small volume in a store this size meant prices had to be higher. A mile was one thing; three blocks was another. This past six months had to have been a struggle.

She wandered into the back, which had suffered damage from smoke and water but not fire. The loading area was empty; the office, bare bones. The computer was darn near an antique, unless its guts had been replaced. No TV or microwave or refrigerator. Either the owner had never had any of the comforts back here, or he'd moved them out before he'd torched his place.

Abby put her vials and bags of evidence along with her Minolta into the trunk of her car, then rang doorbells half a block each way. The stories she heard confirmed her suspicions.

"He was going out of business. Had to be," one gruff, graying man with a paunch declared. "Who the hell was going to pay what he asked?"

"Even the freezers didn't have much in them the last time I was there," a housewife said. "I bought milk, but the date was a little past. Mr. Joseph said a delivery had been delayed, but I wondered."

"Yeah, I saw him and his old lady moving a TV and microwave—I think that's what it was—out the back two days ago," said a neighbor, whose backyard abutted the alley. "Mr. Joseph said the TV at home had gone kaput. But it makes you wonder..."

Abby's cell phone rang and she excused herself.

"Patton," she said in answer.

"Hi, it's Meg. Have you heard from Ben?"

Abby was annoyed to realize she felt mild disappointment that the caller *wasn't* Ben Shea. Of course, their one date had been a flop. He wouldn't be asking her again. She didn't want him to ask her out again. But she had hoped for news about his door-to-door questioning.

"Nope," she told her sister. "You?"

"Not a word." Meg puffed out a sigh that expressed acute frustration. "If I didn't feel about as mobile as a moose stuck in deep snow, I'd go back to work part-time. Darn it, I don't know how seriously Ben is taking this."

Abby tried to be fair. "Pretty seriously, I think. He listened to me. Come on, Meg. You've never had reservations about his work, have you?"

"No..." her sister said grudgingly. "I just... Oh, I feel useless. I hate it!"

Abby leaned against the fender of her car. "Meg,

you're having a baby in a few weeks. What could be more productive?''

Her sister took a few audible breaths. "You're right," she finally said. "I know you're right. This is what I want to do. But I'm not used to twiddling my thumbs!" The last came out as a cry.

"I know, I know." Abby did her best to be soothing. Oral back-patting. "Renee's worried you're going to have twins."

This sigh had an exasperated note. "I've gained a normal amount. *All* women in their ninth month look like walruses wallowing on the beach. At least, all women whose babies are probably going to weigh eight or nine pounds.''

"It's you Renee's worried about. She doesn't want to lose you again.''

"She *told* you that?" Meg sounded surprised.

"I pried it out of her.''

"That's not like you.''

Stung, Abby asked, "What's that supposed to mean?''

"You usually avoid any emotional issues,'' her sister said bluntly. "I'd have expected you to make an excuse to *avoid* having that kind of conversation with Renee. Not push for it.''

"She was crying!" Damn it, why feel hurt? Meg was right; Abby usually did evade sticky, weepy situations. There was nothing wrong with that. She just wasn't good at them.

"You mean, you walked in on her crying?''

"No, we talked about you, and then I suggested that maybe she wasn't worried about twins, she was scared of losing you, and—'' Abby stopped. Swallowed. ''I care.''

Her sister's voice softened. ''I know you do.''

''Anyway, you might talk to her.''

''Okay. Sure.'' Meg paused. ''Why don't I call Ben, too?''

Quickly—too quickly—Abby said, ''No, *I'll* do that. You're on maternity leave. The case is mine, anyway. I'll let you know if he's learned anything.''

Feeling grumpy, she had to get in the car and hunt through her leather folder to find Ben Shea's card. Why hadn't he gotten in touch with her? Why was she having to beg for information?

His cell phone was either turned off or he was out of the area, a mechanical voice informed her. Voice mail told her Ben Shea wasn't available. ''But leave a message!'' the chirpy canned voice encouraged her.

Abby did, short and to the point. ''Call me,'' she said tersely.

He did. An hour later. She was back in her office, writing up a report on the mom-and-pop grocery incendiary fire.

''Shea, here. Don't have much to report,'' he said. ''Sorry I didn't get to you sooner.''

Considering they had dated the night before, she thought that was pretty brisk. *How are you? Hope you had fun last night, would have been nice.* This was not the way to get the girl, Abby thought derogatorily.

Of course, maybe he didn't *want* to get the girl.

Which was fine with her.

''Nobody paid any attention to the traffic?''

''One guy heard a motorcycle pass about the right

time. He was shoveling manure behind the barn, couldn't see the road, but he admitted that his dream is to buy a Harley-Davidson when he retires. He figures he and his wife can see the country on it.''

For no good reason, Abby was diverted from the point. "What's *she* think of that?''

"Not much, from the rolled eyes I saw in the background.''

She snorted. "Why would he expect anything different? Who wants to stare at a man's back for hours every day?''

"You'd want to be the one gripping the handle-bars, wouldn't you?'' An odd tone infused his voice.

"Darn tootin' I would.'' Abby wasn't ashamed to admit it. Why should men get all the fun while women went along for the ride?

After a brief pause Ben mused, "Seems a shame. The guy looked so wistful.''

"We all have dreams.'' And she didn't want to talk about ones that were doomed.

"Yeah, well, the point here is, he noticed the growl of the motorcycle because it triggered a brief fantasy of him eating up the miles on a hog. The one he heard wasn't a Harley—something smaller, less powerful.''

"And easier to lift into and out of the bed of a pickup truck.''

"You got it.''

"So now what?''

"Unless forensic evidence shows us something—and I'm betting it won't—we're out of luck. You know that.''

"Until something else happens," Abby said slowly.

"If it happens."

"If," she agreed.

"I don't like it." Shea was silent for a moment. For the first time he sounded human, even intimate. "I'm sorry, Abby. I wish there was more I could do."

"No. No, that's okay. I know there isn't. I was just hoping…"

"Would you have dinner with me Friday?" he asked abruptly.

A rush of relief disconcerted her. She just didn't like feeling rejected, Abby told herself.

Perversely, she didn't say, "Yes. Please." She didn't tease or flirt. Oh, no. Those were ways to land the guy. She didn't want to land this one.

"Last night wasn't a great success," she said instead. "I could tell that wasn't your scene."

"Friday night, it'll be my choice."

"Which is?" she asked, immediately suspicious.

"Haven't decided yet. What do you say?"

Her eyes narrowed. "How about you decide first."

"What, you're a coward?" he mocked. "I won't take you skydiving, if that's what scares you."

"I took skydiving lessons a couple of years ago. Not much scares me."

"And here I thought you'd say, 'nothing scares me.'"

Just like that, anger blossomed in her chest like a water balloon smacking down on the pavement. "You don't think much of me, do you? Why did you ask me out in the first place?"

He was silent so long, she almost ended the call. The anger spread down to her fingertips, burning as it went.

When Shea did speak, the timbre of his voice had changed; the mockery was gone, leaving something quiet and too solemn in its place. "I think I would like you, if you'd let me get to know you."

"What do you call last night?" Abby asked tartly. "Did we exchange ten words?"

"We were supposed to be having fun."

"My eardrums still hurt."

"Like I said, I could tell it wasn't your scene." She sounded brittle, even to herself. "Which suggests we don't have much in common."

Anger to match hers sparked in his voice. "I'd say we have a hell of a lot in common. We do the same kind of job. We have to live with having seen things other people never do. We care about the same things. We both live alone, isolated partly by our jobs. We probably shop at the same goddamn grocery stores. We could exchange recipes."

She was fighting a losing battle; she could feel it. But "stubborn" was Abby's middle name. "That's one more thing we don't have in common. I'd have to tell you my favorite microwave dinners."

"You don't cook?"

"Not if I can help it."

"I like to cook. See? We're made for each other."

She laughed. She couldn't help it. "All right, all right," Abby conceded. "Just let me know whether to wear shorts or a strapless dress, okay?"

"I will." Amusement played a bass note in his slow, deep voice. "As soon as I decide."

"But tell me one thing, will you?" Get it out front, she decided.

"Sure."

"Why?"

"Why?" Shea echoed. Although he asked, "What do you mean?" he sounded wary, which meant he'd guessed.

"Why me? Why are you so determined? Is it just the challenge?"

Again he was silent for a long moment. Again his voice had changed, although this time she couldn't quite tell what he was thinking. "No. I like a challenge. But...no."

"What, then?"

"You're beautiful."

"No more so than plenty of other women. Most of whom are easier to get along with than I am."

"You look lonely."

"Lonely?" Abby gave a derisive laugh. "You're seeing things."

"I don't think so."

"And if I am? So what?"

"I thought we might...connect. That's all. Do we have to analyze our relationship already?"

She let out a sigh he wouldn't be able to hear. "No. I just wanted to find out whether it was my charm that had gotten to you."

"That was it," he agreed.

"Friday," she said. "Call me before then."

ABBY HAD A LATE DINNER: a spinach salad and microwave penne pasta. Afterward she tried to read, but found her attention wandering. TV seemed like an idea, but nothing on tonight grabbed her. Using the remote control, she turned the television off just as her telephone rang.

"Abby, Scott here," Meg's husband said. "I'm up at the ski area. Just leaving. I need you to look at something. Can you come?"

"Up to Juanita Butte?"

"I'm sorry. I know it's late." He sounded grim. "But I really think you need to see it."

A chill stirred the hair on her nape. "What is it?"

"I'd rather you see for yourself," Scott repeated.

"Is this something like the fire?"

"Yeah. But uglier. Or maybe it just got to me personally, I'm not sure."

"All right." She was already slipping her feet into canvas sneakers. "Don't move. I'll be there in twenty minutes."

The clock on the dashboard said 9:04. Here at midsummer, night was just settling, the first layer like purple gauze, the next denser and darker.

The mountain loop highway climbed fast, bare at this time of year. Abby rolled down her window and breathed in the distinctive scent of pine and earth ground from red lava. The air was cool, dry; it became cold as the elevation rose. In the shadow of the mountain, nightfall came more drastically. She switched on her bright lights, noting how little traffic she met.

The ski area parking lot opened before her, huge, bare and empty, a paved sea that looked alien in the middle of nowhere. She could just make out the bulk of the lodge and the first lift towers rearing above. Patches of snow still lay up there, where plows had formed towering banks during the winter. Her high beams spotlighted Scott McNeil's Jeep Cherokee, parked in its usual spot behind the lodge. He was half sitting on the bumper.

She parked next to him and climbed out, flashlight in hand. "What is it?"

A big man with dark auburn hair, he nodded toward the driver's side of his Jeep. "Over there."

She circled the back bumper, then stopped, shock stealing her breath.

A child's car seat sat beside the driver's door, facing the parking lot and highway. Just as Emily's car seat had, the freezing cold night when she had been abandoned.

A doll was buckled into this seat. Abby trained her flashlight beam on it, wanting to be mistaken about what she was seeing.

The doll was plastic, the kind with arms and legs and a head that attached to sockets in the hard body.

This one was missing its head. From the empty, blackened socket, trickles of red dripped down the pink dress.

CHAPTER FOUR

IN THE BRIGHT illumination from the headlights of his Bronco, Ben Shea squatted beside the child's seat. Abby overheard his muttered profanity.

"I shouldn't have called you," she said to his back. "I know there won't be any fingerprints, and there sure as heck aren't any witnesses." She glanced involuntarily around at the dark parking lot. "I didn't think. I assume this is connected…"

"The doll's neck socket is seared." He sank back on his heels and shot her a look. "Why wouldn't you call me?"

"You were home…"

"Staring at the boob tube. Trust me, you didn't interrupt anything." Ben stood in a lithe movement. "This is some scary bastard. You're probably right. We won't find fingerprints. But I needed to see this. I'd have been fried if you hadn't phoned."

Abby could hardly look at the mutilated doll. How must Scott feel, having found this obscene echo of the past?

Emily had been abandoned here in her car seat two and a half years ago. Scott and Meg had found Emily's mother, murdered, the next day. Somehow she must have persuaded her killer to leave the baby where Scott would find her. But he had admitted once to Abby that he still had nightmares about having bunked down at the lodge, as he used to do sometimes. In his dreams he came out to his car at dawn to find the little girl dead. Frozen, eerily pink in the morning light. He'd shuddered when he described the nightmare.

Abby stole a look at Scott now, standing behind the Jeep, staring at the night. Was he, like Abby, wondering whether somebody sick enough to create such a macabre tableau was capable of carrying through on the implicit threat? Was Emily in danger? Will? Or Meg, too pregnant to defend herself from attack?

Were they all?

"Okay," Ben said, startling her from her dark thoughts. "Scott, I wasn't here the night you found Emily. Tell me about it. What did this guy get right? What did he get wrong?"

They discussed positioning; both times, the child's seat had faced the parking lot and highway, so that Scott had been looking at the back as he approached.

"Which may have been chance, with Emily," Abby pointed out, "but tonight you know darn well this SOB did it so Scott couldn't see what was in the seat until he got here. Suspense and shock value."

Scott grunted. "Otherwise, this is a different kind of car seat. It's been around the block. Look at the tears. They didn't make ones like this anymore even when..." his hesitation was barely perceptible "...when my ex-wife and I had our little boy. I think these were designed for babies up to six months old or so. Most of the seats nowadays are convertible."

Ben made a note. "We'll check secondhand

stores. We can talk to people that had garage sales this past week or so, too.''

"The...doll isn't dressed anything like Emily was that night.'' Scott rubbed his chin. "Maybe he didn't feel the need to bother with details. God knows, the general message has plenty of punch.''

"You could say that,'' Ben agreed dryly. "On the other hand, maybe our friend was dependent on what was printed in the newspaper. Anybody remember how much was written about Emily?''

"Not that much,'' Scott said. "Remember, we didn't find Shelly's body until the next day. By the time reporters heard about Emily's abandonment and made the connection, nobody was asking what Emily had been wearing. The focus was on Shelly's murder and her heroism in saving her daughter. Somebody might have mentioned that Emily was warmly dressed. I don't remember.''

None of them could help looking at the doll, her bare plastic legs sticking out from beneath the skirt of the pink dress. Socks on both feet, one shoe.

No head.

Ben seemed to shake himself. "Let me get some pictures, and then I'll take the seat. We'll let the crime lab go over it. The guy had to have touched the doll. Maybe he was careless.''

Abby doubted it.

The flash created bursts of brilliant light as Ben worked. After he was done, he put on latex gloves and lifted the whole child seat into the rear of his Ford Bronco. When Scott wasn't watching, Abby saw Ben lift the doll's skirt. Earlier, before he came, she had done the same. Thank God the creep who'd wrenched the doll's head from the socket, who'd dripped fake—or real?—blood from her neck, hadn't committed any outrage with a sexual connotation on the realistic plastic body. She was equally grateful that Scott, who didn't spend his days dealing with the scumbags of the universe, hadn't even considered such a possibility.

Or else he'd checked before Abby's arrival.

Ben peeled off the gloves and held out a hand to Scott. "I'll let you know what we find. I'm sure I don't have to tell you to keep an extra close eye on Emily."

"Have Will be careful, too," Abby added. "Make sure Meg locks the doors even during the day."

A muscle jumped in Scott's cheek. "You can be sure of that."

"Has anyone told Murray what's going on?" Ben asked. "I assume Will spends time with him."

"There's more than that." Ashamed to be responsible for excluding Jack Murray—who was, after all, Will's father as well as the sheriff—Abby admitted, "He's pretty closely connected to us. As much as Daniel's mother."

"Because of Will?"

"Because he dated Meg." She added deliberately, "And me. If…if this is someone who knew us back when…"

"Does Meg know…" Scott hesitated, giving a brief cough. "I'm sorry. It's none of my business."

"No. She doesn't know I dated Jack." Abby heard the bite in her voice. "Why would she care?"

Looking stiff, Scott said, "I spoke out of turn."

"Tell her." Abby gave an elaborate shrug and

turned away. "Suit yourself. It's more Patton history. We know how to write it."

"You can tell her," Scott said quietly. "If you choose to." He touched her shoulder. "Thanks for coming, Abby."

She watched him climb into his Jeep Cherokee and slam the door. A moment later, he backed out.

Aware of Ben, a silent witness to her admission, Abby said, "Well? What do you think?"

"That you're pretty steamed at your sister. Care to tell me why?"

"Why's a good word." She hugged herself, the chill of a mountain night penetrating her bones. "As in, why would I? Like I said, it's ancient history. Which means it's none of your business."

Sounding brusque—which she deserved—Ben said, "Unless it has something to do with these cute little messages you guys are getting. Or with the fact that you're mad at me for no reason I can see."

"I'm not mad…" Abby bit her lip. She hated having to apologize. Hated knowing she had behaved so gracelessly. "I'm sorry. This scares me. I don't like feeling scared. I'm taking it out on you."

"Tell me straight." Ben hadn't moved; his voice hadn't softened. "Do you think the fact that you and your sister both dated Murray has anything to do with these threats?"

She walked a few steps, closed her eyes. Sighed. "No. Who knows what set this guy off? Not some guy my big sister and I both saw."

"Just don't hold back on me."

Abby whirled around. "I haven't yet! I wouldn't. It's not me I'm scared for."

He moved then, taking a step toward her, lifting a hand as though to touch her but stopping short of doing so. "This was symbolic. We have no reason to think this guy intends to hurt Emily."

"Maybe not," Abby said tautly, "but there's a pretty strong suggestion of violence here, wouldn't you say?"

"We'll find him."

"Will we?" She didn't let him answer. "It's late. I really do appreciate you coming, Ben. Call me."

"I will." He watched her get into her car. Just before she backed out, he knocked on the window. Abby rolled it down a few inches. "By the way, forget the strapless dress. Wear a bathing suit and shorts. We're going rafting. I'll bring a picnic."

"Rafting." It was almost a physical wrench, this transition her mind had to make from the bloodied headless doll, from the man she and her sister had shared. Blankly, Abby said, "You mean, Friday."

"As early as you can get off work."

"White-water rafting?" Maybe he was a man after her own heart, after all. The physicality, the adrenaline rush, of battling the river sounded like just the panacea she needed.

"Nope. We're going to drift. Listen to the birds and the breeze, soak in some sun. Maybe swim. Spend a lazy couple of hours."

Die of boredom.

He smiled as if he'd read her thoughts. "Trust me. It'll be fun," he said with gentle mockery.

Abby's heart lurched. No, she doubted if she'd be bored. Not with Ben Shea. Irritated, maybe. Defensive, uncomfortable, maybe sexually aroused. But definitely not bored.

"Right," she said, and rolled up her car window. He slapped it with his palm, and walked away.

His headlights were in her rearview mirror all the way down the mountain. She could hardly wait to turn off the main road and escape him.

Why, oh, why, had she agreed to go out with a man who made her feel so edgy?

RENEE ASKED MEG and Abby to meet her the next day for lunch. Abby had a suspicion she knew why.

Meg was the last to arrive, waddling into the café on the main floor of the antique mall. They often had lunch there. The minestrone soup and berry cobblers were unbeatable. Abby, for one, rather enjoyed the irony in the old police station where Daddy had reigned. His office now held shelves and nineteenth-century armoires overflowing with quilts and antique lace. He wouldn't have minded old guns. Lace he would have hated.

Today the three sisters talked about the doll in the car seat and what it meant until the waitress brought their orders.

Renee didn't even look at hers, waiting only until they were alone again. "I'm pregnant," she announced.

Meg lumbered to her feet. "Oh, Renee! Congratulations!"

They hugged and squealed a couple of more times. Abby felt like a fifth wheel.

But when they stepped back from each other and she saw their wet cheeks, she found her own eyes were stinging. Rising to her feet, she said quietly, "You'll be a great mother."

Renee sniffed. "Thank you."

"Funny, isn't it," Meg mused as they resumed their seats. "The idea of us as mothers."

"I wouldn't know how to begin," Abby heard herself say. "Being a mother, I mean. You're so patient, Meg."

"I guess I'm lucky," she said. "I remember Mom the best. She was gentle, always willing to listen or to admire the latest artwork or whatever. I can still hear her giggle, as if she was a kid at heart. She loved us."

"I can't even picture her face." Again Abby was startled to discover she was the one speaking. She often chose to tune out these conversations. "I mean, now I have pictures," thanks to Meg, "but they're all I see when I close my eyes and try to envision her. Sometimes I have this feeling…" She frowned. "Feeling" wasn't quite the right word. Fleeting impressions: a brush of a soft hand, a scent, a murmured voice telling stories, a warmth and sense of security. Even such amorphous memories always ended up swallowed by emptiness and loss, as if her later hurt had acted as WiteOut, obliterating her mother's existence. In frustration and anger at herself, Abby blurted, "I was old enough when she left. I *should* remember."

Meg touched her hand. "Maybe the memories will come back. After I had Will, I found myself thinking about Mom all the time."

"But you'd just seen her," Renee argued.

"Yes, but…" Meg shook her head. "It's as if

she's two different people for me. The mom from our childhood, and the one I watched die. I...never linked them, not really. Does that make sense?''

Her sisters nodded. Sandwiches sat untouched.

''The one I remember is *Mom*. Our childhood mother. I say something to Emily, and I think—Mom said that, too. Or I have little ways of doing things, and I realize that I'm imitating her. Have you seen that poster that says, 'I looked in the mirror and saw my mother?' Sometimes that's how I feel. As if she's part of me.''

Renee nodded solemnly. ''We're imprinted. Like goslings.''

''Right.'' Meg leaned forward, elbows on the table, silverware clinking. Her face was alight with enthusiasm. ''And you are, too, Abby. You *were* old enough. Your conscious mind can block some things out, but I'll bet motherhood will trigger your subconscious. Through your own words and behavior, you'll recover her.''

A sharp slice of pain tightened Abby's voice. ''Do I want to?''

Meg's eyes held warmth and understanding. ''She loved us.''

''She left us.''

''Yes, she did, and I've never forgiven her.'' Meg looked inward for a moment and then laid her hands on her belly, which shifted and bulged briefly. Voice soft, she asked, ''But does one betrayal, however huge, discount everything that came before it?''

Once Abby would have said yes without hesitation. Once she would have been certain she didn't *want* to remember her mother's touch, her mother's face. Daddy hadn't been perfect, but he'd been there. The first rule of parenting: you must be present in your children's lives.

But perhaps Daddy had been there for the wrong reasons, and their mother gone for the right ones. Or at least for ones that a grown-up Abby could understand. Even forgive. She wasn't sure yet, but she was coming around.

"I don't know," she said now, to her sisters. "I don't remember what came before."

"You will." Meg smiled comfortably. She touched her swollen belly with clear meaning, the tenderness she felt for her unborn child expressed in the small gesture. "I know you will."

Abby swallowed a lump in her throat and gave a brief nod. Then she turned to Renee. "What did Daniel say to your news?"

"Hallelujah." Renee grinned and at last reached for her sandwich. Around a big bite, she said, "You know I'm the one who wanted to wait to have children. He'd have been happy if I'd been pregnant the day after our wedding."

"Or the day before," Meg murmured, devouring her lunch, too.

Renee poked her. "Are you impugning my virtue?"

"Yup." Meg's mouth was full.

Without interest, Abby moved the greens of her salad around with her fork. "Meg, did Daniel talk to you last night when he got home?"

Her sister gave her a strange look. Once she'd swallowed, she said, "Well, of *course* he talked to me. Unless... Oh, God. He didn't tell me something.

Was there a note? Or…'' Horror crossed her face. ''Not something really perverted?''

''Nothing like that,'' Abby said hastily. ''I meant…about me.''

''Did he talk about you?'' Both sisters stared at her. ''What do you mean?'' Meg asked carefully.

Oh, Lord. Now they probably thought she'd confessed to poor Scott that she was madly in love with him.

''Nothing like you're thinking. No, don't tell me what you're thinking. I don't want to know.'' Abby concentrated on arranging the slices of cucumber along the rim of the plate. ''It's about Jack.''

She felt Renee stir. God, this was complicated. Jack Murray had gotten Meg pregnant in high school, had later dated Abby, and had become Elk Springs police chief and been Renee's boss. Abby had told Ben the truth; Jack's life was inextricably tangled in the Pattons'.

Meg set down her sandwich. ''What about Jack?''

''I've never told you this, but I dated him for a couple of months. After I graduated from high school.''

''From high school?'' Meg sounded poleaxed. ''But he's my age. You'd have been…eighteen? Nineteen?''

Abby made a face and looked up. ''Oh, it wasn't right away. I was maybe twenty. You're not Methuselah, you know. Jack was only…twenty-five or six.''

''Well…I guess that's true.'' The plain facts, ma'am, didn't make Meg any happier, clearly. ''But…Jack?''

Old defensiveness sharpened Abby's voice. "Is it so unlikely that he'd find me attractive?"

Her sister caught on and said quickly, "No! No, of course not. It's not you I'm thinking about."

It wasn't her Jack had been thinking about, either. Oh, no. It was always Meg.

"You mean Daddy, don't you?" Abby tried to make her shrug careless. "But you see, Daddy *was* the point. I finally got that. Jack had to have one of us just to prove to himself—and to Daddy—that he could. I didn't get it at first. The time he called me 'Meg' was something of an eyeopener."

"You're angry because you think he was using you as a substitute for me."

"Yup." She imitated her sister's offhanded way of saying it.

"You blame me."

"No." Abby thought it was true. Now. "Back then, I resented your perfection. All I ever heard about was how beautiful Meg was. How smart. How sure of herself. So I have my first big romance, and I find out that the guy wished I were you. Which made me feel…unworthy, in comparison to you."

"Abby…" Meg lifted her hands and then let them fall, as if she didn't know what she'd intended. "I can't help it. I have nothing to do with what people said, or what Jack did."

"You made everyone love you, and then you left." Oh, how childish she sounded!

"So we're back to that," Meg said unhappily.

Abby sighed. "No. I'm just telling you how I felt. It was my own stupid fault for getting involved with Jack in the first place. The truth is…" She hesitated, having only recently understood this for herself. "The truth is, I think I started dating him because I wanted to…be your equal. Prove I could be as good as you were. Do you see? So I was setting myself up for Judgment Day: 'No, you aren't. You can't be Meg.'"

"Because you're Abby," her big sister said quietly.

"Lucky me."

"Abby…"

"No." Her smile twisted. "I was just kidding. Most of the time, I like myself fine. I'm just trying to explain why I never told you about Jack. I…had lots of complicated feelings about it, and him."

"And now?" Meg asked.

"He's history." To her surprise, she realized it was true. She had a sudden image in her mind's eye of Ben Shea bending down to talk to her through her car window.

"Good." Meg bit her lip. "What did our esteemed father think about you dating Jack? I mean, considering he'd beaten the crap out of him because he had sex with me."

Abby grimaced. "Daddy approved. Which I suppose was what Jack wanted. Funny, because *I* wanted Daddy to be mad. *I* was trying to walk in your footsteps. Daddy wouldn't even let me do that."

"I guess Jack had redeemed himself by that time," Meg said wryly. Looking at Renee, she asked, "Did you know all about this?"

"Vaguely," Renee admitted. "But remember, *we* didn't know everything that had happened with Jack and Dad. All those undertones, we were missing."

Meg made a face. "Gee, what a shame."

"It really is history," Abby said, abruptly tiring of the whole business. "You want to hear current events instead?" At their nods she said casually, "I'm going out with Ben Shea. He's taking me rafting tomorrow night."

Both sisters whistled at the same time, then grinned at her.

"He's hot," Renee said cheerfully.

"And nice," Meg agreed. "Go, girl."

Abby nibbled on her salad. "Has he been married?" she asked, probably not fooling either sister with her casual tone. "Do you know?"

"Do I know?" Her sister gave her a look. "I'm a detective, remember? I asked. He said no. Having a nature like a two-year-old who's programmed to ask endless questions, I said, 'Why?' Man's man that he is, he shrugged and grunted."

"Ah." Renee turned bright eyes on Abby. "A mystery."

"Probably not one I'll bother with," Abby said airily. "It's not as if I want to marry the man."

Renee smiled cherubically. "Hey, don't knock it till you try it. I've had almost three years of experience, and let me tell you, marriage ain't half bad."

"I'm having a pretty good time myself," Meg said. She scrunched up her nose. "I had a better time when I was a little more athletic. If you know what I mean."

Abby's eyes widened. "You aren't still… That is, you don't want to…"

"Yup. I am. I do. The spirit is willing. If only the flesh weren't so bulky."

They all giggled, a sound of unexpected harmony.

Over the rest of lunch, they talked about how morning sickness and the duties of the Elk Springs police chief would mix.

"At least," Renee said, "my office is at the end of the hall closest to the bathroom!"

"Good, because you're going to need to pee all the time a little later along." Meg sighed. "I wish I hadn't thought of that. Now I have to go."

Renee reached for the check. "I've got to get back to work anyway."

"Yeah, me, too." Abby handed her sister some bills. "Listen, I'll call you both if I hear anything from Ben. About last night."

The reminder sobered them all, tainted the mood. She was sorry to have reminded them, reminded herself.

"Group hug," Renee said unexpectedly, and it felt both awkward and comforting for the three grown women to hold each other, if only for a moment.

"IS THIS THE LIFE, or what?" Ben's strong throat rippled as he tipped his head back and swallowed a swig of soda. "The river, you, me..."

The sun warm on her face, her fingers trailing in the cool water, Abby couldn't complain. The rubber raft formed a firm but supple back support, just enough breeze played over her skin to keep the late afternoon heat from being uncomfortable, and Ben Shea was sprawled a couple of feet away, wearing only shorts.

What more could a woman want?

"Mmm," Abby murmured. A cove of reeds

passed on one side. On the other, pines and manzanita climbed above the riverbank. The campground where they had launched the raft slipped out of sight around a bend. "A little white water would be fun, though," she said wistfully.

"I get enough excitement during the day." His mouth tilted into a wicked smile, although she couldn't see his eyes behind dark glasses. "Not that I couldn't use a little at night, too."

"White water is just as good."

He lifted his brows, voice a sensuous rumble. "Oh, I don't think so."

Warmth unfurled in her belly, and her mouth was suddenly dry. He was...beautiful. Solid with muscle, but not the kind sculpted in front of a mirror. The golden hue of his skin hadn't come from a tanning booth, either, she'd have been willing to bet. His hands were clasped behind his head, bunching the muscles in his shoulders, elongating those in his stomach. Dark hair dusted his chest, vanishing lower, although if she were to unbutton the waistband of his shorts, she would be sure to discover...

Heat crept over her cheeks, and he smiled with the arrogance of a man who knew what a woman was thinking. She tried to be unpredictable, but this time...

"You don't drink beer?" She nodded at the cooler as if her imagination hadn't been stripping him.

"Booze eats holes in my stomach."

"You have an ulcer?"

The yellow raft bumped up against a gravel bar, and Ben handed her his can of pop, then lazily levered himself up and stepped out to free the raft.

"Not according to the doctor." He guided it back out into the slow current, wading until the water was knee deep before he half rolled back in. "He says my guts are processing stress."

Abby contemplated that. "Is this a chronic problem?"

"I have to be careful, but I can live with it. As long as I take a few hours like this now and again."

"Stress." She swallowed the first chuckle. The second escaped, rolled into outright laughter.

"What's so goddamn funny?" he growled.

"It's just..." She was laughing so hard, her eyes watered. "Me. I mean, you have trouble with stress..." Giggles overcame her. "And then you ask me out! Me!"

He didn't like being laughed at; what man did? But after a moment, a reluctant grin tugged at his mouth. "Yeah, you've got a point. But I thought you'd be *fun*. Isn't that what you promised me?"

Abby hiccuped and corralled more giggles. "No, *you* were supposed to be fun. *I* didn't make any promises. I said we'd be too much alike, remember? That's why we should never have gone out."

"Are you telling me you have ulcers?"

"No, I get headaches," Abby told him.

Groaning, Ben let his head flop back onto the air-filled rim of the raft. "Maybe you were right. We weren't meant to be. We should end this here and now. Out. Out, damn spot!"

He rose like a tidal wave from the sea and snatched her up. Abby was swearing and laughing both when she hit the water. Swearing because he'd thrown her; laughing because she kept a good grip on his wrist and knew he was coming, too.

The river was an icy slap. She sank three feet to the bottom, feeling the eddy as Ben hit, too. Abby surfaced like a mermaid, loving the cold rush of current, the slippery rocks underfoot, the hot sun on her shoulders as she emerged.

Ben shot up as fast as she did, water slicking his dark hair to his head, glittering in beads on his skin. He stood, his wet shorts outlining lean hips and the bulge in front. "You were the one who was supposed to be walking the plank," he said, moving purposefully toward her. "I was the captain. Now you'll pay."

Abby scrambled backward, slipped, splashed and finned away from him. "Yeah, yeah," she mocked. "Men always like to be the captain. They like to *think* they're in charge. Maybe you're wrong. Maybe *I* was the captain."

"Do you ever let anybody else be the captain?" Suddenly he was serious.

Suddenly she was, too. She told the truth. "No."

"You were right." A groove in his cheek deepened. "We have too much in common. But I'm going to kiss you, anyway."

Abby rose fluidly to her feet. "Good," she said breathlessly.

The hands that gripped her upper arms were icy cold; his lips took hers with the same shock as the tumble into the cold river water. But this kiss would have melted a thousand-year-old glacier. No ice could have survived.

Their mouths warmed one another. Their bodies

met with a smack, building heat where wet flesh pressed wet flesh. His tongue thrust aggressively into her mouth; she felt a stab of sensual pleasure/pain in her belly, as if he had entered her more intimately, more completely, at the same moment. Abby circled his tongue, tasted his mouth, with hers. A groan shuddered through him; through her. His hands gripped her buttocks, lifted her so that she felt him pressing, seeking, demanding.

She arched her back and met him in that way, too, until at last he wrenched his mouth from hers.

"We're going to make love in the middle of the goddamn river if we don't stop right now."

Abby lifted his sunglasses so that she could see the fire in his eyes. "If we don't stop right now," she said breathlessly, "we may never catch up with the raft."

"Catch up…?" Comprehension came; he swore and swung away from her until he saw the yellow raft bobbing downstream. Swore again. "Damn it, woman! Why didn't you say something? It's getting away!"

Abby smiled, oh, so sweetly. "But aren't we having fun now?"

The dangerous, slow grin he gave her packed as much wallop as the kiss. "Oh, yeah. We're having fun. But—blast it!—I borrowed the raft, so I'd better fetch it."

"Yes, Captain, sir."

Another profanity floated over his shoulder as he splashed, thigh-deep, through the river water.

Abby laughed.

CHAPTER FIVE

SOME THINGS had to be done. Abby sat at her desk, making a call she didn't want to make.

Jack is really steamed, Meg had told her. Meg, of course, hadn't told him, "Abby is the one who thought we should keep family business from you." She'd taken the heat. Abby couldn't let her do that.

Abruptly a ring was cut off. "Murray, here."

"Jack, this is Abby Patton."

The small silence gave away his wariness. "Abby. What's up?"

Dive in. Her philosophy. "I'm the one who kept Meg from telling you about the creep who seems to be stalking us. I...didn't think it had anything to do with you."

"Or my son?" His voice was gritty.

"Or Will." She wouldn't let him intimidate her. "After the first incident, I figured I was imagining any connection to my family. But when the doll... Well, I should have called you."

"Why didn't you?" he asked uncompromisingly.

Why didn't she? *Truth or dare.*

Truth. "I'd never told Meg you and I dated. I...tend to avoid the subject of you."

"This has nothing to do with you and me," he growled.

"Maybe it does." She stared unseeing at her bulletin board. "We don't know what it has to do with. Like it or not, you're messed up with us in more than one way."

His grunt could have been a rueful laugh. "Messed up with. That's one way of looking at it."

"I told her."

Caught off guard, he repeated, "Told her?"

"Meg. About us dating. About you calling me 'Meg.'"

He swore. "It was a slip. I knew who you were. You look alike."

But one Patton sister wasn't as good as the other, she ached to say. *Why wasn't I as good? Why Meg? Why not Abby?*

But what was the point? He'd say the same things he'd said back then, the same things he was already saying: a slip of the tongue, it meant nothing.

She shrugged, as if he could see her. "Water under the bridge. I just didn't want you annoyed at Meg. I asked her not to involve you. Now you need to be involved, so I owned up. Hey, as if any of us care anymore."

Only *she* cared. Or thought she did. But again she saw Ben, this time rising like a phoenix from the river, droplets shimmering on his bare skin, and she wasn't so sure this slice of her past held the same sting it once had.

"It was a long time ago," the county sheriff agreed, and if his voice sounded hollow, that, too, was probably in Abby's imagination.

"I WISH I had better news." Ben slouched beside Abby on the park bench, facing the river; velvety green lawn sloped down to the water. Two weeping willows dipped toes in the slow currents beside the bank. A concrete Depression era bridge built by WPA workers spanned the Deschutes just downstream.

Today he and Abby had met for a paper bag lunch at the downtown park. This stretch of river was civilized, bounded by homes and parks, in contrast to yesterday's wilder banks. Unfortunately, the park didn't allow for any privacy.

An asphalt path followed the river. Ben idly watched the parade of energetic souls jogging, in-line skating or cycling as they passed.

In response to his discouraging news, Abby sighed. "Thank the guys at the crime lab for working overtime on this one. No, I'll thank them myself. And, to tell you the truth, I'd have been stunned if they *had* found any prints."

He grunted his agreement. This bastard was a smart one. He knew how to set a scene, and he knew how to do it without leaving any trace of his own presence. Since so far there wasn't a murder—hell, so far there wasn't a *crime,* except for motor vehicle theft—Ben's hands were tied as to how much time he could devote to this investigation.

Yesterday, when he argued, his lieutenant had shrugged. "Shea, you know how many weirdos are out there. Ninety-nine percent of them are never going to do more than send nutso notes."

"This one has gone further than that already."

"He hasn't personally contacted anybody."

Ben set his jaw. "Yet."

"We've got to do a 'wait and see' on this. You know that."

Yeah. Ben knew it. He didn't like it, but he knew it. He might even have said the same thing, if he were assigning manpower.

Now, Ben crumpled his lunch wrappings into a ball and lobbed it at the nearest garbage can. With a muffled ring of metal, the paper ball dropped in.

"Oh, you're good," Abby teased.

"Not good enough." He laid an arm along the back of the bench and faced her. "I checked out the old newspaper articles. The one about Emily..." He grimaced. "It could have been a play-by-play for our guy. The journalist had interviewed Scott, who talked about walking out to the parking lot that night, thinking somebody had left a box beside his Jeep because the back of the car seat was toward him. He was right: there was nothing about what she was wearing."

Abby said thoughtfully, "Chances are, this guy would have had to read old reels of the *Journal* at the library. He wouldn't have wanted to ask at the newspaper office."

Ben could tell where she was going with this; he cut her off. "You don't have to ask at the library. The paper is on microfilm now, and all you have to do is sit down at one of the machines. The *Journal* and half a dozen other newspapers are available on the shelf above the microfilm reader. I had to wait my turn. Somebody is probably sitting at the damn thing all day long. The librarian wouldn't have noticed any one individual."

Abby huffed out a frustrated breath.

"There is also the possibility this creep has been keeping a scrapbook on your family. Assuming he's had a grudge long."

He felt her shiver, knew what it would feel like to learn that a stranger had been collecting mementos of your life like family photos in an album.

Abby didn't want to buy it. "Remember," she argued, "that when Scott found Emily, he had no connection to us. He and Meg didn't marry until four months later."

"Their wedding announcement was in the *Journal,* too."

She shivered again. "What if he's not watching the newspaper? What if he's watching *us?*"

Their reflexes involuntary, Ben and Abby scanned the park. Only one man was even glancing idly toward them, and he laughed suddenly and scooped up a little girl who raced into his arms. Nobody was watching.

But then, this SOB was careful. They already knew that.

"Let's not get paranoid," Ben suggested gruffly.

"Right," Abby agreed, too briskly.

Ben stretched; he had to get back to work. "Another possibility. This guy may be getting a charge out of scaring people. Maybe not you or your sisters in particular. Have Renee see if anything with the same tone has been reported recently. I'll do the same at the sheriff's department."

"Okay." In exact imitation of him, Abby wadded up the paper bag that had held her sandwich and lofted it at the can. With a metallic ring, it went in.

"I'm good, too." If her smile looked a little forced, he wasn't calling her on it.

"Yeah, you're good." Even in her uniform, she was sexy as hell. Her blond hair was up in some roll on the back of her head that looked fancy—maybe like a picture of Princess Grace. The simplicity highlighted the elegance of Abby's cheekbones, the lushness of her mouth, the catlike slant of her eyes.

He wanted to kiss her. But he was in uniform himself, and he suspected their employers—and the Elk Springs public—would take a dim view of their police officers necking in front of God and everyone.

"Dinner?" he asked, without much hope. They might have had a good time yesterday out on the river, but he hadn't breached her fences yet.

So he was surprised when she said absently, "Mmm, sure. If you can make it late. I'll be on until at least six. And this afternoon's job will be dirty."

Thus the steel-reinforced boots. They were kinda cute with her relatively dainty feet.

"Call me when you get home," he said.

"Okay." Still she sat there, frowning straight ahead. When he waited, she said finally, "Maybe this *isn't* aimed at us."

"Maybe not." He didn't believe it; too much attention had been given to detail. But he didn't like her worrying.

"You should hear Meg go on. She isn't sure you're going to give us your all."

"She knows me better than that."

"Having Emily in preschool isn't good for Meg. Gives her too much time to twiddle her thumbs and worry."

"She's never been much for sitting around," Ben said with faint amusement. "Or getting twitchy."

Meg didn't fuss. He'd tried to treat her like a woman when they'd first worked together, but she hadn't let him get away with it. A smarter, gutsier cop he didn't know. He couldn't see her being ready to stay home and change diapers.

"No, and heaven help us if she has too much more time on her hands." Abby gave him a sidelong look. "Meg says you've never been married."

"That's right." He smiled. "You asked."

"A girl can't be too careful."

"True." He let himself touch her nape. Delicate wisps of hair clung to his fingertips. "I asked, too."

"You don't hate knowing your boss has had me?"

Her tone mocked; her eyes had the wildling look that had gotten to him before. She was trying to be brazen, but a hint of uncertainty, of nerves, peeked out like the glow of a bedside lamp through the curtains.

"Murray?" Ben named the county sheriff carelessly, but she was right: he didn't like the image of the big man bedding the defiant woman beside him. He wondered if it had been good for her. If she'd had "fun." "I don't mind unless you're pining for him," Ben lied.

"'Pining?'" The uncertainty in her eyes vanished with a choke of laughter. "Oh, yeah. My heart's broken. Can't you tell?"

"I think your heart has been broken," he said slowly. "Was it Murray?"

Her laugh died. "Don't be ridiculous."

"Then who?"

"Nobody. I'm not sure I have a heart to be broken." This smile was cool, flip. "Fair warning."

"Taken."

He walked her to her car, touched her cheek, and basked in her smile, sweeter than she probably realized. Watching her drive away, Ben wondered about his sanity. He'd be drinking antacid the way most people did coffee if he kept seeing Abby Patton.

His mouth tilted up in a rueful smile. Hell, he could get to like the taste of Mylanta. He'd rather drink the stuff than date a woman so bland he didn't need it. You had to give her that much: "bland" was not a word you'd associate with Abby.

The thing he liked about her was her bluntness. Too many women specialized in sugary manipulation. If there was an Olympic gold medal in cracking the whip without raising your voice above a hushed, sweet murmur, his mother would have no competition. Give him a choice anyday. Ben would rather plunge knowingly into corrosive acid than be lured into it like a cat lapping up a deadly pool of sweet-flavored antifreeze.

His guess was that, while Abby might give the impression of being bitter tasting, he was going to find she was as sweet as apple pie on the inside. Everybody had defenses. Hers was: I am tough. I am modern. I am heartless. Unlike some people, she believed her own line, Ben thought.

It was actually pretty touching that she kept warning him off. She was being considerate. Which was one of many reasons he wouldn't take her warnings.

No, he'd find out for himself why a gorgeous blonde with a nice family felt the need to take cover like a Vietnam vet when a car backfired. What had happened to her? Who was she inside that tough shell?

Ben gave himself a shake. He had a day waiting, and he was standing here with his head in a cloud.

Starting down the sidewalk toward his own car, he reminded himself that romancing Abby was fine and well, but keeping her safe came first.

Challenge *numero uno:* figure out who had it in for the extended Patton family. Who blamed them for the ills of the world?

And this guy with a grudge against the Pattons: what did he plan to do about it?

STANDING IN HER DOORWAY at six-thirty that evening, Ben smiled engagingly. "Here's the plan. I have groceries in the car. I come in, cook dinner here. Or you come to my place, and I'll cook there. Your choice."

Alarm thrummed in Abby's chest like the roar of an oncoming avalanche. He was getting cocky. Two dates, and he wanted through her front door. To speak metaphorically.

She pretended to consider. "What if I want door number three?"

"And behind it is?"

"Alexander's." The classiest restaurant in Elk Springs served French provincial and required dressing up. "Or Mario's." The best pizzeria sounded as if it would take less effort.

Ben Shea's face went serious. "You really want to go out?"

"No," Abby admitted. "But I'm not sure I'm up

to having you bustling around my kitchen in an apron.''

''My kitchen is fine,'' he said agreeably.

The man was a mule. He was as bad as her sisters. ''All right, all right,'' she conceded. ''But I follow you in my car.''

''I could run you home.''

''My car.''

He was getting mildly ticked; she could see it. ''I won't hold you hostage. I know how to take no for an answer,'' he growled.

She didn't blink. ''Prove it.''

''You're an irritating woman. You know that?''

Abby laughed. ''I keep telling you, and you keep ignoring me.''

''My mistake.'' He cleared his throat. ''Let's get this show on the road.''

She had to admit—to herself, not him—that she was curious about his place. You could tell a lot about a person by what kind of bed he slept in, what he hung on the walls, kept in the kitchen cupboards, sat on to watch TV. Most men, she could predict: this guy'll live in a condo, modern art on the walls, white bedspread, convenience food; that guy'll be a slob, nailed-up sheets taking the place of curtains, the fridge full of beer.

Ben Shea... She'd be disappointed, Abby knew, to find he lived in an apartment with furniture rented by the month. She wished she'd thought to ask Meg.

What she didn't expect was to find that his home was eight blocks from where she'd grown up. The Bronco ahead of her pulled into the driveway of a small 1920s era house right next door to where her best friend in elementary school had lived. Lots were narrow on this street, the foundation plantings old and dense, overpowering the modest houses.

Ben's was different. A cedar picket fence outlined flower beds and a pocket lawn. A blue-purple clematis in full bloom buried a trellis and girdled a porch pillar. The house itself was painted seafoam green with dark teal and white trim. Home sweet home.

Abby was torn between love at first sight and...what?

Chagrin, because her own place was so sterile in comparison? What did it say about her, that she didn't know how to garden, lived in a condo where pets weren't allowed, didn't cook, checked books out of the library instead of buying them?

And what was she doing, dating a man whose idea of fun was growing annuals from seed or trying a new casserole?

She parked and got out. Ben had lifted the hatch door on his Bronco and was grabbing the bags of groceries. She went to help him.

"You garden." Brilliant.

"Man's got to have a hobby," he said negligently.

She spotted a dainty calico sitting on the porch rail. "And a cat?"

His expression softened as his gaze followed hers. "Cindy—Cinderella—is only sorta mine. You'll see."

As they mounted the porch steps, the cat didn't so much bolt as flow away, there one minute, gone the next.

"Feral," Ben said. "But she's young enough that

I'm convincing her life doesn't have to be a bed of thorns. She lets me pet her now.''

He was coaxing a wild cat to give up her independence. Become as cozy and domestic as the garden and the cute seafoam-green house. Abby's unease increased.

To her relief, the inside was less complete than the outside. Wood floors needed refinishing—she knew better than to think he'd cover them with carpet. A crab pot with a glass top served as a coffee table; a plum velveteen slipcover dressed up a couch with a sagging seat. The warm-colored wood of the dining room table glowed, however. Abby was compelled to trail her fingers over the silky surface as she passed.

"Cherry," Ben said, uncannily reading her mind.

"Oh. It's beautiful."

"Bought it at a garage sale for thirty-five dollars." He paused, nudging open a swinging door with his hip. Beyond was an old-fashioned kitchen. "It was painted red. Olive green under that."

"I haven't been to a garage sale since I was a kid."

"You find great stuff for a song." Putting away groceries, Ben didn't seem to notice her discomfiture. "I have this iron bed—it looks like lace, really cool. Cost ten bucks. I sanded the rust off, primed and painted." Enthusiasm changed the tone of his voice. "And remind me to show you my rolltop desk. I always wanted one of those."

"Me, too." She'd forgotten; all those nooks had appealed to her over-organized nature. And she'd liked the idea of secrets lurking beneath the rolltop.

With genuine curiosity, she asked, "How do you find the time to do all this?" She gestured around. "Strip paint and dig up flower beds and tame a cat."

His big shoulders moved in a shrug; he didn't look at her. "It's what I do. I don't party. I don't drink except for an occasional beer in front of a football game. I like growing things, I like treasure hunting. That's how I have fun."

"Why aren't you married?" she asked bluntly. "This isn't a single guy's house."

A muscle jerked beside his mouth. "It's mine. I'm single."

"I didn't mean..." She swallowed her words. "Can I help? I mean, with dinner?"

"I'm the cook, remember? And I know what you didn't mean." His voice was rough, his expression remote. He pulled a cutting board from a drawer and began chopping green onions. "You sound like the guys in the department. They can't figure out why I don't want to booze until I'm puking my guts out."

She settled on a stool and watched him work, his big hands quick and sure. "Why don't you?"

He shot her a look from beneath dark brows. "Does that sound like fun to you?"

"No. But I'm not sure weeding does, either."

He worked in silence for a moment, lifting the cutting board and scraping the onions into a bowl, then beginning on a stalk of celery. Abby had about decided he wasn't going to answer when he said abruptly, "I never figured I'd marry. No reason not to want a real home, is it?"

"Not marry?" Oh, God. He was gay. Or... But

her imagination failed her. He couldn't kiss her like that, could he, if...

"My parents have a crappy marriage. It didn't inspire me to want to bring home a little woman."

Startled by a stinging sensation in the general area of her heart, Abby wondered in astonishment whether her feelings were hurt. *She* hadn't been planning a stroll to the altar. Why should she mind that he was honest enough to admit now, up front, that his intentions weren't honorable?

"Good thing I'm not a little woman, then." Damn it, she hadn't succeeded in sounding as uncaring as she'd intended. She'd betrayed pique, if not wounded feelings.

He shot her one of his inscrutable looks. "I did use the past tense."

"What?"

Chopped celery joined the onion in the bowl. Peeling a carrot, he said calmly, "When I bought this house, I didn't figure I'd ever marry. I'm not so sure anymore."

The warmth spreading in her chest got sopped up fast by the sponge of her panic. "What do you mean?"

A smile glinted in his gray eyes. "Just that I've finally noticed some people do have happy marriages. I'm not like my father. I don't have to pick a woman like my mother."

"Not exactly a compliment." Rude, maybe, but also the safest thing she could think of to say.

Wham, wham, wham. The knife severed the carrot into perfect coins. "You'd have to meet her," Ben said evenly.

Telling herself she was glad that he didn't want to go into messy emotions, Abby was nonetheless too curious not to ask, "Do your parents visit?"

"Sure." He reached for another carrot. "Mom doubts I could run my life without her...counsel."

Maybe she couldn't remember her mother very well, but Renee seemed to have the same attitude. If nagging was a parental skill, she had it down pat. "From what friends tell me," Abby said, "most parents feel that way."

"Yeah." He paused in his chopping, moved his shoulders as if loosening tension. "Do you miss your folks?"

"I hardly remember my mother. I was eight, but... She's faded. You know? And Daddy..." Her nonchalance sounded faked. "I suppose I should miss him, but the truth is, he wasn't all that nice. I didn't have any trouble with him—I mean, I didn't fight with him the way Renee and Meg did—but we weren't best buds, either. I'd come by to see Renee, and he'd sit in that big recliner of his in front of the TV and hardly even glance up. Except sometimes I'd come over in my uniform and he'd tell me I looked like hell. No. What he'd say is, 'You look like a man.' Which is ironic, because he really wanted a son."

Ben swore softly. "What a fool."

Even with all that had happened, she hadn't really thought about her father in a long time. Not seen him, clear as day, with his feet up in that big brown recliner, a beer in one hand and the remote in the other, lines drawn deep on his forehead, perpetual irritation tugging heavy brows together.

"You know me. I wasn't about to shrivel inside.
I'd say, 'Dang! What a surprise! You've got a son,
after all. Maybe we should hit the bars together.'"
She smiled wryly. "Or maybe I'd say, 'Hey, boys
are better, anyway. I can be one.'"

Abby wished she hadn't remembered the time
she'd said that; she'd toughened up by then, but not
enough. Driven to finish the story, she made a face.
"Daddy being Daddy, he told me if I couldn't even
make a decent woman, I sure as hell wouldn't measure up as a man."

She saw the way the muscles in Ben Shea's jaw
spasmed; heard the rage in his voice.

"May he rot way down under."

"He wasn't that bad," she said in surprise. No,
not surprise. She'd *wanted* Ben to react as he had,
angry on her behalf. She'd wanted him to dislike her
father, sight unseen.

Why, when she was the one always defending
Daddy to her sisters when they summoned bad memories?

For the thousandth time Abby reminded herself
that her father had been there. Nothing was more
important. Maybe he hadn't been a great parent, but
he hadn't deserted his children, either.

"Meg's told me some about him." Ben whacked
the knife down so hard on the chopping board, it
jumped. "You're wrong. He was that bad."

"Meg and he butted heads."

"The bastard hit his own kid. He broke her arm."

Suddenly the room felt close. Claustrophobic. Air
was short. Abby didn't want to think about voices
screaming, tears, trips to the emergency room. Lies.

She hopped off the stool. "Let's skip old times, okay? They weren't that much fun. Can I snoop around your place?"

He gave her another look, but let her get away with cowardice. "Yeah, sure."

The sound of chopping faded behind her as she wandered around the first floor of the small house. The living room she'd already seen, but she smoothed her hand over the cherry table again and took a closer look at the titles of books on his shelves. Some how-to: one on refinishing furniture, half a dozen garden books, one on paint techniques like stippling. She studied it for a moment, intrigued. She'd been planning to paint her bathroom; maybe she should try this rag or sponge thing, layering two shades of the same color.

She snapped the book shut. Oh, right. She wanted to spend all day playing with paint.

Still, the room on the cover looked pretty cool, Abby admitted as she shelved the book and scanned further. Sci-fi, a lot of the fiction that she'd read, too. Some stuff left from college, she'd bet: a behavioral psychology text, geology, art history, Revolutionary War, economics. And literature: Shakespeare, Dickens, Virginia Woolf, Chaucer and Thomas Hardy.

Abby wandered on, studying the watercolor of two children on a foggy beach, then poked her head into the bathroom, tidy, unimaginative and obviously little used. She was just reluctantly deciding it would be rude to go upstairs, when Ben called from the kitchen, "Go on up. The rolltop is in my office up there."

He'd done that rag thing in the hall, she saw, liking

the result. This floor held a bathroom and two bed-
rooms, one of which he'd turned into a home office.
The oak rolltop dominated, but Abby tried out the
leather club chair and hassock and peeked out the
window at the backyard. A big vegetable garden
filled the center, and roses flung long arms over the
cedar fence.

This bathroom was messy and lived-in. A razor
was plugged in, a comb held strands of dark hair,
and a wet towel had been flung over the glass door
to the shower. The sight made Abby wary. He'd
showered for her. Did that suggest he had ambitious
post-dinner plans?

She couldn't resist pausing in the doorway to
Ben's bedroom. He might notice if she pushed open
the door, but she saw enough through the crack to
stand transfixed. The white-painted wrought-iron bed
was beautiful, complemented by a blue-and-white
quilt. Irish chain, she seemed to remember that pattern was called. The bed was neatly made—in her
honor? The effect was somewhat marred by the up-
turned crate serving as a bedside stand.

But the bed… Her gaze wouldn't leave it. Despite
the lacy twirls of iron, the effect was simple, spare.
Plump pillows were encased in navy blue. A blue
rag rug covered the bare wood floors.

She could see Ben sitting on the side of the bed,
hair tousled, wearing…pajama bottoms. Shoulders
and chest bare. She knew what he looked like. He
was groaning, running a hand over an unshaven chin.
Morning.

Or… She gripped the molding. Now he was *in*
bed, pillows piled behind him. Lamplight fell on the

book he read with that intense concentration she knew well. His skin had the golden glow of a Michelangelo painting; she wanted to touch it, flatten her palm against the smooth planes of his chest, touch her lips to his strong neck, feel muscles shift and tighten...

"So," he said from so close behind her she could feel the vibration. "What do you think?"

Abby swallowed. "I think, when you bought that bed, you intended to share it with a woman."

"Maybe." He didn't touch her. "Do you want to be that woman?"

Yes. *Yes!* She closed her eyes, made herself breathe in, breath out. Put him off, she thought frantically.

"Who knows?" She shrugged. "It's early days."

"Is it?" He sounded odd.

She pasted a smile on her face and turned. "Did you come to get me because dinner's ready?"

By the time she fully faced him, his expression had gone blank. No, she told herself, she'd imagined the raw desire that turned his eyes the color of mercury.

"Right," he said woodenly. "Dinner's ready."

As he turned away, she stole a last glance at the bed through the narrow opening. This time, she saw herself in it. Her hair fanned across the pillow. The quilt tangled around her and the man she'd just turned down.

Something that might be regret—couldn't be longing—knotted beneath her breastbone.

He would ask again.

Abby wished she knew what her answer would be.

CHAPTER SIX

RESPONDING TO HER fourth call of the day, Abby pulled into the parking lot of the Fred Meyer store. The fire truck was still at the far end; she'd gotten here only three minutes after her beeper went off.

She parked behind the apparatus and grabbed her camera first thing. The excitement had drawn a crowd, some pushing carts loaded with groceries, others who'd probably been on their way into the store. Abby automatically snapped photographs of the crowd, as she did at the scene of any suspicious fire. Arsonists often liked to watch either the fire itself or the firefighters. That was the whole fun of it.

Later she'd pore over the pictures, look for familiar faces, for expressions that were too avid. Right now, she wanted to see the scene itself. The dispatcher hadn't known what kind of vehicle had been ignited, only that the caller said it must have been deliberately set.

"Excuse me," she said, pushing her way through the crowd, which parted as people saw her uniform.

The first shock was the sight of the blackened bicycle in a rack. Water dripped from it; firemen were rolling up the hose. Soot formed a plume pattern on the concrete block wall behind the rack.

But the real shock came when her nephew Will

broke away from the cluster of cops and firefighters. Relief flooded his face. "Aunt Abby! I said they should call you."

He was too old to hug in public, but she gripped his hand and he squeezed back so hard it hurt. "Is this your bike?" she asked.

The sixteen-year-old nodded. "See, Dad's taking me camping for a couple of days. But he's not coming till three, so I rode my bike down here to pick up a few things." Will took a deep breath. "I locked it up the way I always do. Only, I heard the siren, and when I came out, it was like this."

The lieutenant joined them. "The boy says you're related."

"That's right." She gave Will's shoulders a quick squeeze.

Will asked, "Do you think...well, that this has anything to do with the doll? And that pickup truck?"

He was both scared and excited by being the center of attention, Abby could tell. She remembered being that age, when nothing really bad would ever happen to you.

"Unfortunately, that's a possibility," she said, trying to hide how disturbed she felt. "But let me ask you something, Will. Did you tell any of your buddies about those incidents? Maybe a girlfriend?"

He flushed. "Well, sure. I mean, Jessica... I tell her lots of stuff. And Ron. And I guess a couple of the other guys were there. Why?"

"There isn't anybody who really dislikes you, is there? Like this Jessica's last boyfriend?"

So, have you ticked anybody off recently? Ben's

question rang in her ears. But she often asked some version of the same question. This could be a copycat crime. The fact was, teenagers set half or more of all arson fires.

"Jessica wasn't dating anybody special before me. And…jeez. I don't have any enemies, if that's what you're asking." Will turned to stare at his bike, tires flat, metal seared. "You think somebody would do this just…well, because they thought it would scare me?"

"I think that's exactly why somebody set this fire." Her voice was grim. "All we have to do is figure out who and why."

"It smells like lighter fluid," Will said tentatively. "Scott uses it when he barbecues."

"He's right," the lieutenant said. "Anybody could have put his hands on a can."

Abby sent Will off to call his mother.

"And don't scare the daylights out of her," she said sternly. "Say, 'I'm all right, Aunt Abby will drive me home, but somebody set my bike on fire.'"

"Yeah, okay," he said, and headed for her car.

With the lieutenant watching, she examined the scene of the fire. With no fuel but the flammable liquid—and after a tentative sniff, Abby was inclined to agree that it had been charcoal lighter fluid—the fire would have been quick, hot and brief. It had blackened the metal on the bike, the rack and a circle under it.

"Witnesses?" Abby asked.

"The woman over there called it in." The lieutenant nodded toward an old Buick big enough to substitute for a Hummer. An old lady so tiny she barely peered over the dashboard sat behind the wheel. His mouth twitched. "She'll tell you all about it. And then tell you again."

"You notice anyone special watching? Hanging around?"

"You kidding? Once the smoke roiled up, every shopper in the parking lot joined the gallery."

"Nobody you knew?"

"My sister-in-law." He sighed. "Nobody stood out. Except her. I never have liked her."

"Just so your brother does."

"Never liked him, either." The lieutenant briefly looked morose. "You need us anymore?"

"Nah, I'll take care of it."

"Then we'll roll." He waved, and the truck roared to life. Abby had a rare pang of regret for what she'd given up when she became an investigator. The rumble of the trucks, the siren and lights, the adrenaline rush and the teamwork. Every call was an adventure; you never knew what you'd find, from a hibachi that had sparked a porch railing to a five-alarm fire that might claim lives. The only smoke she smelled these days was the acrid stench that lingered after a fire like a bad memory. The closest she came to danger was the possibility of falling through a charred floor.

But she did like finding answers, and she liked making a difference. She'd discovered a way she could do both. It might not offer the thrill and fear of plunging through a smoky doorway when flames were shooting out windows above you, but then, she didn't have any desire to die young, either.

At peace once again with her decision to leave the

force, Abby walked over to the boat of a car. Ten feet away, she recognized the old lady.

Mrs. Chadwick had taught Abby's third grade class, retiring after that year. Abby had thought she was ancient then.

Bright dark eyes studied Abby with all the sweetness she remembered. The year with Mrs. Chadwick had been one of Abby's favorites. Eighty years, give or take a few, had folded Mrs. Chadwick's fragile skin into intricate creases, reminding Abby of an aerial photograph of a river valley.

Without hesitation, her former teacher said, "Why, it's Abigail Patton!"

Abby crossed her arms on top of the open car door and smiled with surprise and unexpected delight. "You remember me."

"I remember all my students," she said with satisfaction and a brisk nod. "I'm lucky. Age hasn't robbed me of my memory. I taught your oldest sister, too, you know."

"Meg."

"Meggie Patton." She sounded reminiscent. "I read that she married a young man who works at the ski area."

Abby wondered how her brother-in-law would like that description. "Scott is the general manager."

Mrs. Chadwick waved that off. "Nice girl. Behind on her reading, but all she needed was some extra time. Some children are like that. I still volunteer as a tutor at the elementary school. Those poor children probably think I'm going to die when I'm there, just klunk down face-first on the table in the library. I always tell them I'll at least step out in the hall before

I quit breathing! Wouldn't want to frighten them!''
She chuckled in delight at her own sense of humor.

"Mrs. Chadwick." Abby waited until she had the
elderly lady's attention again. "The boy whose bike
was burned is my sister Meg's son. Will Patton."

The creases deepened. "Meggie's son? Why, I
don't seem to recall him. Perhaps my memory is going, after all. Was he a good reader? If I never tutored
him…"

"He has his nose in a book all the time. But you
wouldn't have met him anyway. Meg was in the Air
Force, you know. She raised Will in Germany and
Southern California and Alabama. On Air Force ba-
ses. They only moved back to Elk Springs a couple
of years ago, and by then Will was in high school."

"Well." She gave a birdlike nod. "That does explain it. Thank you. I don't like to think I'm getting
forgetful. And I do try to notice the children of my
former students."

Sweat rolled down Abby's back and baked her
bare arms and shoulders. It was hot as sin in the
concrete parking lot, with no breeze stirring the air.
Every passing driver slowed and stared.

"Mrs. Chadwick," she asked, "did you see the
person who started the fire?"

"What a terrible thing! Why would anyone do that
to a nice boy?"

"I don't know." Abby could be patient when it
counted, and she could tell there was no hurrying her
former teacher. "That's what we need to find out. It
would help if you saw someone running away from
the fire. Or driving away."

"There's so much traffic here," Mrs. Chadwick

said apologetically. "I'm sorry. Now I feel as if I ought to have been more observant."

"He may have been gone before you came along. And this lot is rather out of the way."

The huge Fred Meyer store had four entrances, the busiest one into the grocery section. But they were on the back side, just around the corner from the chain-link fenced garden department, the loading docks beyond. The parking lot was busy, but nobody would have paid attention to someone briefly hovering over a bike. Abby had immediately spotted the small twisted piece of blue plastic beneath the bike rack, which she was quite certain would turn out to be a cheap plastic cigarette lighter. The perp could have poured the lighter fluid all over the bike and ground, then gone back to his car. Flick on the lighter, wrap a piece of tape around it, and give it a toss as he drove by.

Piece of cake.

"Mrs. Chadwick, thank you," Abby said, straightening as she saw Will coming. "If you happen to remember any vehicle you passed on the way into the parking lot, give me a call. Here's my card."

She introduced Will, leaving him to politely listen to reminiscences of his mother's third grade school year. She snapped photos, scraped soot off the bike, gingerly lifted the lump of melted plastic with tongs and dropped it into an evidence bag.

Mrs. Chadwick was still talking, Will still nodding although he rolled desperate eyes Abby's way when she went into the store to speak to the assistant manager. Not real happy about the cleanup involved, he would have progressed into active resistance if she'd given him orders, the way most men would have. Instead she smiled sweetly, batted her eyes shamelessly and asked for his cooperation without implying that she could coerce it—which she could. He warmed immediately and let her persuade him to post a notice for clerks asking them to request names and phone numbers from any customers who mentioned seeing the fire.

Exiting through the hardware and garden part of the store, Abby almost turned around and fled back inside. Oh, God. Not only was Jack Murray standing there with his son, but Ben Shea had arrived, as well. She never wanted to see Jack, and she sure didn't look forward to the combination of both men.

They stood stiffly, both staring at the bike but with a good ten feet between them.

She was too late to flee. As if he'd been keeping an eye out for her, Ben turned the moment she stepped out into the hot sunlight and watched as she walked toward him. This being one of his days off, Shea wore khaki shorts and a faded green tank top that exposed a sinful quantity of tanned, muscular chest and shoulders.

Abby immediately thought about last night's good-night kiss. The sight of Shea's bed during her tour of his house had fueled her desire, which flared hot the moment his mouth captured hers, but he didn't take the kiss anywhere. She'd felt his passion, but he banked it. Groaned, set her away from him, walked her to her car and told her to drive carefully. All without once saying, "I wish you'd stay tonight."

Maybe he thought he'd already asked, and she'd already answered.

Maybe he had, and maybe she had.

But to herself she could admit that she'd wanted to be asked again. Abby hated knowing that about herself. It seemed so coy, so like the games teenagers played. She had always believed she was above that kind of silliness; that she could be straightforward. Yes or no. Why tease?

What she hadn't known was how confused she could feel about a man.

Will spotted her. "Here's Aunt Abby."

"Hell of a thing," Jack said, frowning. "I called Shea. I hope you don't mind."

"No, that's fine. I'd have phoned him myself. How are you, Ben?"

"Good." He touched her arm.

She felt the minor, innocent contact all the way to the soles of her feet. No, not innocent, Abby recognized immediately. He was establishing possession, for Jack's benefit.

"Witnesses?" Ben asked, as though nothing else was going on.

Gritting her teeth, Abby decided to let him get away with it.

Will had already told them about Mrs. Chadwick.

"I'll develop my film," Abby said. "I can show the pictures around to the clerks inside who worked this shift. See who they know, who can be eliminated. You all take a look, too. Could be you'll turn out to know someone."

Jack grunted. "Do your best. I'll take Will home now."

Abby kissed Will's cheek, an unusual gesture for her. "Take care, kiddo. Jack...watch your back."

Their eyes met in a moment of understanding; he nodded, and walked away with his son. Abby watched them go, astonished to realize she felt absolutely nothing for him. He was an old acquaintance; her sister's high school boyfriend; Butte County sheriff. He'd been her first big romance, but she'd blown it out of proportion. Neither she nor Jack had been after real love or even sex; they'd both had agendas having more to do with Daddy than with each other.

Sure, Jack had hurt her feelings. In his eagerness to flaunt a Patton daughter on his arm in front of Daddy, he'd never spared a thought for her.

Or—for the first time she wondered—had he not realized Meg was the one he really wanted? Perhaps he'd fooled himself, just as Abby had.

Because she'd damn near begged him to flaunt her. She'd wanted to prove she could accomplish anything Meg could.

She'd behaved as poorly as he had. Or had deluded herself as thoroughly, depending on how you looked at it.

So why hadn't she let go of her hurt years before? she wondered in vague astonishment before turning to Ben, who was watching her thoughtfully.

Abby didn't give him a chance to get personal. She wasn't ready for that.

Instead she expressed her frustration with the case. "What next? Should we be guarding Emily's swing set?"

"Scary stuff, when a nut targets a kid," Ben said. "Assuming this is our guy."

"I asked Will whether he'd made anybody mad lately."

His sharp glance told her he, too, remembered asking her the same question.

"He says no."

They talked about how this one was set, then Abby's beeper went off. "House fire," she said after calling in. "Nothing to do with us, thank God. But I've got to go."

"Can I come by tonight?"

He sounded...serious. Not as if he wanted to hang out at her house, talk about the day, but rather as if he had something to say. An emotion next door to fear clogged her throat for a second.

"I'll be home," she said.

He nodded and stood by as she got in her car. "See you around seven," Ben said, and Abby drove off.

"ED PATTON was a hell of a cop. I don't care what they tell you." Vince Feist drained his can of beer and tossed it toward the plastic recycling bin on his front porch. It clattered short, but he didn't even turn his head. "These young guns, they want to think they can do it better, but they're nothin' but a bunch of pansies." He gazed blearily at Ben. "Pansies, you hear me?"

"I hear you." Ben pretended to take a swig of his beer. It was going warm and flat, and he rolled it on his tongue before swallowing as little as possible. The retired police sergeant didn't seem to have noticed that Ben wasn't popping tabs as fast as he was, and Ben would just as soon keep it that way.

Feist staggered to the kitchen and back, the screen door slamming behind him. "Too bad I don't have a little lady to fetch and carry for me. Had one once. She left me for a mechanic. Hated my work. Always hated it."

With a grunt he settled back into an Adirondack chair. His small house was neat but devoid of personality. The woman's touch was what it lacked, some men would have said; Ben wasn't one of them.

"The ladies aren't tough enough to stay married to a cop, and now they're trying to *be* cops." The balding, paunchy ex-sergeant shook his head in disgust. "Not just cops. Police chief! God Almighty!"

From where he slouched on the broad porch railing, Ben observed mildly, "Our new police chief is a Patton."

Feist flicked the tab off a new can of beer, seemingly unaware of foam spilling over his fingers onto his skinny legs. "She's a girl! Might be Ed's daughter, but she's a girl, anyway. He'd be the first to agree with me. Women don't belong in uniform." He took a swallow of beer, wiped his mouth with the back of his hand and swore. "Ed must be rolling over in his grave."

Ben surely did hope so. He liked the idea of Ed Patton resting real uncomfortably. A bed of nails would be about right.

"You know many people who feel the same way?" he asked, keeping his tone idle, conversational. He hadn't considered the possibility that the guy setting the fires might be a disgruntled ex-cop, say, who was targeting the Pattons only because they were women police officers.

"That a woman shouldn't be wearing that badge?" Feist worked up a wad of spit and let it fly. "Goddamn right, I do! Anybody who served under Ed would feel the same. I'll bet even Jack Murray would agree, for all he's in the Patton girls' pockets. He's not a man wants to take orders from a woman. Hell, Jack Murray learned at the master's side."

Ben's impression was that Jack Murray was a decent guy who probably had no problem with a cop who happened to have breasts instead of a dick. But he wanted information from Vince Feist, not an argument.

"Was Ed ever involved in any cases that involved fire?" Ben asked. "His youngest girl is an arson investigator, you know. She was talking the other day, said she thinks one of her cases must have something to do with her dad. Somebody who holds a grudge, maybe."

Feist gave a bark of laughter. "Might be plenty of those! What cop doesn't leave a trail of grudges?"

"True enough," Ben agreed easily.

"Fire." The ex-sergeant rubbed a hand over a bristly chin. "Sure. I can think of a few, off the top of my head. One that sticks in my memory was this nutso, thought he'd get his girlfriend back if he torched her house then rescued her. Ed was a patrolman, then—must've been about 1975. Yeah, I remember when his youngest was born. Anyway, a neighbor spotted this guy with the gasoline and called it in. Ed got there just in time to see the stupid bastard light a match. Boom." He paused to contemplate. "The girlfriend was pissed at Ed. Former boy-friend is fried to a crisp trying to torch *her* house, and she's screaming at Ed for not stopping him. Go figure."

Domestic violence cases were every cop's worst nightmare for this exact reason. A wife might be try-ing to stab her husband one minute, but let a cop grab the husband and haul him off her and she'd turn the knife on the cop. On the other hand, Ben had to wonder: what if Ed Patton held back and *let* the idiot light that match, and the girlfriend knew it?

"Before that there was the house Ed burned down. Guy was holed up in there, see, taking potshots at every cop who stuck his head out. Ed shoots back, and next thing we know fire's flickering in the win-dow. Later they figured out he'd hit the bastard, who fell into the fireplace. Dead of winter, did I mention that? Late 1969-'70. Lit his clothes, and next thing the rug and drapes were blazing away." He shook his head. "By the time we worked up the guts to storm the house, that baby was roaring away. We could see he was dead, but we couldn't get to him anyway."

"Anybody else killed in that one?"

"Don't think so. Though somebody probably holds a grudge," he said the word with peculiar em-phasis, savoring it, "over that one, too. Figures we oughta called a shrink or something. Let the SOB shoot until he'd worked out his anger, maybe. Who knows?"

"Works that way, doesn't it?" Ben was increas-ingly disgusted by Vince Feist, who clung to his in-tolerant views and his memories of a time when men were men. Had he thought it was okay when Patton's daughter wore a cast because Daddy broke her arm? Did women get what was coming to them in Feist's opinion, too?

"Oh, and a real messy one." The retired cop gestured broadly, knocking his can of beer off the broad arm of the chair. He wavered bending over to pick it up. "Damn," he muttered. "Good brew down some worm gullets."

"Use 'em for fishing."

A crack of laughter. "Goddamn! You've got it right! I'll raise super worms!" With a drunk's care, he poured the rest of the beer through a crack in the floorboards. "Catch me the biggest rainbow trout ever with beer-fattened worms!"

Ben waited with croding patience as Feist staggered back into the house and came back with two cans of beer. Ben caught the one tossed at him.

He waited until Feist had cracked open what must be his eighth. "A messy one?" Ben prodded.

"What?" Feist blinked. "Oh, yeah. Fire. Hot damn, that was an ugly one. Woulda been about…" He had to think hard. "Say, '85? Somewhere 'bout then. Hey, what do you care when these were, anyhow?" He peered suspiciously at Ben.

"Somebody is threatening one of Ed's girls. He might not want them to be cops, but he wouldn't want 'em hurt, would he? His family?"

"Hell, no, he wouldn't!" Feist took a long drink. "Where was I?"

With some more prodding, Ben got him back on track. Fellow was threatening to kill himself and his family, the ex-sergeant said.

"Ed didn't hold with going easy on that kinda jackass. Talking all day, gettin' 'em psychiatric help..." Feist shook his head and kept shaking it, as if he didn't know how to stop. "Ed razzed him, you know? Just kept pushin' and pushin'. Figured the guy'd come charging out of the house. Or put a bullet in his own head. Ed thought if he made him mad enough, he'd forget about the wife cowering in the corner, or the kids upstairs."

"But Ed was wrong," Ben said slowly. This one sent chills up his spine. It was the kind of story he'd been looking for.

"Yeah. Son of a gun." Feist still looked puzzled, as if no one could have foreseen a tragic end to the story. "Guy squirted gasoline everywhere and lit it. Later we found out he'd shot his wife and one of the kids first. Then he lit the fire and swallowed the gun."

"There were other kids?"

"Yeah, one other. Firemen got him out an upstairs window. Kid was okay. He'd hidden from his father."

And heard it all, every word. His dad screaming for help, and a cop egging him on. He'd have heard his mother's cries, the three shots that left him alone.

He'd have reason to hate.

Bingo, Ben thought.

CHAPTER SEVEN

BEN STOOD on Abby's doorstep and stared at her front door. His hands stayed at his sides. *Not a good idea,* he warned himself.

He was an idiot to put pressure on her. Ben knew that, and he was going to do it anyway.

He had to. He was getting in deep, and he had to make sure he wasn't alone.

Letting out a long breath, Ben rang Abby's doorbell.

She opened the door and said, "Hi," sounding a little shy. Her hair was wet and slicked to her head; she wore a pair of denim shorts over a racing-style bathing suit that was so snug he could see her nipples.

Ben couldn't seem to tear his gaze from her chest. Her breasts were small, high and perfectly shaped to fill his hands. "Hi." He had to clear his throat. "Uh, can I come in?"

"Oh." Her voice squeaked. Her tongue touched her lips in an endearingly nervous gesture. "Yes. Of course!" She stepped back. "Um, I was going to take a quick shower and get dressed. Do you mind waiting?"

He wanted to peel that bathing suit off, step into the shower with her and watch the hot water sluice over her pale silken skin. He wanted to brace her against the wall of the shower and fill her, watching the surprise and pleasure in her eyes.

He didn't ask. He intended to ask for as much as he figured she was ready to give. Maybe more. But he wouldn't push his luck.

"No," he said, sounding scratchy even to his own ears. "No. Go ahead."

Not taking her gaze from his, Abby backed toward the stairs behind her. Stumbled over the first one. Cheeks turning pink, she nodded to her left. "The living room is over there."

"Can I look around?"

The idea unsettled her; unease flickered in her eyes. But she pressed her lips together and nodded. "Turnabout's fair play."

"I won't open drawers." *Make you bare your secrets.*

"I didn't, either."

True enough; she hadn't pressed him when he cracked a few emotional drawers, so to speak. He'd been kind of hoping she'd give a tug.

He heard the shower start only seconds after she vanished up the stairs. Ben began in the living room.

The furniture was modern, spare. Different than anything he'd have chosen, but the soft simple pieces in black leather suited Abby. He'd expected modern art, the kind with a black canvas and one splash of red. Instead, a watercolor hung above the couch. Shades of gray showed a foggy day at the beach. Only the muted yellow of a man's—or was it a woman's?—rainslicker added color. The figure in the picture had pants rolled up despite the obviously chilly morning—and Ben was sure it was morning, although he couldn't have said why. Something bobbed just out of reach on a wave. A Japanese float, maybe, the glass ball having astonishingly survived a journey across the Pacific Ocean. Now it tantalized, drew the morning walker into the cold fingers of surf.

The painting said a great deal about Abby. It held a mystery. The man or woman was alone on the beach; even lonely, like her. Ben had sensed the bleakness in her, but also the willingness to reach for something magical.

Satisfied by the insight, he moved to the dining room, tiled in terra-cotta, dominated by French doors that led onto a small patio where she tended at least a few pots of geraniums and verbena and nicotiana with its night fragrance.

In the kitchen, white cupboards and pale rose countertops were standard "condominium." The row of antique glass bottles on the windowsill weren't. Light poured through the amber and purple and green glass, casting a rainbow on the cream floor. The bottles came in myriad shapes, squat, delicately rounded, narrow-necked; some were embossed with writing, one with the outline of a horse's head.

More magic.

He could live here, Ben thought with relief. He'd been afraid he couldn't, that they would be too far apart.

Her collection of bottles would look glorious on his windowsill, too.

As she would in his bed.

Ben felt her presence rather than heard her arrival. He turned to see her watching him from the kitchen doorway, apprehension in her eyes like a ghost whose existence she would deny.

"Pretty," he said, nodding toward the bottles.

She looked past him toward the window. "They're...nothing special at night. But in the late afternoon or summer evenings, like this, the color is so wonderful I feel like a painter must. I move them around, replace them when I find a new one I can't resist. I've always loved bottles."

"Are you hoping for a genie?" Ben asked softly.

Her smile was wry, even a little sad, although he guessed she would have denied that, too. "I found that bottle on the end—the amber-colored one— when I was a kid. I was cutting across the yard of an abandoned house, and for some reason the lip of the bottle sticking out of a rubbish heap caught my eye. I took it home, soaked it for days, and then when it glowed like Spanish gold from one of those wrecked galleons, I rubbed it and made a wish."

"Which probably didn't come true."

Her laugh had a rueful ring. "Actually, it did. It was a minuscule wish, all I dared make. Something like, 'Please let Dad be in a good mood today. Please don't let him and Meggie fight.' But you see, there must be a genie in the bottle, because Dad was, and they didn't. So I kept making wishes. Sometimes they came true, but often not. So I thought, maybe every bottle held a genie, but they were only good at granting certain wishes."

As she came toward him and the glorious array of bottles in the window, she had the expression he'd seen on faces of children at a carnival. As if she were still hoping.

"And you're still collecting," Ben observed.

As if with a physical wrench, she looked away from the bottles. Her tone became offhanded. "So I am. But only because I think they're pretty. They let me be an artist. I've outgrown wishes."

"I'm sorry," he said, and meant it.

"Oh, for Pete's sake!" She boosted herself onto the counter and swung her feet like a careless kid. "Are we mourning the loss of childhood? Sorry, but mine wasn't so terrific I can join you wearing the willow, as the Victorians put it. I'm glad to be all grown up."

"Do you want children of your own?" This was edging near his reason for coming, but the question came of its own accord, from pure curiosity, not as part of a planned progression.

"I don't know." She made a face. "I worry a little that I wouldn't know how to be a mother. And…oh, diapers gross me out." She shrugged. "What about you?"

"Yeah, I think I would." He saw them, these mythical children: a stocky dark-haired boy and a skinny blond girl with merry blue eyes.

"But you said your parents don't have a very good marriage. Right? Would *you* know where to start?"

He hid his satisfaction; she'd given that tug.

"They loved me. They might have done some things wrong, but they got that right."

"Nice for you." This time her scrunched nose was meant to hide remembered hurt.

"You love your sisters."

"Yeah?" Her gaze challenged him. "So?"

"Then why doubt your capacity to love a child?"

"Oh." She didn't want to look at him anymore. "I didn't say that I did. It's just such a huge responsibility. I couldn't live with walking out like my mother did."

He smiled. "You're not a quitter."

Her chin shot up. "How do you know?"

"Instinct."

Abby rolled her eyes. "Men always say that."

"Have you had dinner?" he asked.

"No." She hopped down. "It's a microwave night. Want to pick one from my store?"

"You're offering me dinner?" Ben pretended to look astonished.

She grinned, and he saw the imagined little girl in her. Had Abby lived her entire life with fear and a sense of inadequacy? Had she ever really been a little girl?

"I have a big microwave."

"Ah. Sure, I'll take a look."

He chose a penne pasta with sun-dried tomatoes; Abby a beef burgundy frozen dinner. While the microwave hummed, she dug in the refrigerator for salad makings. "No, I can do this much," she insisted, when he offered to help.

She poured them both milk, apologizing because she had no beer or wine to offer.

"Like I said, I'm not much of a drinker." Ben carried the glasses of milk to the table.

Abby followed with place mats and silverware, which she set out. "See? I'm being fancy for you."

"I'm honored," he said gravely.

Her gaze flitted to his; flitted away. She hadn't asked if he'd wanted to come over this evening for a reason. Maybe it hadn't occurred to her that he'd be stupid enough to try to corner her.

Over dinner, she told him about the house fire, which she was reasonably sure had started in a dining room light fixture. "It had those little clear bulbs. The homeowner said she always buys the forty watt ones, and the fixture was designed for twenty-five watts max. People always do that. They never look. You put seventy-five or a hundred watt bulbs regularly in your average socket, sooner or later you're going to have a fire."

"So it wasn't arson."

"Nope. Definitely not."

"You talk to Meg?" he asked.

Abby nodded and set down her fork. "She was pretty upset. Will may be six feet tall, but he's still her little boy. She wants me to find somebody who saw something."

"Do you think you will?"

"Nope." Abby sighed. "If some good citizen had actually seen the guy light that baby, he'd have reported it. Either nobody saw, or somebody did who doesn't like cops, or..." She gestured helplessly. "Teenagers wouldn't want to rat on each other. You know that."

Ben frowned. "The guy was taking a chance. A lot bigger chance than the other times."

"He had to have been following Will." Fear edged her voice at the idea. Was this unseen watcher following all of them some of the time? Was he outside the windows now?

Well, let him watch, Ben thought coldly. Let him come close; the closer the better. They'd get the bastard. This was a family of cops; he suspected that even Meg, close to nine months pregnant, was still packing her gun.

Ben said thoughtfully, "You did ask Will whether he noticed any car a couple of times? Maybe turning ahead of him? Pulling into the parking lot?"

She shook her head. "Nothing."

They ate in silence for a moment. Both knew the reality; they could do little but wait, stay sharp.

He told her then about his visit to Vince Feist.

"I remember him." She shivered. "He was one of Daddy's cronies. They hunted together. I haven't seen him in ages. He was a pallbearer at the funeral. I think—" her gaze became far away "—he mourned our father more than Renee and I did. Which I suppose says something about us."

"Or about him," Ben said, hiding his intense dislike.

Her eyes focused on him again. "What did he say?"

When he told her, Abby remembered a couple of the stories vaguely. "The guy who shot his wife and daughter and then set his house on fire... That one was all over the papers. The girl was my age. We weren't in the same class, but I knew who she was. It gave me the willies. I used to..." Abby stopped abruptly.

Ben lifted a brow. "Used to?"

Her gaze touched his, darted away. "Wonder whether my father would do the same, if he ever decided to kill himself. Sometimes, when he was drunk and mad, I'd hide. Like..." She stopped again.

Frowned. "Like Debbie Price's brother. I remember that. She had a brother."

"That was the name? Price?"

"Yeah." Abby nibbled on her lower lip. "Funny that I remember, but…yeah."

"You don't know what happened to the brother?"

"No." Her fork was suspended halfway to her mouth. "He was younger, I think. I don't remember anything about him. Oh, God. Could this be *him?*"

"Strikes me as a possibility. One of many."

"Will you try to track him down?"

"Top of my list for tomorrow."

Again she was silent for a moment. Ben watched her surreptitiously, and found himself struck anew by the tension that shimmered around her like an aura. Did she know how to let herself be totally vulnerable? Was she too wary ever to trust anyone completely?

He also savored the delicacy of her bone structure, her long graceful neck and high arch of cheekbone, the thick silk of blond hair shoved carelessly behind her ears, the fragility of her collarbones and the pulse that fluttered at the base of her throat. And the shocking, electric blue of her eyes when she looked directly at him.

"You didn't come by tonight to eat a microwave dinner." It wasn't a question, but was one nonetheless.

Ben was surprised, something he rarely let himself be. She read him better than he'd guessed. And, for all that he'd practiced what he would say, he wasn't ready. *Let it go,* he told himself. *Give her time. Space. Don't be a fool.*

He opened his mouth to say, "Just wanted to see you." That wasn't what came out.

Instead, gruffly, he said, "I figured I should ask you something."

Her chin tilted up. "Ask."

"You didn't want to date me. How do you feel about it now?"

"About 'it'?"

"Me." Absently, he rubbed his stomach.

Her eyes shied from his, as they tended to do when she was afraid she'd give away something. "Isn't it a little soon to be declaring our intentions?"

Acid burned in his gut. "Maybe," Ben said. "No. All I want to know is whether we're on the same road. If I'm a drive-by for you, say so now."

He felt her poise for flight without moving a muscle, the way he knew when Cindy would flow out of sight before she even flicked her tail.

"I don't understand. What do you want me to say?"

"That you could fall in love with me," Ben said roughly. "That you won't flit on to some really *fun* guy the second I get a little too close to you."

Her eyes were huge, the pupils dilated. "You want promises."

He stood, the chair sliding back. "I want to know whether I scare you, the way you scare me."

She swallowed. She was breathing quick and shallow, but the closest she came to flight was rising slowly to her feet so that she didn't have to look too far up.

"You scare me," she said, almost inaudibly.

He closed his eyes on the powerful surge of relief

and exultation. She was every bit as gutsy as he'd guessed, and he hadn't imagined the two-way current that raised the hair on his arms when he touched her.

She might not want to fall in love, but she was.

Just as he was, despite the world's best laid plans.

"Good," he said. The word came out with the texture of a chunk of lava. He took a step toward her, and she took one toward him.

The kiss began in a fierce explosion of nerves, as if passion could excuse any admission of weakness. Her lush mouth opened under his, and her tongue met his in a duel as sweet as it was dangerous. He yanked her up against him, and she jerked his head back down to hers when he tried to lift his mouth long enough to taste her throat and feel the pillow of her earlobe between his teeth.

"I want you," he growled.

She froze. One second, passion that ran as hot as his; the next second, she'd turned to a block of ice.

Ben lifted his head. "What?"

If she'd had a tail, it would have flicked. "I'm not ready. If that's what you think I agreed to…"

"No."

"What?" She stared.

He swallowed thickly, dragged his thoughts from bed—where he wanted to take her. "No. I can wait."

"I said I wouldn't make any promises." Tension shivered through her again; she edged back a step, then another.

"I'm not asking for one," Ben said patiently.

"Oh." Abby frowned. "I'm not a virgin."

He was smart enough not to say a word.

"If that's what you thought."

"I'm not one, either."

She lifted her chin in challenge. "You don't care?"

"First doesn't matter to me." Last did, he realized with a sudden, sharp jolt.

"Sex can be fun." She crossed her arms over her chest, as if to protect herself, but her chin was still high, anxiety disguised as defiance in her eyes.

"Sure it can." Ben's sense of satisfaction grew. "But that's not all it will be, when you and I rip each other's clothes off."

She hated to agree; it went against her grain. But she was also invariably honest. "Maybe," she said grudgingly. "That's why I want to wait."

"Until you're sure."

Wariness in her eyes and a pucker on her forehead showed that she didn't like his choice of words, either. Did "sure" speak of promises, wedding rings, a lace veil and the permanence—and confinement— of marriage?

"Are you done eating?" she asked abruptly.

Ben braced himself. Now was when she asked him to leave. He'd crowded her. She wanted space, the illusion that he didn't loom in her life.

"Yeah," he said. "I'm done."

She surprised him again. "I feel like ice cream. You want to buy a girl a sundae?"

He smiled. "Hot fudge?"

"Banana split." Her grin stole years from her face. "Gotta get those fruits and veggies somehow."

"Right." He took a chance and a step, kissing her before she could retreat. Her mouth softened, while her body melted against his. Only momentarily, but he knew he hadn't imagined it.

Then she gave his chest a firm, hard push. ''I'll get my shoes,'' she said, and fled.

Ben felt himself smiling like an idiot. Just the way he had the first time Cindy let him stroke her.

The most primitive part of him reveled in his discovery: Abby Patton wasn't hopeless any more than the little feral cat had been. All a man needed was kindness, patience and determination. And a taste for taming wild creatures.

''LOOK AT ME,'' Meg groaned. ''It's practically noon, and I'm still in my bathrobe.''

''Scott take Emily to day care today?'' Abby accepted a mug of coffee from her sister, who eyed it wistfully.

''Yes. Maybe I wouldn't be so tired all the time if I could have caffeine.''

''I thought doctors had decided it wasn't so bad.''

''They still don't recommend it for pregnant women. And I don't want to do anything to hurt him…'' Her hand touched her belly.

''Him?'' Abby asked. ''Do you know?''

Meg made a face. ''No. Scott didn't want to find out. And I don't care one way or the other. But I really think the baby is a boy. It just…feels like one.''

Abby laughed. ''ESP, huh?''

''*You're* in a good mood,'' her sister observed. ''Anything to do with Shea?''

''Oh, Ben…'' Abby took refuge in a sip of scalding dark coffee.

"What's *that* mean?" Meg's blue eyes, so like Abby's, were bright with curiosity. The rest of her didn't look so hot.

She'd admitted to having stayed in bed until nine-thirty. "I'm just so *tired!*" she'd exclaimed. She wore a baggy pink nightgown and a bathrobe that wouldn't close over her belly. Her hair was tangled, her face puffy, her movements slow and awkward. Nobody would hire her today to be a model for one of those upbeat magazine articles on pregnancy. She looked too miserable.

Abby watched as Meg shuffled over to the stove and poured herself a cup of herb tea. When her sister returned to the table in the breakfast nook off the kitchen, Abby decided to indulge her.

"Ben is getting serious on me," she said carelessly. "He's trying to pin me down. Make sure I don't think of him as a 'drive-by,' quote unquote."

Meg sloshed her tea, swore, and dabbed at the wet spot on her chest. "So, is he?"

"Is he what?"

Her sister gave her a withering look. "A drive-by?"

"Shooting?"

"Not a bad analogy," Meg said thoughtfully, "considering the string of boyfriends I've seen come and go in your life over the past three years. Do they ever last more than a couple of weeks?"

"I get bored." True enough.

"Does Ben bore you?"

She shifted, wishing suddenly that she hadn't stopped by on impulse to see her sister. "No. He doesn't bore me."

"Will he?"

Abby realized the inquisition had to do with Meg's fondness for Ben Shea. The two had worked together off and on ever since Meg came home to Elk Springs. Together, they'd investigated the murder of Emily's mother. Apparently Meg was afraid her little sister was going to hurt the big tough cop.

"I don't know," Abby said, meeting her sister's eyes with stark honesty. "How can I know? I've never felt anything more than a passing crush for some guy. How *do* you know when it's more? I mean, what if you get out of bed tomorrow and realize you don't care how Scott's day went? Decide you have a headache when bedtime rolls around? You're supposed to love him forever. What if you don't?"

Meg's voice was gentle, her gaze compassionate. "Love goes deeper than being bored. Sometimes I tune Scott out. He's probably getting really tired of listening to me whine about how I feel like a beached whale. Momentary boredom doesn't mean you don't love somebody, that you wouldn't do anything for them. Also, I suspect sometimes, once you've made the commitment, you need to work at keeping your relationship interesting. We haven't needed to yet…" Pink blossomed on her cheeks. "We still, uh, find each other interesting…"

"Oh, God, I don't want to know about your sex life!"

"Isn't that part of what you're asking?"

"I don't know! I…" *Am scared. Confused.* "Oh, I suppose," Abby admitted.

"The thing is, people find it all too easy to give

up at the first sign of trouble. *Or* boredom. Move on. Why not? But we Pattons take commitments seriously. Maybe because of Mom. I don't know. But we do. That's why you're scared, isn't it?''

Abby took immediate offense. ''Who said I was scared?''

''Me. Meg. Your sister. I know you.''

''I'm not scared,'' Abby said with unnecessary force. ''Just...wondering. Which is different.''

''Uh-huh. Well, here's my best answer.'' Meg spread her hands. ''Look at me. What man would be thrilled to come home to me right now?''

''You don't look that bad.'' Abby did her poor best to sound convincing.

Meg made a face. ''Liar. But it doesn't matter. I'm not worried that Scott doesn't love me just because I look crappy. Maybe that's when you know it's forever. Not when he turns you on, or vice versa, but when he does something really disgusting or he's bleeding and looks like hell, and you know it would break your heart not to see this man every day for the rest of your life. And you know, deep down inside, that he feels the same. That he's looking past your boobs and your pretty face—'' she grinned ''—to *you*. So tell me—does Ben do that?''

Oh, God, Abby thought again. He did. That, in a nutshell, was what scared the daylights out of her. He saw beneath the carefully crafted surface, to where she was still a frightened child hiding under the bed.

She bit her lip. ''Do I have to answer that question?''

''Only for yourself.''

Abby nibbled on her lip. "We haven't talked about Jack. I mean, the fact that I dated him."

"No. We haven't. I figure it's none of my business."

"It was stupid." Abby shifted restlessly. "He was trying to prove to Daddy that he could have a Patton girl if he wanted. I was trying to prove I was as desirable as you were. After a few weeks, I knew he wasn't seeing me, not the way Ben does. I'm not sure he ever realized that he wasn't the point for me. Just as well."

Meg stared down at her hands. "Do you still feel that way about me?"

"No. Oh, no!" Abby felt her cheeks heat. "I suppose I was mad at you, after you left. And Renee talked about you all the time. You were daring. Smart. Beautiful. If…maybe if Daddy had ever once told me I did something right, I wouldn't have felt so inadequate. As it is…" She hated admitting to something as dumb as this. "As it is, I think I tried to blame you for everything. If you hadn't been so perfect… If you hadn't left… If I could be like you…"

"Oh, God." Meg squeezed her eyes shut. "I'm so sorry. I should have called. I should have…"

Abby reached over and took her hand. "No. If you'd never gotten pregnant, if you'd never left, Daddy still would have been a bastard. No matter what, he wouldn't have thought any of us measured up. You'd have gotten a job and your own apartment and moved out, anyway. I just…wanted to blame somebody. You were handy, because I thought you'd deserted us. But you did what you had to. My life wouldn't have been that different if you'd stayed.''

"I'm not so sure," Meg said sadly. "But I can't change the past now."

Abby smiled. "Hey, we didn't come out so bad, now did we? Daddy—oh, heck, why do I call him that?—he was the fool."

A slow smile dawned on Meg's face. "Yeah. He was. I'm glad you see that."

"Father." Abby made the title a stone, hard-edged. "That's what I'll call him from now on. Like you do."

"Why pretend affection we don't feel?" her sister said simply.

Right. Why *had* she bothered? Abby wondered. Even when he was alive, no pretense would ever have made him a real, loving father. "Daddy" he never had been; never would have been even if he'd lived to be ninety-two. Another delusion, Abby realized: if she sweet-talked him, called him "Daddy" like the other girls did their fathers, he'd be magically transformed.

Too bad it had taken her twenty-seven years to see through her own delusions.

After a moment of silence, Meg heaved herself to her feet. "I've got to take a shower. I can't stand it if noon strikes and I'm not dressed. Do you have time for lunch? Maybe Renee could meet us."

"Sure." Abby had to laugh. "I don't mind being seen with you even if you look like hell."

Her sister gave a puckish grin. "That's because you love me." In a rare physical gesture of affection, she bent and kissed the top of Abby's head.

Abby was shocked to feel the sting of tears. "Oh, go take a shower. I'll call Renee."

Meg laughed. "I'll hurry." She sighed and pressed the small of her back, adding over her shoulder, "Or not."

Renee, answering her cell phone, agreed that she could manage lunch. They arranged to meet in forty-five minutes.

Upstairs, the shower stopped. Restless, Abby wandered into the living room and poked in the magazine rack. *Parents* magazine was not what she had in mind. A very pregnant woman who looked incredibly athletic and perky hoisted a toddler on the cover.

Jeez, Abby thought idly. Why didn't Meg look like that? Maybe if she exercised more...

Upstairs, Meg swore. A floor away, Abby heard her sister's shock and fear in both tone and the use of a word she never said.

Abby spun around and raced for the stairs.

CHAPTER EIGHT

ABBY BURST INTO her sister's bedroom. "What's wrong?"

Meg sat on the edge of the king-size bed, naked but for a towel wrapped inadequately around her breasts and belly. Hair dripping wet, mouth working without a sound coming out, she pointed at an open dresser drawer.

A bra hung down the front of it. A nursing bra, Abby noted with half her mind. A holstered gun lay atop the bureau among framed photos, cosmetics and a tray that held coins and a set of keys.

Abby approached the drawer warily. Her nose had told her nothing was on fire; nor did it catch the distinctive sickly odor of blood. But something had shocked the hell out of her usually unflappable sister, pregnant, sure, but still a cop at heart.

Surrounded by the lace and silk of Meg's lingerie was an eight-by-ten photograph. Abby recognized it. Last year Meg had been honored for her work with teenagers. She wore her uniform, was ponytailed and solemn.

And someone had burned two holes where her breasts should have been.

Abby, too, muttered an expletive.

"Look and make sure there's nothing else," Meg

said behind her, an edge of hysteria in her voice. "Open the other drawers."

Abby got a washcloth from the bathroom and used it to edge open each drawer, finding heaps of disordered clothes. "It's a mess," she said. "Did he ransack your drawers?"

Meg, pink and flushed from the shower and from dawning anger, was now peering over Abby's shoulder. "No. I'm a slob."

Using a mascara tube so as not to mar fingerprints, Abby lifted the photograph. Beneath it were more panties.

Abby glanced at her sister. "Uh, normally I'd say we shouldn't touch anything, but you'd better grab some clothes."

"He was in *my* drawer." Meg stared down at the photograph. "That bastard. How dare he come into my house?"

"And when did he do it?" That was the part bothering Abby—the idea of this sick SOB here in this bedroom maybe when Meg slept only a few feet away.

"Oh, God." Meg swallowed, as though her stomach had taken a lurch. Backing up, still clutching the towel around herself, she sank back onto the edge of the bed. "Something woke me this morning. About eight. Scott was long gone. I just…you know when you hear something. I thought it was the telephone, but then it didn't ring. I lay there listening, but I didn't hear another sound, and I drifted back to sleep. Do you think…"

Abby sat, too, taking her sister's hand. "When were you last in that drawer?"

"Yesterday morning."

"Were you out of the house yesterday at all?"

Thinking about it calmed Meg. "Yes. For a couple of hours. I had a doctor's appointment, and I went to the mall. Shopped for baby stuff."

"It's more likely he broke in then," Abby suggested, although she wasn't so sure. He was taking bigger chances, maybe enjoying the risks and not just the taunting. Standing here with Meg asleep in the big bed might have given this guy a real charge.

"You're right." Meg's voice strengthened with relief. "If he was watching the house, he'd have seen me leave, and known that nobody else was home. That would've made sense."

"Okay," Abby said, giving Meg's hand a squeeze. "I'm going to call Ben. You get dressed. Try not to touch anything you can help."

Meg lifted a brow.

Abby smiled faintly at her sister's irritation. "But I guess you know that, don't you?"

Meg gave her an exasperated look. "Get out of here. Let me have some privacy, okay?"

Abby phoned not only Ben, but Renee, as well. By the time the two arrived at almost the same moment, Meg had dried her hair and was dressed in a denim maternity jumper over a T-shirt. She'd put on some makeup. "No," she had said when Abby saw her, "not from on top of the dresser. That's just extra stuff. For fancy occasions."

Renee rushed to hug Meg, then followed Abby and Ben upstairs while Meg remained in the kitchen brewing more coffee.

Ben's obscenity pretty well expressed how all of them felt.

"You searched the other drawers?"

"I looked in them," Abby corrected him. "I didn't lift anything except the photo, and I didn't stir things around. I figured we should fingerprint first."

"Yeah, yeah." His tone said what they all knew: there would be no prints this time, either. He looked up. "Okay. What's the thing with the breasts? Meg hasn't had, um, silicone implants or anything, has she?"

"Our mother died of breast cancer." Renee sounded shell-shocked. "Meg was with her."

"Is this public knowledge?" he asked grimly.

"No..." Renee began.

"Yes," Abby corrected her. She'd had time to think this through. "Meg spoke at that benefit for Breast Cancer Awareness Day last year. The paper featured her along with a couple of the other speakers."

He swore again. "Okay. Let me go get my camera, and then I'll have an evidence technician come by and dust for prints. See if you can figure out where he got the photograph."

That one was easy: Meg found the empty frame downstairs in Scott's office.

"So he didn't come prepared." Abby pushed out her lower lip while she thought. "Maybe he assumed he'd find a picture here."

"Most people have a photo album, at least," Renee said. Her eyes glittered with rage as she paced the kitchen. "What does this bastard want with us?"

"To hurt us." Meg sat quietly at the table, sipping herbal tea. Her voice was calm, quiet.

"So far, all he's done is try to scare us," Abby pointed out, aware of Ben listening from the kitchen doorway. He'd just shown an evidence tech in.

"That's what he's *doing*," Meg said, her calm almost eerie, "but he wants more than that. He wants to burn us. He'd have liked the blood in that pickup to be Dad's. He'd have liked Emily to die that night. He wants us to suffer."

Renee started to protest, but Ben stepped into the kitchen, effectively cutting her off. "I agree. Whether he'll act on what he wants, I don't know. So far, he hasn't tried. Maybe he's waging an inner battle. If he really wanted to kill you all, he wouldn't be warning you over and over. He wants you to hurt the way he hurts, but so far something is stopping him from making sure you do."

His bluntness brought silence in its wake. Just then Scott arrived home with a bang of the back door, demanding explanations.

Meg was herself again, angry more than scared. She sat with her sisters at the kitchen table; Scott stood behind her with his big hands wrapping her shoulders.

Involuntarily Abby looked from her brother-in-law's hands to Ben's. He had good hands, large, tanned, blunt-fingered, but not so calloused as to be insensitive. They were strong hands. She knew how they felt touching her in desire. What would it feel like to have Ben claiming her as Scott was claiming Meg; reassuring her, comforting her, offering silent love and a promise of safety?

But Scott wasn't a cop. To him, his wife was a woman first and foremost. Would it ever occur to Ben to feel protective of Abby? Did she want him to? Could a man feel protective and also respect a woman as an equal? Why did she have this sudden longing to feel his hands gripping her shoulders, sending a thousand unspoken messages?

Had she really let this creep terrorize her to the point where she felt the need of a bodyguard?

Abby lifted her gaze from Ben's hand, holding a coffee mug, to meet his eyes. He was watching her as she watched him. He didn't smile, but he looked back at her without reserve, his stillness so profound she felt as if she were gazing at a deep, quiet pool she remembered in a crook of the Deschutes River. The river current had seemed to leave it untouched. Shadows shifted in the depths but never stirred the green water. The air had been hushed, the leaves still. Not even water bugs skittered on the surface.

Looking into Ben's eyes, she felt the same kind of peace. As if he were touching her. Trying to tell her something. His gaze never wavered until she dragged hers away.

What was wrong with her? Abby wondered on a ripple of new fear. She had never in her life looked to a man for reassurance. Her sisters…maybe. But not to a man. They were all, on some level, her father. All violent. All selfish. They could be handled, sure. Trusted, never.

What made her think Ben Shea wouldn't hurt her?

Abby found herself studying Scott McNeil. It surprised her to realize that she was beginning to believe he would do anything for Meg, that Daniel Barnard would do anything for Renee. That her sisters could trust these men they loved.

That all men were *not* her father.

If Scott and Daniel were different, why not Ben?

She might be sorry if she didn't give Ben a chance.

The others present had been talking while she brooded. Abby tuned in to hear Renee say, "The trouble is, I don't think we can assume that the case necessarily involved fire. Probably it did. But maybe our perp is ticked off, and he happens to like fire. A lot of emotionally damaged people do. Maybe the fire isn't the message."

"It's just his preferred M.O.," Meg concluded.

"Maybe," Ben said, frowning, "but my gut feeling is that he wants you to burn because he was burned, or someone he loved was, and he blames you. We can't look at every case your father ever handled. I say we focus on the ones that involved fire, where somebody got hurt."

"Yeah, okay." Renee stood. "I've got notes in my car. Let me grab them. I've come up with almost two dozen cases so far. And I've hardly begun. I've got to tell you, he handled everything head-on. No sympathy, no patience. You go in after 'em. That was his philosophy. He liked gas canisters, he liked sharpshooters. He hated negotiators."

Abby remembered the relish with which Ed Patton would talk about taking some bastard down. That was how he always put it: "taking him down." As if it were a duel, or a wrestling match. A contest. And he could triumph only by physically over-whelming his opponent. The more battered and bloody he had left his adversary—and it was always personal from his point of view—the happier Chief Patton was, the more pleasure in his voice as he rambled at the dinner table. He liked it when the perps fought back; if they were "goddamn wusses," as he put it, he was disappointed. He never talked about the wives or children or victims, and she had always secretly known why. He had no sympathy for the weak. They were *asking* to be victims.

It was why she had never let herself be at anyone's mercy. Only her sisters could hurt her, and she had known from the cradle that they wouldn't. Even Meg's desertion had made sense, in a way; Meg was fighting Dad, which was okay. She'd chosen a stupid way of doing it, in Abby's opinion. It was so easy to convince him to do what you wanted him to do, if you cajoled and smiled and puffed him up. Why butt your head against a brick wall if you could oil the hinges and open a gate with the lightest of touches? But Meg was stubborn, and in her own way she was obeying the Patton girls' number one rule: never be weak, or you, too, will be a victim. He might hit them, but as long as they fought back, whether covertly as Abby did or overtly as her sisters had chosen, they were opponents, not victims. Meg had left because she had to. Now that Abby knew her sister had been pregnant, she especially understood: Meg would have been at their father's mercy if she stayed. She would have been a victim.

Renee came back into the kitchen and handed out copies she'd made of her notes. Some cases were major busts, some minor, but all were ones that might have left someone bitter.

A man who'd been lighting fires in waste bins at

his company—penny ante stuff—was not only going to lose his job, he'd have to stand trial. He'd blown himself to bits with a shotgun and left two children rather than face the humiliation.

A burglar who had been shot as he ran—or so claimed the boy's sister in an abusive tirade afterward. The evidence wasn't conclusive; the bullet had entered the heart through the eighteen-year-old boy's side. Perhaps Officer Patton had had good reason to believe the boy was turning with a gun. Probably the kid had only been looking over his shoulder as he fled. Supposedly he'd been angry at the store owner, who'd busted him for shoplifting. The owner claimed he caught the kid with a gas can in back trying to torch the place, but later investigation showed the can actually belonged to the neighbor across the alley and was empty. The storekeeper had yelled at the kid, who ran. By bad luck, Ed Patton, only two years on the force, had been walking into the store to buy a pack of gum.

The list went on and on. Abby marveled at it. These days, any police officer who had pulled a weapon this many times, much less used it, would have been investigated, suspended over and over, probably fired eventually. Ed Patton had been given medals. Promoted. If you committed a crime and weren't scared Ed Patton would come after you, you should be, trumpeted the *Journal*. Abby remembered the satisfaction in his voice, the swagger in his stride, and felt sick.

She didn't want to think about him as her father. Why should she and her sisters have to take responsibility for his cruelty? No matter what Ed Patton had done to him, the creep who'd slipped into Meg's bedroom and left that obscene photo in her underwear drawer didn't deserve any sympathy.

"Let's divide up the list." Abby realized too late that she'd interrupted somebody. "Oh, sorry."

"No problem," Ben said, his eyes keen on her face.

"Let's each take five cases, see if we can find survivors. Ben, are the ones you told me about on Renee's list?"

"One is. The other couple aren't. I'll follow up on them, too."

Meg took the lion's share. "I've got plenty of time," she said wryly. "I'm good on the telephone."

Renee would continue to go through case files hunting for ones where Ed Patton had wronged someone.

"I wish it were like hunting for a needle in a haystack," she muttered. "Unfortunately, it's more like fishing for trout in the Deschutes. All you have to do is have a little patience. Plenty of them there." She sighed. "Well. To work."

Abby rose, too. "Meg, when is Will getting home from his camping trip?"

"Tomorrow. But I'm okay."

Scott's eyes met Abby's. "She won't be alone."

Meg didn't protest, only rolled her eyes.

Abby started out of the room, shaking her head. Big sister Meg had been born so fiercely independent, the family story had it that she'd punched their mother when she tried to swaddle her. Now Meg— Meg!—was letting a man swaddle her.

Go figure.

The crunch of a footstep on gravel gave her a second's warning before Ben's hand on her arm stopped Abby in the driveway. "You okay?" he asked.

"Why wouldn't I be?"

"You had a funny look on your face earlier. I thought maybe this shook you up."

He still gripped her arm, his hand warm and strong. Protective.

Panic singed her throat. "I'm not shaken up. I'm angry. Big difference. Bastard can pick on a kid and a pregnant woman. Let him tiptoe into *my* bedroom."

Ben's jaw clenched. "I'd like to be there."

"Sure you would," Abby said with light mockery. "But, sorry, I'm not so scared I'm planning to invite you to join me anytime soon. If that's what you had in mind."

His eyes narrowed. "You know damn well that's not what I was suggesting."

Shame flushed her cheeks, but that fear she hated to acknowledge kept the acid in her voice. "Do I?"

Ben released her arm and stepped back. "I'm wasting my time with you, aren't I? You're not going to let anyone close enough to get a crack at hurting you."

"Is that what you were planning?" She held on to the mockery though her voice felt tremulous. "To break my heart?"

"You know better than that, too."

Damn him! If only he would sound angry. Anything but sorrowful.

Her cheeks burned now. "Oh, God, Ben." She squeezed her eyes shut. "I'm sorry. I—I suppose I am...shaken." Admitting it was as hard as tugging her gun out of the holster that first time in training. The stiffness of the leather and the weight of the weapon combined with the emotional knowledge of what she was doing. Of what it meant. Could mean.

He'd gone still on her again, unreadable. Abby waited in agony. She'd chased him away. Had done so with malice aforethought.

No, she hadn't thought. Had only lashed out.

As her father had done when he slammed one of his daughters against a wall over some little thing, because he was boiling and she was there, handy. Vulnerable.

As Ben was to her, she sensed. She despised herself for taking advantage of the feelings he'd confessed. Worse, she despised herself for lashing out with bitter words as Daddy had done with a heavy hand. The minute she let herself feel something, she became as bad as her father. Had she learned *nothing?*

"Why *are* you wasting your time with me?" The words burst out of her. "I can be so…awful. Why would you want me?"

His face softened, although she hadn't been trying to play to him. "What if I said it's your eyes—" he touched her eyelid "—your mouth—" his fingertip traced the swell of her lower lip "—your long, long legs…"

Somehow she had come to be against him, her head tilted back so she could look up.

"Would you believe me?" he murmured.

She shook her head dumbly. "I'm…nothing special."

"You're beautiful, and you know it."

"I don't..."

"You carry yourself like a beautiful woman. You've got it, and you flaunt it."

She liked seeing a spark in a man's eyes, liked knowing she'd put it there. Liked moving him to excitement, then dousing his excitement with a brush-off as chilly as a bucket of water.

Another reason to dislike herself.

"But you're right," Ben said. "That's not why I want you."

"Then...then why?"

His fingertip gently touched her eyelid again. "Sometimes I see a lost, lonely little girl looking out at me. She reminds me of the ones I have to pick up after their parents abandon them at neighbors' houses."

Abby swallowed.

The pad of his thumb caressed her lip. "Sometimes your mouth trembles, and I want to kiss away your troubles."

She stared, mesmerized, into his eyes, so dark a gray right now they were almost black.

"And then I see you walk, with that long swinging stride, as if the world's your oyster." His hand gripped her hip. "Or you wipe away the fear in your eyes with a laugh and a toss of your head. I want you, Abby Patton, because of all those contradictions. Because you need a best friend and a lover. Because someone has to teach you how to trust. And because you're gutsy enough to survive no matter what."

She was paralyzed. Body. Vocal chords. The whole shebang.

Until Ben kissed her, when she came to life with a hot exhilarating surge, as if electrotherapy had brought color back to a gray, depressed world.

She wrapped her arms around his neck and kissed him with pent-up longing and fear and hope. She strained against his tall strong body even as he drove a leg between her thighs and lifted her in a way so suggestive, heat liquefied in her belly.

The sound of more footsteps on gravel mean nothing to her, but Renee's amused voice did.

"Uh, I don't mean to interrupt, but I can't leave until Ben does."

Eyes glittering, he held Abby away, his gaze never leaving hers. "Yeah, okay, Patton." His voice was rough. "Give me a second here."

"Sure, sure." Renee's voice and footsteps receded. A car door slammed.

"Can we take this up later?" Ben asked, still in that oddly thick voice.

"Um..." Abby felt disoriented. "I suppose we have to, don't we?"

A muscle jerked in his cheek. "What's that mean?"

"I...not what it sounds like." Whatever that was. "I just...need to think. Okay? Can...can we talk tomorrow?"

"Tomorrow."

"Is...is that okay?" She sounded so meek, tentative.

One corner of his mouth tilted into a wry smile. "You know it is." He backed away. "I'll, uh, call you."

She was going somewhere. Abby looked vaguely

around, recognizing her own car without the sight meaning anything.

"Ben?" she said.

He stopped. "Yeah?"

"You're nicer to me than I deserve."

He scowled. "No. You deserve nice. Don't let your son of a bitch of a father convince you any different."

"That's what Meg always said." She smiled wistfully. "I missed Meg."

Ben took a step toward her. Stopped with his hands knotted into fists at his side. "You're sure you want to be alone tonight?" He gave an irritated look over his shoulder when Renee tapped the horn.

"Yeah." To Abby's surprise, her smile broadened into a real grin. "I wouldn't want to give in too easily, now would I?"

Ben laughed, as she'd known he would. "Nah," he said. "You wouldn't want that."

"Besides, we've got work to do. I'm going to spend the evening in the company of the telephone and directory assistance."

"Right." He didn't move.

"Ben." She smiled again. "Go. I'll see you tomorrow. I promise."

"And something tells me," he said thoughtfully, "that you do keep promises."

"Oh, yeah," Abby agreed. "My one virtue."

Ben went, and left her to long bitter reflections on how much she had in common with the man she'd called Daddy. Why, he kept promises, too, Abby thought that evening, as she hung up the telephone after the twentieth fruitless inquiry. When Ed Patton said he'd be there, he was. When he said you'd be sorry, you were.

He had told her she wouldn't even measure up as a decent woman, and danged if he hadn't proved to be right. She didn't know how to fall in love. Wasn't even sure what it felt like. What woman didn't know something so elemental?

But it seemed she wouldn't make much of a man, either, or else she wouldn't be craving Ben Shea's protective presence and touch the second something scary happened.

So what did that make her?

Abby glanced down at her notes and reached for the telephone, but didn't pick it up.

Rephrase, she told herself. It wasn't what did *that* make her, but rather what did *he* make her? *He* had always wanted her to fail. Even his relationships with his daughters had been adversarial. *He* could win only if they lost. And damned if she'd let him.

So. What he had created was a daughter— no, three daughters—who wouldn't back down.

"Well, *Father,*" Abby murmured, "maybe I can be a decent woman, after all. I wouldn't want you basking in the warmth down there, thinking you were right, would I?"

Chief Patton didn't answer; by this time, he was no more than a heap of bones in the fancy coffin she and Renee had bought out of a sense of obligation and an awareness that townsfolk were watching. So why was she still letting him ruin her life, as he'd ruined too many lives?

It would be easy to feel sorry for the one victim of her father's who was lashing back, Abby reflected.

Well, she wouldn't go that far; he had no business visiting the sins of the father on three innocent women and their families. But she did understand. Ed Patton could twist people as if they were made of clay, letting life be the kiln that baked them in their skewed form.

But if she continued all her days that way, twisted up emotionally, why, her father would have won. And one thing she'd never been was a fatalist. She always fought back. What was going to be, didn't have to be. Now did it?

All of which was a fancy way of deciding she was going to make love with Ben Shea the next time he asked.

When the telephone rang, Abby reached for it.

CHAPTER NINE

"MR. JOYCE? This is Detective Ben Shea." Ben slouched low on his couch, the phone cradled between his ear and shoulder. Notes littered the cushion beside him. He listened to the other man for a moment. "No, no," he said hastily, "this call has nothing to do with your daughter. I'm sure she's fine. No, this has to do with ancient history."

"What do you mean?" the man asked with deep suspicion.

"I'm hoping you have some recollections of the incident during which your father died."

Dick Joyce gave a harsh bark of laughter. "*Incident?* Talk about a mealymouthed way to put it. Kinda like 'passed away.'"

Ben said ruefully, "You're right. That was a euphemism. Sometimes I find, uh, that people are offended if I'm too direct."

"If you were being direct, what would you call that 'incident'?"

"A fiasco." Ben let out a breath, his mouth twisting. "But I don't know what to call it. I've read the police report and heard the story from a retired officer who was present. I was hoping to hear the family's side from you."

"Far as I'm concerned, my father was murdered."

Dick Joyce grunted. "He was crazy. I won't deny that. He wouldn't stay on medication and my mother had left him. Thank God, or we'd probably all be dead. But did they have to kill him?"

"He was shooting at police officers."

"Because they had surrounded his house and were yelling through a bullhorn demanding that he come out with his hands up." Joyce was breathing heavily. "Dad was schizophrenic! The whole thing started because a neighbor called the cops on him. I guess he threw rocks at some teenagers who cut across the lawn. So what do the police do but send some kinda SWAT team. He probably figures 'they' have come to get him at last. Of course he shot at 'em! So they killed him."

Ben weighed the response. Joyce sounded angry, but no more than seemed reasonable. After reading the police report, Ben personally agreed: the cops had come on too heavy. Joyce hadn't done anything to deserve being shot for.

Still... How angry was Bernard Joyce's son?

"Do you know which police officers were involved?" Ben asked.

A brief silence. "You mean, names?"

"That's right." Ben had practiced his cover story. "I'm investigating that and several other incidents in which police response might have been...inappropriate."

"Yeah, well, it's about time somebody did." Joyce was silent for a moment. "I'm trying to remember. My mother blamed one guy. Jeez. I know he ended up as sheriff or police chief or something.

That made her mad. But I don't remember his name. She died a couple of years ago. Is it important?''

"No, sir,'' Ben said. "I do know what officers were present. I just wanted to get your perspective.''

"Why?'' Suspicion had resurfaced. "After thirty years?''

"We're looking at a pattern.'' True enough, unfortunately. "Your father's death is one of many cases I'm scrutinizing.''

Joyce bought it.

The woman Ben called next didn't.

"After twenty-five years? I don't think so,'' she said flatly, and slammed down the phone.

He drove out to see her. Same address, Ben was interested to note, as in the police report; not many people stayed put for so many years.

The white bungalow was typical of Elk Springs, modest but solid. Small yard, but a couple of crab apple trees shaded a neatly tended lawn. Two kids' bikes leaned against the porch. Ben nudged a soccer ball aside as he climbed the steps and went to the front door.

It opened before he rang.

"Let me guess.'' The woman who stood with her hand on the door stared at him with open hostility. "You're that guy who just called.''

"I'm Detective Ben Shea. That's right, ma'am.''

She shoved back hair that was overdue for coloring and perming. Dark roots were stubbornly straight in comparison to the brassy yellow curls. "Nobody listened to me then. Why are you here now? And don't feed me none of that crap about 'patterns.' The son of a bitch is dead. You can't slap him on the wrist now. So why're you all fired up?''

''Mama?'' A girl who might be nine or ten peered around her mother, eyes big and anxious. Her whisper was clearly audible. ''Why is a policeman here?''

Lori Weaver hushed her daughter. ''He's just asking about somebody. Nothin' for you to worry about. Now, you go back to cleaning that kitchen.''

The girl flashed another frightened look at Ben and vanished.

''I hope I didn't scare her,'' Ben said quietly.

''Then maybe you shouldn't have come.'' Tiredness rimmed Lori Weaver's eyes more emphatically than did her eyeliner.

Some impulse—a cop's instinct—made Ben opt for honesty. ''Somebody has threatened Chief Patton's daughters. We're looking into cases where he might have left somebody angry.''

She hooted, the sound more bitter than amused. ''Bet they're not hard to find.''

''Unfortunately not,'' he admitted.

Her face hardened. ''Well, I read the paper. I know his girl is getting sworn in as chief. I didn't like it, except I've never heard nothin' bad about her. Or the other ones. I've got two girls of my own now, and a husband, although he drives a truck and it seems like he isn't around enough to be any use at all—he never even wants to mow the lawn when he is here. Anyway, even if I was some kinda crackpot, I got no time to cut letters out of the newspaper and glue 'em together like they do on TV shows so's the handwriting can't be identified. How would that pay the bills or get the kids to swim lessons?''

Ben cracked a smile. "I don't expect it would."

"So, is that all you wanted to know?"

"I just wondered why you were angry at Ed Patton when he wasn't the one who set your house and himself on fire."

She gripped the door frame so hard her knuckles showed white. "Because I saw the cop car pull up five minutes or more before I heard the whoosh and Jimmy's scream..." Ms. Weaver shuddered. "I never heard nothing like that before. Or since, thank God! Anyhow, I saw that policeman get out of his car and kinda stroll up the walkway, only then he didn't come onto the porch. He went around thataway..." She jerked her head toward a big lilac blocking one of the front windows. "He was moving real careful. Real quiet. Last I saw, he had his hand on his gun. It scared me. You know? I made sure the front door was locked and then I sort of ran and sort of tiptoed into the kitchen and checked the back door, too. After that I stood in the hall halfway between, where no bullets could hit me if somebody was trying to break in and the cop started shooting. But nothing happened for the longest time." She looked right through Ben, seeing the past. "I swear I could hear my heart pounding! I just stood there and stood there. I remember getting dizzy—I musta been holding my breath or something. And then I heard it. A whoosh and a roar and this scream worse than anything! I could see flames through the kitchen window, so I went running out the front door, which I guess, thinking back, was stupid—I mean, I didn't know what was going on, but I just went. You know? You ever do something like that without thinking?"

"Yeah," Ben said wryly, remembering his first domestic violence call, when he'd jumped in and wrestled this guy with a gun to the ground, and afterward it was all a blank—he had no idea whether he'd acted reasonably, thought about risks or whether he should call for backup. He'd just…done it.

Her gaze became unfocused again. "I tore around the house, and this cop swung around and pointed his gun at me. I near peed my pants, I can tell you that! 'I live here!' I yelled. He holstered his gun and nodded toward the fire, which was just out of my sight, with the shrubs, you know."

Ben nodded, since she seemed to expect a response.

"And he says, 'Is this man known to you?' Just like that. Kind of formal. So I take a couple of steps, figuring Jimmy would be lying there on the grass in handcuffs. He'd quit screaming by then. I knew it'd be Jimmy, because when I threw him out he said I'd be sorry. He said somethin' would happen. Like maybe my house would burn down." Her tongue wet her lips.

"But he wasn't handcuffed," Ben prompted, his voice low and gentle.

This shudder racked her whole body and she closed her eyes momentarily. "He was on fire. Dead, I guess. Crumpled facedown. He was black, and melting… I threw up. And then I saw that cop was smiling. 'Well,' he says, 'I guess you can't recognize him, can you?' What kind of monster was he?"

Ben stared back at her, letting her see on his face a mirror to her shock. "I don't know," he said slowly. "I wish I could tell you."

"Jimmy wasn't any too smart. I guess he poured gasoline all over the back porch and then lit a match. Of course, that's what Officer Patton claimed. But I always kinda wondered. I mean, either he stood there in the shadow of the bushes and watched Jimmy, knowing the whole time what would happen, or..." She stopped; her mouth trembled. "Or else somehow he caused it. Not excusing Jimmy, who had a bad temper and shouldn't've been back there at all, but you know what I mean?"

"Mama?" one of her daughters called from inside the house. "Mama? Is somethin' wrong?"

"No!" she yelled. "You just stick to your chores." She scrubbed a hand across her eyes, smearing mascara. In just above a whisper, she said, "I went crazy. I threw myself at him and tried to scratch his eyes out. I'm the one who ended up hand-cuffed! There's a joke! Jimmy tries to burn down my house, and instead of arresting him, the police officer lets him fry and cuffs me!" She let out a careful breath. "So, why was I mad? Now you know."

"And you complained about him."

"Damn straight I did!" She was back to being steamed again, her eyes smouldering. "Nobody would listen. I could tell they didn't believe me."

Ben held her gaze. "I believe you," he said quietly. "Ed Patton enjoyed seeing pain and fear. He probably figured your boyfriend had it coming. He was the kind of bastard who probably told sick jokes about it. I'm only sorry he didn't come to a worse end."

Shock was chased by satisfaction across Lori Weaver's tired face. "And his daughter? This one who's taking his place?"

"Is a good cop and a nice woman. You have my word."

She searched his face, finally giving a small nod. "These threats… What do they say?"

"We wish we knew." He shook his head when she opened her mouth. "I'm afraid I can't reveal the details. Once we make an arrest, I expect you'll be reading all about it in the newspapers."

Ms. Weaver nodded again. "Well, you tell Renee Patton that I don't blame her. Heck, I feel sorry for her, having that kind of father! And I hope you hurry up and find this person before somethin' bad happens."

"Thank you, Ms. Weaver," Ben said gravely. He held out a hand; they shook. "I appreciate your time. And I am sorry for what you went through."

Night had come while they talked. He had to turn his headlights on during the mile drive back to his house. On the way, her story kept replaying in his head, and he saw it with stunning clarity: her huddling in the hall, heart pounding as she listened for an intruder, for shots, for footsteps. And the scream—Ben had heard someone once, trapped inside a wrecked car that burst into flames. Once in a while, he still woke up sweating with that scream echoing in his head. And Ed Patton, just standing there in the shadows, the way she'd said. Watching. Probably grinning, because he knew what was going to happen to the stupid bastard. For a man like Patton, it was probably akin to watching a spider popping out of a crack in a log you've just thrown on a campfire. The way it would panic, run back and forth. If there was no way to reach across the flames, or if the spider raced away from your hand, sooner or later the flames licked it up.

Only, Patton hadn't reached across the flames. He'd smiled and watched and waited.

Ben Shea had never hated anyone with such ferocity as he did Ed Patton right this minute.

He pulled into his driveway, the headlights catching the cat bolting around the corner of the house. In the daytime, Cindy would watch him come and go from her spot on the fence post or the porch railing. At night he and his vehicle assumed monstrous proportions in her eyes. He understood even as he regretted the fact. Nights were when his house seemed emptiest, when he most would have liked her company.

Tonight he let himself in the back door, turned on the lights and cracked open a window. Cindy had food and water bowls out back, beside the garage, but he opened a can for her every morning. At first he'd given it to her beside her kibbles. Then he'd moved her treat to the porch. Lately he'd taken to calling her and setting the bowl on the floor of the dining room, just inside the window he opened for her.

Tonight, on impulse, he chose a can of gourmet tuna and mackerel. Standing beside the window, he called, "Cindy! Here, kitty, kitty. Dinnertime." He held the can up and peeled back the top. Cindy could hear that distinctive sound a mile away. Whether she'd come at a strange time, in the dark, was another story.

But as he stooped to dump the cat food in the bowl, he heard the small thud of her paws landing on the sill. Still crouching, Ben waited.

The dainty calico oozed around the leg of a dining room chair, eyes big and dilated.

"It's okay, little one," he murmured. "Come and eat. I won't hurt you."

She inched forward. He kept murmuring silly nothings, which seemed a comfort to her. At last she reached the bowl only a foot away from him and, after a brief hesitation, began gobbling.

Ben reached out slowly. Cindy paused in her eating, thought about what kind of danger he represented, then wolfed down another bite. He stroked her back. Once. Twice. Several times.

At first he thought he'd imagined the way her spine arched and her small body seemed to undulate against his fingertips. But then she did it again, her tail poking straight into the air when his scratches reached her hind end.

Hardly daring to breathe, he kept stroking. She ate more slowly than usual. Once she tilted her head to one side so he could reach a sensitive spot beneath her ear. She licked the bowl clean, arched once more against his hand, and then leaped for the windowsill, leaving behind—Ben realized only then—a faint hum on the air.

A purr.

"I SAW YOUR CAT out on the porch when I pulled in," Abby said. "At least, I think it was yours. She ran when I got close."

Ben had asked her to dinner, of course. Not just

dinner, she knew that, but he couldn't say, "Wanna spend the night?" without wrapping it up prettier. So here they sat across his cherry dining room table from each other, nibbling at a delicious dinner, chatting like two strangers stuck next to each other at a conference—they had something in common, found each other agreeable, but would probably never meet again. The upcoming presidential election had provided fodder for fifteen minutes of conversation; from there, they'd moved on to local politics. Abby's mention of the cat was as personal as they'd gotten.

Now Ben tore a roll in two. "A calico? Yeah, that was Cindy."

"Does she come in the house?" *Does she sleep curled against you?* Abby wondered, shocked to feel a sting of jealousy.

"She's pretty scared. She comes in once a day, just long enough to eat some canned food. Last night she purred for the first time for me."

The jealousy vanished in a wash of pity and a strange sense of kinship. "You let her come and go?"

Ben looked at her oddly. "I wouldn't shut her in. She is what she is."

"You could get a friendly cat." This seemed important. "I see ads all the time."

"I know." He watched her. "I like Cindy."

He was trying to tell her something. But was it the same thing she was asking? Abby didn't have the courage to say, *What if I'm scared? What if I can't stand being too close? Will you be mad if I don't move in cozily? Magically become a cook and a gardener? A housewife and mother?*

It was too soon to ask those questions, anyway, she told herself. Maybe what happened here tonight would be a flop. Maybe he'd be an insensitive lover. Or the whole thing would just be awkward—fumbling, inept, elbows bumping ribs, grunts and sweat and dissatisfaction. Or it might be good sex, but not special. Physically pleasurable, but not emotionally transforming.

No, she was definitely worrying about something that might never come to pass.

Abby took another bite of the stir-fried chicken and snow peas. "I followed up on about half my share of cases already. I didn't find anybody likely."

"Me, either." Lines in Ben's forehead deepened. "But I heard some damned ugly stories."

She hadn't been able to sleep last night, not after the earfuls she'd gotten. In an instant, anger sprang out of her, full-fledged. "Next time you say grace, you'll have one more thing to be thankful for."

His brows rose. "Which is?"

"He wasn't your father."

His clear gray eyes held compassion. "You survived."

Damn him. He saw more than she wanted him to. "Did I?" she asked quietly.

Suddenly they were more than two strangers; he had once again violated her acute sense that she stood apart. *I am an island,* she had always believed in defiance of what was said. She usually drove intruders from her shores.

Yet with Ben the connection felt less like an enemy landing and more…like a bridge. Mysterious, not quite solid, shimmering as if it might be a mirage.

But sometimes she was tempted, like now, to take a step onto it, test the footing. If it was sturdy enough, she might go farther. Perhaps it wouldn't be so bad not to stand alone in gray, gale-whipped seas.

How melodramatic! she scoffed at herself. She liked to be independent, that's all. Love meant leaning on someone else, a dangerous business if the support was yanked away.

Perhaps he feared the same. *You do keep promises,* he had said, as if that ability meant something to him.

Ben Shea, she suspected, liked solid footing, too.

He spoke now, having bided his time as though he were reading her mind.

"You're more than you think you are. I told you that."

She went still. "Just so *you* don't think I'm something I'm not."

His dark, lean face looked meditative. "I'm not big on preconceptions. I tend to come at people the way I do an investigation. There's a puzzle there. You don't jump to conclusions because of one clue. You sift through the facts, let people give themselves away. You don't act until you *know.*"

"Have I given myself away?" She couldn't help but ask.

His mouth tilted into a smile. "Tends to work that way. Haven't I?"

"But you weren't trying to hide anything."

"Wasn't I?"

Abby had to think. When he first asked her out, she supposed he was. But he was honest with her, as she'd tried to be with him. That was partly what she liked about him.

Unless he was obliquely suggesting that he *hadn't* been honest. She didn't like the realization that hit her in the face, but she couldn't deny it: so far this relationship had all been about *her*. What scared her. What she wanted. How he would affect her life. How many protective layers he'd peeled back; how deeply he saw into *her*.

Ashamed, she wondered if he'd yet seen how self-centered she was.

She'd sworn she wouldn't change anything about herself for any man, but now she knew better. If tonight, awkward or not, had any hope of going anywhere meaningful, she needed to quit worrying exclusively about herself.

"What did you try to hide?" she asked straight-out.

He evaded her gaze. Ripped that half a roll into inedible shreds. "Nothing earthshaking."

"What?" she persisted.

His smile was humorless. "I was hoping it would take you a while to notice how boring I am."

"Boring?" she echoed, staring at him in astonishment. "You're kidding."

"You haven't noticed."

"Boring?"

"Jeez." He scowled. "Don't keep saying that."

"You're the one…"

"Okay. Forget it."

"You're a cop," she said. "I've heard stories from Meg."

He flushed.

"You must have a couple of medals hung in a display case."

"Stuffed in a drawer," Ben muttered.

"Why?" Abby asked, tilting her head to one side. "Real men can brag, you know. I mean, you shoot something and hang it on your wall, that's bragging, right?"

He uttered a strangled swear word. "I didn't shoot 'something.'"

"Well, I wasn't suggesting you stuff a bad guy and mount *him* above your fireplace." Abby had begun to enjoy herself. "Just the medal." She waved him to silence. "Forget it. The point is, you've done heroic things. The kind of stuff girls like."

"Being a cop is my *job*."

She pushed out her lower lip thoughtfully. "Oh, I get it. You're sexy on the job, but once the uniform is gone, what's left is as dull as the financial page."

She'd anticipated some irritation. Or amusement. Not misery.

"You're the one who said it. I'm not a fun guy."

Her temper sparked. "Drop it with the 'fun,' okay? That was an act. And you know it darn well!"

He looked flabbergasted. He *hadn't* known, Abby realized in amazement. He had really, truly, thought her life ambition was to dance to loud music every night.

"I garden," Ben said.

A non sequitur. Except it wasn't, she knew immediately.

"What's wrong with that?"

He was starting to feel foolish, it showed in his glower. "Real men don't pamper roses."

"Oh, for Pete's sake. You can't shoot bad guys twenty-four hours a day."

"I cook."

"And very well, too." Even if dinner was getting cold on her plate.

"That's me. My idea of a fun evening is putting my feet up and reading a good book."

It was sinking in: Ben Shea genuinely didn't know what an incredible catch he was. A calendar-handsome hunk, a tough guy on the job, he was sensitive about the fact that he liked to cook and prune roses. Apparently he figured he ought to be bellowing at the umps on his TV set and spitting tobacco juice instead.

Her own insecurities were so massive, she hadn't been able to see past them to his. Now that she could, the sight struck her as comical. A fact he would not appreciate.

"It's a good thing one of us can cook," she said practically.

"Yeah." His voice sounded hollow. "A good thing."

Abby stood and went to him. "Otherwise," she said, "we'd either starve to death or else we'd have to be ordering pizza all the time. That's what I do."

He shoved his chair back in time for her to settle onto his lap and wriggle comfortably. Speaking roughly, Ben said, "You're not shaped like someone who eats pizza all the time."

"I swim it off."

"Uh-huh." He either had a frog in his throat, or she was getting to him.

"See, tonight I got my vegetables," she continued innocently. "I don't usually, you know."

He smoothed hair from her face, ran his thumbs over her cheekbones.

"So, tell me one more time," she said, her own voice taking on a husky note. "Why am I supposed to be bored by a guy who puts great food in front of me?"

"Women like to go out." He massaged her neck beneath her fall of hair.

"I used to like to go out." Now she sounded faint.

He tugged her head down until their mouths met. The kiss was closer to a whisper than a shout, but she never had liked loud voices. Closing her eyes for a moment, she metaphorically took another step onto that bridge. Like a pier, it quivered underfoot but felt secure.

"You'll want to go out again. Evenings at home will drag."

"How about if we compromise?" Abby whispered. "You'd go out with me sometimes, wouldn't you?"

He nipped her lower lip. "Maybe. Sometimes."

She cradled his face in her hands, saving the textures of shaven jaw and hard muscles playing under her palms. "I might learn how to fertilize roses."

"You don't have to."

"I know," she said on a breath of air. But making him happy wouldn't be so hard.

His hand was on her breast, rubbing gently, and she sucked in a breath, arching her back involuntarily.

It might be awkward, she tried to remind herself. Nothing special.

But she knew better.

They could compromise, she had said. She could have *this*—she gasped when his mouth closed over her breast, dampening her thin shirt. She could have that illusory sense of connection to another human being.

And it wasn't as if it would be so hard to convince him that he was happy. She knew how to handle a guy; hadn't she secretly despised her sisters because they refused to learn?

She'd just never wanted to bother before.

Now she did.

She smiled at Ben when he came up for air. Gripping the hem of her T-shirt, she peeled it right off and reached for the hook on the front of her skimpy bra, chosen with great care for this occasion.

"Why don't you try that now?" she suggested throatily.

His grin was fierce and male. "I just might do that," he agreed. "Although I suggest we take this upstairs."

Remembering the lacy white iron bedstead and the plain navy sheets, Abby wasn't sure she could walk up those stairs.

But she saw the intent in his eyes and scrambled off his lap. Oh, no. No man would carry her like some conquering warrior bringing home a prize. No, if she was going to climb into a man's bed—and she was—it would be under her own steam.

"What's keeping you?" she asked brazenly, and fled one step ahead of him.

CHAPTER TEN

ABBY RACED UP THE STAIRS, giggles floating behind her like the wisps of a jet trail. Ben caught her right outside his bedroom door. He planted his hands to each side of her, pinioning her between the wall and his aroused body.

"I've never had a beautiful blonde lure me into my own bed," he said thickly.

Her eyes were wide and so deep a blue they made him think of the velvety darkness of pansies. "But then," she murmured, "you've never had me before at all, have you?"

He kissed her lightly, a mere taste. His blood heated at the touch of her lips, as plush as her breasts had felt under his palms. His brain was fogging. He hoped like hell Abby wasn't going to change her mind.

"Are you nervous?" he asked.

A quiver ran through her. "Yes."

"If you don't want to do this, say so now." A cold shower wouldn't do it. Maybe he'd slam his fist through a wall. Pain might dent this mindless desire.

She smiled with deliberate, sensual warmth. "I want to do this."

A flood of relief was indistinguishable from the pummeling of raw hunger. Ben growled something wordless and captured her mouth with the brutal intent of a cop kicking down a door to enter a house.

Abby didn't melt against him; she grabbed on tight around his neck and kissed him back as desperately, making breathless little sounds to weave a duet with his groans. She squirmed until he gripped her buttocks and lifted her to cradle his painfully hard erection.

"Damn." He wrenched his mouth away. "Why'd you have to wear jeans?"

"Next time," her voice was high and breathy, "I'll wear a skirt. With no panties underneath."

He had to kiss her again, just to give himself strength to last until he could peel those jeans off. Unzip his own. His thoughts were muddled, slow-moving. *Take her here* fought with the need to make this good, ensure she felt no regret.

Her mouth was swollen and red, her eyes cloudy. Ben gripped her thighs and hoisted her higher yet, until her legs clasped him around the waist.

But her fingers bit into his shoulders. "I want to walk," she squeaked, and he heard alarm.

"Why?"

"I just do."

He groaned and closed his eyes, but lowered her to the floor. She slid down his body, the denim seams at her crotch scraping him with the exquisite taunt of fingernails over his bulging fly. Damn. He couldn't bear it.

"I'm not chickening out," she whispered. "I just swore... Never mind."

She gripped his hand and pulled him after her into

the bedroom. She stopped right beside the bed and began undoing the buttons on his shirt.

Ben stared down at her intent face, tongue caught between her teeth, lashes forming dark fans against her cheeks. Abby's inner toughness was belied by the delicacy of her features, the satin veil of golden hair parted simply in the middle. He could have looked forever, if every button she tackled hadn't meant the tickle of her fingertips caressing his skin.

"There!" she said in triumph, sliding his shirt from his shoulders and running her hands over his chest, seeming to savor the contours. Her voice became throatier. "Now..."

Heaven help him, she was working on the button at the waist of his jeans. Slowly. Another little cry of pleasure told him when she had conquered it. The scrape of metal and an easing of the constriction was followed by the sweet agony of her slender, strong hand gripping him.

His head fell back and he made a strangled sound, closing his eyes as he fought for control.

"Can you..." She sounded hesitant. "Can you take off your own boots?"

He sucked in air. "Yeah."

"Are you...all right?"

"Never been better." His voice didn't sound like it. He clenched his teeth and opened his eyes.

She was staring anxiously up at him. Her throat was long and golden tan, but her breasts were creamy white, perfectly formed, crowned with taut pink nipples.

"You're beautiful." He wished he could think of

something more original to say to her, but the truth was, he couldn't think at all.

Her jeans had a button fly; each popped free as he tugged. Belly button. Creamy firm stomach. At last, silky curls as gold as the fall of straight hair that cascaded over her shoulder when she shivered.

Ben wrapped his hands around her hips and eased the jeans and a tiny pair of high-cut blue panties down. Her legs went on forever. By the time his hands were wrapped around her calves and she lifted one foot to step out of her jeans, he was on his knees in front of her. Just at the right level to nuzzle those sunny curls.

She squeaked when he rubbed his cheek against her. "Ben?" she cried.

He surged upward, lifting and depositing her on the bed, her legs apart and him right where he wanted to be: between her thighs. He kicked off boots and jeans both, following her down.

Of course she wouldn't stay passive. She reached up for him and kissed him as frantically as he kissed her. Their legs tangled; they rolled until the bed groaned. When he had her flattened on her back, he entered her, feeling the shock and pleasure vibrate to his bones. Her core gripped him as fiercely as her hands did his shoulders. She was strong and lithe and long-limbed, her voice a cascade of amazement and joy that severed his last threads of control.

He withdrew, agonizing inch by inch, plunged back into her. Over and over, lifting her hips so he could go as deep as his first memories. Her hips met each thrust and she gasped for breath, huge blue eyes fixed on his as if she had to see his face until the end. As if they were connected by the sight of each other as much as by his penetration of her body.

He saw the astonishment flood her face even as her body rippled and squeezed around him. His own climax went on forever, like nothing he'd ever felt. By the end of it, he would have sworn he'd died and been reborn.

She could do with him what she willed. He was hers for life.

HIS CHEST WAS SLICK beneath her cheek. The thunder of his heartbeat was slowing so one didn't crash into the last. Abby had never felt so boneless, so relaxed, so…happy. She felt giddy, as if she'd inhaled an overdose of laughing gas at the dentist's. Somewhere underneath that delicious languor, there must be the dull ache of pain. She'd never lived without it.

Enjoy the moment, she told herself, even as she began probing for the pain. She felt incomplete without it.

She kissed Ben's chest, tasting the salt. "Was that as good for you as it was for me?" she asked lightly.

"Better." He yanked her atop him so he could look into her eyes. "It wasn't 'good.' It was a piece of heaven on earth."

Yes. That's exactly what it had been. A firm skeptic, Abby had never glimpsed heaven before.

"If you say so," she heard herself say, and wondered why she couldn't confess how she really felt.

His eyes narrowed for a second. "You need some more convincing?"

She hadn't found the ache yet. Maybe a callus, but nothing sharper, rawer. Could a person be cured in the space of half an hour? Was being happy this easy?

Abby pretended to be thoughtful. "I guess I must. Need convincing, that is. Think you're up to the challenge?"

The grooves in Ben's cheeks deepened with a wicked grin. "Oh, yeah," he said huskily. "How hard can it be?"

A giggle popped out of her mouth like a hiccup. "Is that a pun?"

"Hell, no. It was a question."

"Oh." She batted her eyelashes and wriggled experimentally. Pursing her lips, she said, "Not very hard."

Male ego affronted, he growled, "Yet."

"Well, how can you convince me, if..."

"Like this," he murmured and, framing her face with his big hands, pulled her down for a slow, sweet kiss.

No teeth or tongue, no edgy hunger, just a loving caress, a savoring of texture and intimacy.

It jump-started her fear.

Hands on his shoulders, she shoved herself to a sitting position. Smiling deliberately, she lifted her hair and gave her head a toss. She arched her back just enough to draw his eyes to her breasts and narrow waist.

"Whaddaya think, big guy? You going to let me be on top this time?"

Hands cupping her breasts, his thumbs playing over the nipples, Ben didn't seem to notice how she'd broken off the kiss. She couldn't imagine that he'd guess why.

She didn't know.

Why was a kiss even more powerful than sex?

Sex? Who was she kidding? What they were doing was way more complicated than that tiny word suggested.

This time, Ben had more patience. He played with her body as if he were a connoisseur rolling a good wine around his mouth. A touch here; a delicate flick of his tongue there. He had her weak and helpless by the time he was done.

No. Not quite helpless. She got in her own shots. His muscles jerked under her hands. His eyes were hot with need by the time he rolled off her and lifted her astride his body once again.

"You want to be in charge?" he said roughly. "Go for it, girl."

A bitter thought, barbed, hooked her somewhere around her heart. Of course she wanted to be in charge. She was too big a coward to learn what it felt like *not* to be.

She managed to pry the barbs from her skin and pretend they hadn't left droplets of blood. After all, how else could she have *fun?* Wasn't that how she was trying, really hard, to look on this experience?

"That's it, love." Ben groaned as she poised above him, starting to lower herself, stopping, backtracking. "Torture me. This is your chance."

One she'd fully meant to take. But the fcel of him, thick and heavy, filling her, was more than she could bear. *Sex* let her tease, enjoy her power over a man. This was something else. Something that drove her to an urgency she didn't understand, couldn't deny.

With a sigh that came out as a whimper, she sank

onto him, taking him in deep. Eyes closed, head back, she paused for a second, savoring the incredible sensation of having Ben inside her. *This wasn't sex,* she thought again hazily. It was neither awkward nor smooth and practiced; it was the completion of something they had been heading toward from the moment she had scrambled, sweaty, up onto the road and faced the big dark cop. They were coming together, as somehow she had always known they must and would.

She opened her eyes and drank in the sight of him. His face was taut with need and a fierce, burning intensity. She wanted to see exultation transform the hard lines, soften him.

Abby wanted to please him, as she had never wanted to please before.

This brand of need was new to her, unsettling but possessing an urgency that would not let her do anything but give in to it.

Inner muscles tight, she rose deliberately, sank back. She kept the pace slow but steady, watching Ben's eyes glaze, savoring the rough sounds he made, the feel of his hips driving upward.

How ironic that pleasing him excited her to the point where she quit thinking, only felt. She whimpered, faltered, lost control of the pace, and gloried in his big hands gripping her hips and taking charge.

Yes! Faster, harder. Exquisite tension coiled inside her, tighter, tighter.

"Ben?" she whispered. Begged.

"Let go," he said hoarsely. He plunged upward. Teeth gritted, Ben panted, "I...need...you...to fly."

His voice was the last sensation, on top of the

others, as if he had touched someplace inside her that was more sensitive than any nerve-ending on the surface.

White-hot pleasure imploded in her belly, ran like rivers of fire to her fingertips and her toes. Abby screamed from the shock and pleasure.

On a guttural sound, Ben joined her, the spasms deep inside her, part of her own, as he was part of her.

She collapsed, sure she couldn't have moved if a gunman had burst into the room. Ben's arms wrapped around her convulsively; he took great, harsh breaths that seemed to fill her lungs with his.

Her stunning sense of completion, of wholeness, was not something Abby could accept. It meant she *wasn't* whole on her own, and that thought was terrifying.

It chilled her skin with astonishing speed. Not moving a muscle, she withdrew into herself. Probing inside, she found the ache beneath her breastbone. As if it were a crystal ball, she focused on it, cupped it in her hands, searching for herself in its cloudy depths. *This* was who she was. Ben Shea would shatter this glass heart if she let him, and she would not be a woman who lived for a man rather than for herself.

Willpower alone slowed her breathing, let her clutch at a sense of distance. Allowed her to raise her head and smile, as if nothing of significance had just happened.

Allowed her to say insouciantly, ''Well, you kinda convinced me there. But heck, maybe we'd better do it again.''

Allowed her not to see that she had hurt him.

"I'VE FOUND ZIP," Renee reported the next day in a quick phone call. "Or maybe I should say, I've found too much. Ol' Pops ticked off plenty of folks."

"So I'm discovering," Abby agreed dryly. She ignored the blinking light of another phone call. "And here we always thought the man was revered by everybody but us."

"No kidding." Renee was silent for a moment. "I'm getting scared, Abby. Half the time I'm puking in the toilet, and here I'm supposed to be a police chief, and meantime someone's out to get us. I can't deal with everything."

"You *are* dealing with everything," Abby said stoutly. "I talk to Elk Springs officers all the time. They like you. They respect you."

"Really?" Her sister sounded hopeful.

"Would I lie?"

Renee let out a puff of air. "Probably."

Abby had to laugh. "Come on. If anything, I don't know how to keep my big mouth shut."

"Except with men."

That stung, and a few months ago Abby would have responded hotly. Renee was the one who had a problem dealing with men, she'd always believed. Who'd have thought Renee would end up happily married, while Abby never got to first base?

Only because she didn't want to, she told herself too quickly.

Hadn't wanted to, she corrected herself.

It rankled to admit to herself that Renee might

have been right all this time and Abby wrong. Maybe the way she'd coped with Daddy *wasn't* healthy.

Getting clobbered on a regular basis wasn't healthy, either. So maybe neither of them was right or wrong. Just different in how they survived.

"Men like smiles," Abby said now. "They're not usually big on honesty."

She braced herself for what would be a chiding comeback. Renee was still determined to play mom. Still sure her little sister needed guidance.

But for once, Renee surprised her. She dropped the subject of Abby's conduct altogether.

"Do you think we're going to find this guy before I get sworn in? It'll give me the creeps having a crowd pressing around when I know *he* might be in it. Maybe with a gun."

"Not a gun." What would he do? Abby worried. "This guy has fire on his brain. He'll have something spectacular in mind."

"Oh, I feel so much better."

The other light on Abby's phone quit blinking, and she had a spurt of guilt. She *was* on the payroll right now. And Lord knew she had plenty waiting to be done.

"Listen, I've got to go," she said. "You're doing great, Renee. You saw Meg go through this. The nausea will pass and you'll feel fine. Just be careful, okay?"

"Thanks, Abby," her sister said, sounding almost meek. "The pep talk's appreciated."

Weird, Abby thought as she hung up. All of a sudden, she was the strong one. Meg and Renee were both calling her for reassurance, crying on her shoulder. Was it just because they were pregnant and therefore felt more vulnerable? Or did they? Maybe instead their relationships had fundamentally changed in some way she didn't understand.

Or—here was an even stranger thought—maybe they always *had* called her, depended on her, as she did on them, and she just hadn't noticed. Her insecurities had convinced her, once Meg came back to town, that Renee loved Meg most. And of course Meg was closest to Renee; after all, Abby had been a little girl when Meg left. Whenever either sister called her, Abby had secretly believed she was second choice.

Maybe that, too, had never been true.

The phone rang. Abby, shaking off a dazed feeling, took the call from an insurance agent returning her earlier one. He confirmed that the owner of a fancy toolshed—or so the owner claimed, putting a price tag on it of twenty-two hundred dollars—had only added coverage on it six weeks ago. No, the agent hadn't gone out to look at it. He couldn't confirm that, before the fire Abby was investigating, the shed had been anything more than the ramshackle lean-to a neighbor claimed was all that had ever stood on the spot. Making notes, Abby thanked him, promised to let him know the result of her inquiries, and ended the call.

Sometimes she swore that all any cop did was hunch over a desk gabbing on the telephone. Maybe her right ear was flatter than her left one. As an arson investigator, she knew darn well that she spent a heck of a lot more time on the phone than she did in the field. She was best friends with clerks at credit agencies, title companies, banks, the county assessor's office—never mind insurance brokers.

The "how" of arson was easily established, but juries wouldn't convict unless the "why" was laid out in great big strokes like a child's crayon drawing. Stick figures only, please; subtle washes of color only confused jurors. The trouble with arson was that there were rarely witnesses to the crime itself.

Her job was to show that the owner—of the burned grocery store, for example—had been so desperate, he'd had almost no alternative but to torch the place. The business was failing; banks and suppliers wanted their money back; and there was no way on this green earth he was going to be able to sell that store. She wanted to lay it out so plain, jurors would be nodding and thinking, "Yeah, of course he's the one who set the fire. If I didn't have a superior moral conscience, I'd have done it myself in his place."

Today, in between calls about a half dozen current cases, she followed up on some more of Daddy dearest's enemies. Ben had passed one over to her in hopes she could discover more than he'd been able to.

This was a winner, she remembered from an earlier conversation with Ben: a suicidal, drunken, angry man had been holed up in his house with the wife who wanted to leave him held hostage and two scared kids huddled upstairs. He was going to burn the damn place down, he had threatened.

Lieutenant Ed Patton—he hadn't made police chief yet—hadn't called for a negotiator. Hadn't tried to soothe, coax, suggest alternatives. No. Instead he'd goaded, told Richard Price he didn't have the balls to kill himself, that he'd never do it, that he might as well crawl out now because sooner or later he would.

This one sent shivers down Abby's spine, because she'd known the girl. Just by sight, they weren't friends, thank God. But her death, along with her mother's and father's, was all over the newspapers and local newscasts by the next day. At school, counselors came to each classroom to talk to the kids. Abby would never have made an appointment to see one of the counselors, even though Debbie Price's murder gave her nightmares. She might slip and tell more than she should about her own dad. But it scared her. A lot.

Ben had tracked Debbie Price's little brother into the state foster care system. Two years after his parents had died, the paper trail on David Price had petered out.

In the meantime, Ben had been handed two new murder cases. A drunk, beaten to death in an alley behind a Dumpster, and a sixteen-year-old girl, raped and strangled in a small park within shouting distance of her home. Sounding harassed, he'd called Abby and asked if she could try to locate David Price.

In a way, the conversation was a relief, because it had been businesslike. After she had slipped out of his house in the predawn hours to come home, shower and get dressed for work, she'd half dreaded their next meeting. Would Ben make assumptions because they'd had sex? Would he figure a wedding cake and two point five children were in their future now that she'd lowered her guard so far?

The disconcerting part was, Abby didn't know which to hope for: that he took their lovemaking in the spirit she'd intended it—fun; or that he assumed it meant a diamond ring and forever. The cowardly part of her hoped for the first; her foolish feminine side hoped for the second.

The trouble was, she was never going to believe in "forever." How could she? Fate had a way of snatching it away the second you started believing in it. You had to be an idiot to expose yourself to that kind of pain over and over again.

One thing Abby wasn't, was an idiot.

But Ben would walk out of her life if she didn't start trusting him.

It didn't help that he was offering the same in return. She didn't want that kind of power any more than she wanted someone else to have it over her.

But she would miss Ben Shea. She was becoming uncomfortably certain that the freewheeling, superficial life she'd been living wouldn't satisfy her again, not after knowing Ben.

Damned if you do, and damned if you don't, she thought unhappily. Her instincts had screamed "no" from the beginning. She should never have gone out with him.

Then she wouldn't have known what she would be missing.

Thank heavens the phone rang and saved her from further brooding.

Abby grabbed the receiver. "Arson Investigations Unit. Patton speaking."

"Ms. Patton, this is Jennifer Kramer in Children's Services. I've done some further research on David Price, as we were discussing."

Abby went on full alert. "Yes?"

"What appears to have happened is that his foster family moved out of the state. California, at least initially. In those circumstances, we always have to weigh the benefits of having the child stay with a family against the risk inherent in handing over a dependent child to authorities in another state. In this case, apparently the move was allowed and custody transferred to the State of California."

She had tracked down phone numbers and the last known address for David Price's foster family. After thanking her profusely, Abby plunged into the morass of child services in California. Nobody was eager to spend precious time hunting for records so old.

"He's no longer a minor," a social worker said in a tone of exaggerated patience, as if Abby hadn't figured out something so obvious.

She explained again, and knew the woman on the other end of the line was groaning inwardly. Abby even understood. What public employee wasn't overwhelmed by too many cases, too much paperwork, too many needy, desperate people?

"I'll try," she was promised.

Somewhat to her amazement, the woman phoned her back just before five.

"The foster parents moved again," she reported, "but this time they weren't interested in taking him. He acted out in the next home. Nothing real serious—fights, bad language, that kind of thing. They asked us to find him a new placement. After that he went in and out of half a dozen homes. The usual sad story. Custody was discharged when he turned eighteen.'' Abby heard paper being shuffled. ''Amazingly, he'd graduated from high school, but I have no address or further information after that.''

Abby took down the phone number of David Price's last known foster parents. Perhaps they'd know of high school friends he might have stayed in touch with.

But the Cronins, too, had vanished. Checks on driver's licenses and motor vehicle registration failed to locate them. They'd either died or moved out of state, as well.

Frustrated, Abby went to work on a case she'd just begun investigating: a rental house that had burned down two nights before. She'd look into insurance first, then the owner's debt load. See whether he'd advertised for new tenants to replace those that had given notice two weeks ago. She made a note to remind herself to call the tenants' association and find out whether anyone had registered complaints against this landlord, who owned several other rentals, as well. Was he not responding when problems developed? ''Bank,'' she added to her list—a quick infusion of insurance money might be needed to help him over a cash flow problem.

All the while she was debating whether it was worth trying to hunt down David Price's last foster family. She could check with neighboring states... But he'd only lived with the Cronins for a year. What were the chances they'd maintained close ties? And it wasn't as if she had any reason to think he was the one. Heck, Daddy had ruined dozens of lives. David Price had been a mere incidental.

No. She wouldn't waste any more time trying to track him down.

If she felt disquiet at her own decision...well, she was a good investigator because she made a habit of questioning herself. A little uneasiness was as familiar to Abby as the clutter on her desk.

Something she frequently had to ignore.

CHAPTER ELEVEN

ABBY ARRIVED at Ben's house wearing blue jeans and a faded T-shirt that still managed to cling in all the right places. If his mood hadn't been so dark, he would have pulled her across the threshold, closed the door and ripped the T-shirt right over her head.

As it was, he finally managed to wrench his gaze from her tiny waist and narrow hips only because he smelled something damn good—and it wasn't her.

Abby lifted the bags she held in each hand. "Dinner," she said simply. "I figured you'd had a tough day, and you shouldn't have to cook."

"You made dinner?"

Her smile was impish, nose crinkled. "You don't have to worry. This is takeout. The good kind. Straight from The Great Wall."

"You're a sweetheart," he said, and meant it. Even opening a can of soup had seemed like more effort than he wanted to make. He was so damned tired.

If there was one kind of crime that got to him, it had to be the murder of a kid. He'd been stoic all day, but every time he closed his eyes he saw an image of that girl's dead body, naked and sprawled obscenely under a shrub on the bare dirt.

Abby waved him back and scooted in, using her

hip to close the door behind her. "You sit down. I'll get dishes."

"Did I sound so bad when I called earlier?"

"No. But I guessed."

He moved uncomfortably. He'd told her the once that he sometimes cried, but that had been an unusual admission for him. Cops couldn't afford to let their job get to them. They were supposed to expend their rage and pain in tracking down the killers, the rapists, the scums of the universe. They were supposed to be able to compartmentalize what they felt. How else could they go home to wives and children?

"I hate it when the victim's a kid."

"Me, too." She touched her hand to his cheek, the softest of gestures, and he closed his eyes momentarily and rested against her hand. Until, burned into his eyelids, he saw the girl.

He swore and scrubbed a hand across his face. "She was sixteen years old. Some bastard raped her. Can you believe it? Her mother says she'd never even been on a date. Sweet sixteen and never been kissed. Now she's dead."

"You'll find him." Abby's voice was a balm.

"Damn straight."

"But not tonight. Tonight—" she gave him a firm look "—you're going to go sit down at the table and let me wait on you. Then maybe a bath. With bubbles. There's something to aromatherapy, you know."

"Yes, ma'am." On the drive home, he'd wished like hell for a hot shower, a home-cooked dinner and Abby to hold him close under the quilt in his own bed. If he had to go to work tomorrow smelling like lavender, so be it.

Besides...she was being so sweet, so kind, so unlike her usual tart self, he knew she was trying. "Give me a few minutes to change."

She walked past him into his kitchen. "Make it snappy. Dinner's getting cold."

Upstairs he stripped off his uniform and dressed in gray sweatpants and a T-shirt as faded as hers. His anguish hadn't faded, and he hadn't expected that it would. But side by side with it, he had a fleeting thought: life was good. Abby made all the difference.

He wasn't surprised that she'd chosen spicy entrées such as Mongolian beef.

As he ate, Ben let Abby's chatter wash over him. He didn't say much in return. Abby would understand; she'd seen things as bad as that girl's body. That was one thing about dating another cop; you knew she had sights as horrific etched in her memory.

She gave him quick, anxious glances; twice the delicate flutter of her hand touched the back of his. When they finished dinner, she put on a CD and tugged him into the living room, where she melted against him, the sway of her hips holding his dark thoughts captive.

Afterward, she went up the stairs with him as though she did it every night. He decided to skip the bath, his mind on her. Beside the bed, he bent his head to kiss her, but she moved away.

"Take your clothes off."

"What?"

"You need a back rub." Her expression was sweetly serious.

He ripped his shirt off, tossing it aside. "Darling, you can make me a happy man."

"I know I can."

Ben caught something peculiar in her tone, but she was untying the drawstring at his waist and giving him a shove back onto the bed, so he didn't dwell on it.

She turned off the overhead light and a moment later followed him onto the bed in the glow from the bedside lamp. She stradled him, her strong, clever hands finding every knotted muscle, untying tension and making him groan with pleasure. He closed his eyes for the first time without seeing the dead girl. Humming under her breath, Abby kneaded his lower back, worked her way methodically up his spine, finally massaging his scalp.

By that time he couldn't have strung two words together. He felt boneless, as if he were floating in a warm dark pool. He ought to roll over, pull her down to him, kiss her, make love to her. But he couldn't seem to find the energy.

He tried to murmur something, but she shushed him. Her hands gentled, soothed...sent him to sleep.

The next thing Ben knew, it was morning, and he was alone in bed.

JACK MURRAY hadn't been sheriff all that long. Ben had known him casually for years; the Butte County Sheriff's Department worked closely with the Elk Springs Police Department. Ben had heard all the gossip, and paid closer attention to it than he usually did, because it involved Meg.

Murray and she had been teenage lovers; she'd fled him and Elk Springs. No one was quite sure whether he'd known he had a son before she came back to town two and a half years ago with a four-teen-year-old kid in tow who looked just like a young Jack Murray. Ben hadn't asked Meg for the scoop; he and she weren't friends, just colleagues.

He did know that the sheriff had taken to parenting like a duck to water. Will had gone camping with his dad last weekend.

Ben had heard other stories, too, the ones that sug-gested Jack Murray was a modern-day version of Chief Ed Patton: quick of temper, uncompromising, uncompassionate.

Ben didn't buy those stories, not wholly. He didn't figure Meg was the type to pretend she liked her son's father if he was that kind. Still, Ben had been wary, as had most of the department, when the new sheriff took over the reins.

So far, so good. Jack Murray had soaked the county council for a desperately needed boost to the budget. He gave speeches and shook hands in the right places, making deputies more popular in a few quarters. He'd added two K-9 units to the depart-ment, something that had been wanted for years. He'd suspended a cop for a drinking problem, which had caused some grumbles, but Ben thought it had been necessary.

Ben might have been ready to relax around the guy, if Abby hadn't mentioned their past. She'd laughed at the idea she was pining for Murray, but their relationship sure as hell had consisted of more than a few casual dates and a roll in the hay, or she wouldn't have sounded so brittle about it. She wouldn't have thrown it out there so defiantly, with that edge of anger and hurt.

Ben also had a feeling that Abby wouldn't be impressed if he confronted Jack Murray, maybe drummed his chest a few times and laid it on the line. "My woman." He grinned faintly at the idea. Hell, maybe he should piss on the post supporting her mailbox while he was at it.

His reflections about his boss weren't more than a few hours old when the man himself knocked on the glass insert in Ben's office door and walked in.

"Got a minute?" Murray asked. Since Ben was sitting there to all appearances doing nothing but rubbing his stomach and staring into space, the sheriff could be forgiven for the note of irony in his voice.

"Huh?" Ben swiveled in his chair. "A minute? Oh. Sure. Have a seat. I was just thinking."

"About?"

"The sixteen-year-old who was raped and murdered. Damn it, her stepfather has what should be a rock-solid alibi, but I don't like him. There's just something about the way he's pretending to grieve..."

Murray's face hardened. "Then find a hole in the son of a bitch's alibi."

"He's a vice-principal at the middle school."

Murray breathed a prayerful obscenity. "All the more reason. If you're wrong, I'll back you up."

Grudgingly pleased, Ben studied the sheriff. Today he wore a suit that must have cost more than Ben made in a month. Pale gray fabric draped beautifully. A white shirt was paired with a deep red tie. Black shoes gleamed. Murray looked like a politician, which is what he mostly was these days.

But he was still a cop, as his willingness to walk out on shaky ground showed.

Ben popped a couple of antacids. "What can I do for you?"

"Just wondered what you've come up with on this bastard stalking the Pattons."

Ben snorted. "Too many possibilities. We've been looking into people who'd have a grudge against Ed Patton. But we either can't find 'em, or they claim they wouldn't hold Chief Patton's sins against his daughters." He contemplated the sheriff. "You knew the man well. What did you think of him as a cop?"

Murray shoved his hands in his pockets and lounged back against the door frame. "He was smart, aggressive—maybe too aggressive—and he didn't like 1990s sensibilities. Hell, you put the guy behind bars, you didn't worry about his rights or even the victim's trauma. He'd mellowed some by the time I joined the force; I heard stories about the early days. I was never quite sure whether they were true or not."

"They were true," Ben said shortly.

Murray's dark eyes met his. "Tell me."

Ben gave it to him, half a dozen of the worst cases. The sheriff listened, face impassive. Only at the end did he close his eyes and squeeze the bridge of his nose.

"God Almighty," he murmured.

"I hear you were his protégé." Ben tried not to sound judgmental.

Murray's mouth twisted. "Yeah. You could say that. For a while there, I figured that's how a man acted." His gaze briefly met Ben's. "He and I had a past, you know."

"I guessed."

"He broke my nose. Cracked a couple of ribs. Had me down on my knees begging. I felt lower than a louse. Seventeen years old, and the only way I could figure to regain my self-esteem was to one-up him." Murray's laughter was humorless. "My own father was ashamed that I'd let myself be beaten up. I could see it in his eyes." He shook his head. "May God help me, I tried to be like Ed Patton."

"But you didn't succeed."

"No." He was silent for a moment. "But I re-spected him. I never saw anything like you're telling me."

Ben clasped his hands behind his head and rocked back in his office chair. "Abby and her sisters aren't surprised by any of this. He hurt them, you know."

Jack Murray growled a word that was probably obscene. "I didn't know then. Renee told me just a few years ago, after he was dead. Back in high school, Meg lied about broken bones and bruises. I bought it." And didn't forgive himself for his cre-dulity, his expression said.

Ben studied his boss. "Why are you telling me all this? This stuff about you and Chief Patton isn't common knowledge."

A nerve jumped under his eye. "I know you're involved with Abby. I want you to understand."

"What you saw in her?" Ben asked, tone hardening.

"The whole picture." Murray shoved himself away from the door frame. "You can't help Abby or any of the others if you don't know the past."

"You know it. Why aren't you more involved in this investigation?"

"I'd do anything." Murray's voice was hoarse. "But I'm too close. Meg and I get along okay, but Abby doesn't like having me around. Renee and I—there's always been some tension there, too. I thought maybe she blamed me for Meg's leaving. Or resented me taking over as chief after her dad." He shook his head. "But if I can help, let me know."

Ben stood and held out a hand. In an obscure male ritual, they solemnly shook. With Murray gone, Ben sank back into his chair with a rueful grunt. Well, hell. He guessed they'd come to an understanding of some kind.

Easier than a pissing contest any day.

ABBY WAS AS SWEET as peppermint candy again that evening, even though Ben had had to call and upset their plans, warning her he wouldn't be home until eight or nine.

"You'll probably just want to go straight to bed," she'd said promptly, with no hint of being miffed.

"Maybe," he said. "But only if you're in it."

"You're sure?"

Oh, yeah. He was sure. If he'd thought she was ready, he would have suggested she move in with him. He'd even slowed his steps in front of a downtown jewelry store yesterday. A solitaire sapphire had caught his eye, the rich blue making him think of Abby's eyes. The ring would look perfect on her finger.

Now *that* he knew she wasn't ready for.

But he did succeed in convincing her to come for dinner and as much of the night as her restless nature let her stay.

She arrived with grocery bags this time. Ben was touched that she worried enough about him to want to pamper him. In the kitchen she triumphantly produced steaks and salad makings from the brown paper sacks, insisting on doing the cooking.

"I'm not totally inept," she said, flapping her hands at him when he tried to take over. "I may have given you the wrong impression. The idea of putting dinner on the table at five on the nose, day in and day out, for the rest of my life leaves me cold. But I did learn the basics. Truly. Now sit down and talk to me. How was your day?"

He told her about his efforts to crack a suspect's alibi, without being specific; even with her, he wasn't going to name names and then find out he was wrong.

She offered a couple of ideas, but tentatively, without her usual force. Maybe because she sensed he was holding back. Or maybe, he thought with a twitch of the mouth, she was afraid of damaging his fragile self-confidence.

After dinner they cleaned the kitchen companionably, then went upstairs where Abby insisted on the bath he'd foregone last night.

The bubble bath wasn't lavender scented; it was lemon. Somehow it suited Abby. On her knees, she checked the temperature one more time and turned off the hot water. "There," she said, smiling gently up at him. "Now, you just relax. I'll read in bed."

"I don't think so."

When she rose to her feet, he tugged her T-shirt free from her jeans and shimmied it over her head.

Her eyes widened. "But...there's no room..."

"We'll make room." Ben tossed her bra over his shoulder.

"I wanted you to relax." But she didn't fight him as he unzipped her jeans and slowly eased them off.

"Don't wanna."

"Ben..." Her earnest expression made him want to laugh.

"Yes?"

"You're making this hard."

"Is that a pun?"

She giggled. "Well, no, but..." She pressed a hand to her mouth and tried to stifle another giggle. "Now that you mention it..."

Grinning, he lifted her into the tub and stepped in after her. Foaming water splashed onto the floor as he sank down, cradling her between his thighs.

"Oh!" she said, when he scooped up handfuls of iridescent bubbles and plastered them to her breasts. She murmured contented sounds as he played with the bubbles, popping them, building mountains, plunging his hands inside them to find the pink flesh.

"Now this," he whispered in her ear, "is relaxing."

"Mmm."

Making love in the bathtub wasn't as easy as he'd imagined, although she was more compliant than she'd ever been in bed. With her astride, her knees cracked against the porcelain sides. It was too short for him to lay on top of her. By the time Ben turned her around and entered her from behind, half the water was on the floor and they were both laughing between moans of frustration.

But, oh, the completion was sweet, and the laughter as they drained the tub and dried each other sweeter yet. As Ben turned out the bathroom light, he smiled like an idiot at the sight of Abby's toothbrush hanging in the holder beside his. There was a permanence in her leaving a toothbrush here that he liked.

More than liked.

He was a happy man when he fell asleep half an hour later with a damp Abby tucked in the curve of his arm, the scent of lemon in his nostrils.

So why wasn't he as happy the next night, when Abby wrinkled her nose and denied any desire to go out?

Okay, he thought at first, letting his uneasiness go. He alleviated the stress of the last days by layering a complicated lasagna and adding garlic bread and a green salad, but then realized he was doing most of the talking at the dinner table. Damn it, she was agreeing with every word he said, which was downright unnatural.

"You know, I'm okay," he said pointedly. "I arrested the son of a bitch today."

"I know." Abby smiled and raised her wineglass. "To a shining example of good police work."

Ben lifted his glass, as well. "May he rot in isolation."

"Amen." She sipped.

"You've been treating me as if I'm made of glass," he continued, refusing to be distracted from his point. "What's the deal?"

This smile was as gentle and mysterious as all the other ones he'd seen from her in days. "No deal. What, you want me cranky?"

"Will you marry me?" he asked, stunning himself.

Her smile slipped. "I... Do you mean that?"

"Yeah. I think so."

Her tongue touched her lips. "I don't know, Ben. Maybe. I...hadn't gotten that far yet in my dreaming. Can we talk about it later? You'll give me a few weeks?"

"Yeah," he said roughly.

It scared him that he was relieved. Unlike her, he had been traveling that road in his daydreams. But all of a sudden, something wasn't right. He couldn't believe she'd so easily lost her wariness, forgotten to feel threatened.

She just wasn't herself. He had this sense that he was dining with a clone of Abby Patton. Without the reluctant honesty and the sting, she was so damned serene, he kept wanting to shock her into some kind of real reaction.

Hell, he thought. That's why he'd asked her to marry him. Not because he wanted an, "Oh, yes, please, Ben," but because he'd expected to get a reaction.

It was like having Cindy stroll into the house, hop up onto his lap and purr the night away. He'd spend the whole time staring down at her wondering if some other cat who looked just like her had wandered into his house.

This was Abby, all right, sitting across the table from him taking dainty bites from her crunchy garlic bread. But in another way, it wasn't *her*. He knew it; he just couldn't figure out why or even when the transformation had happened.

"Are you having to bite your tongue often?" he asked.

Her face was so blank when she looked up, he knew damn well she understood what he meant. "Excuse me?"

"You haven't told me off in days."

Her mouth curved. "Have you deserved it?"

"Probably."

"You've had a stressful week." She held out a hand. "Can I dish up some more lasagna for you?"

"No, goddamn it! I don't want lasagna!"

"What do you want?" she asked, sounding puzzled.

"You," he snapped.

"I'm here."

"Yeah?" He shoved his plate away. "I'm not so sure."

Hurt flashed in her eyes. "If you want me to go home…"

"You know I don't."

"Well, then, don't be grumpy!" she said with more spirit than he'd heard in days. "Tell me what the fallout is going to be on this arrest. Does the girl's mother believe her husband killed her daughter?"

The mother didn't *want* to believe it, and who

could blame her? Ben found himself talking again, with Abby making encouraging noises and prompting him now and again.

Not until later, after they'd made love in his white wrought-iron bed and Abby had fallen asleep, did Ben think again about the conversation. She'd wriggled out of explaining herself as deftly as a con man evades a cop. Somehow *he* had felt in the wrong; a grump.

Ben broke out in a cold sweat. He knew what had happened: he'd been hooked and gutted, just as his mother had done to his father.

No outsider would ever guess that Elizabeth Shea was anything but a sweet little homemaker, supporting her husband's career and following her son's. It had taken Ben years to see what she was doing to Dad. A little chuckle, a comical roll of the eyes, and she'd slide the knife between his ribs.

"You can't really mean to do something so silly," she'd say, when he thought of taking up painting. Or, "Why, you know you'll never get that job," when Dad talked about applying for a promotion at Cranston and West, the huge office furniture manufacturer where he had spent his entire career. "Hugh, dear, I hate to think that people might be ridiculing you."

By that time, everything Dad suggested was tentative, his voice hesitant, as he waited to see what his wife would say. Ben could always predict Mom's response: it would be gently dismissive, hinting that Dad would fail anyway, that he should be content with his modest successes and leave anything bigger to those more capable.

Dad never made decisions at home. Mom would appear deferential, smiling so sweetly, while she made up his mind for him.

She liked to talk about the career she would have had if she hadn't married Hugh Shea. She'd been a buyer at a big clothing store when they met. In her memory, she had been on the brink of rising to department head. Of course, she would be a regional manager for the chain of stores by now.

"But Hugh likes to have me at home," she would tell strangers, smiling as she patted her husband's arm. "I'm sure he's right. Although things at Cranston and West haven't turned out the way he hoped. But who knows?" Her laugh would gaily show she held no bitterness. "Maybe I wouldn't have gone as far as I'd hoped, either." Her tone always made plain that of course she would have, but she didn't want to hurt her husband's feelings.

The teenage Ben had come to wonder how his father functioned at work. Was he as timid there, always waiting for someone else to make the tough decision? If so, no wonder he hadn't gotten any of the promotions he'd talked about over the years.

Or perhaps he was a different man during the day, as he was on the rare occasions when he and Ben went to a ball game or fishing without Mom. It was then that Ben had come to know the man his father might have been, if he hadn't married Elizabeth Glassner.

Ben had gone through a stage of despising his father even as he detested his mother. But no relationship was ever as simple as it appeared even from a son's perspective, he had learned. Mom had been orphaned at the awkward age of eleven and had been reluctantly taken in by an aunt. Dad, in turn, had perhaps been hiring a manager when he married a woman made of steel more than porcelain.

Could be, neither had gotten what they wanted from the marriage. Dad might have thought Mom would be his foundation rather than a wrecking ball. Mom might be right that Dad didn't have the grit to take on tougher jobs. In the end, they'd brought out the worst in each other, not the best.

But Ben had always known one thing: he wouldn't get involved with a woman who wasn't plain-spoken. He wouldn't be manipulated, and he wouldn't let himself be crippled for the sake of love.

And suddenly, he had the ugly feeling that Abby had manipulated him at dinner, and that he'd knowingly let her. Her sometimes stunning bluntness had given way this past week to smiles and gentle suggestions.

He had no idea what had triggered the change in Abby, or what to do about it. Push until she got mad? Let her have her way? *Like Dad had let Mom have hers.*

All he knew was, he didn't want to lose Abby, but he wasn't going to reprise his father's life, either.

CHAPTER TWELVE

ABBY HADN'T MEANT to spend the night. She'd never been able to sleep soundly with a man's arm lying across her. She tended to be testy until she'd had cereal and a cup of coffee, and she didn't like the idea of having to make nice before breakfast. The other nights with Ben, she'd slept for a while, until he snored or rolled heavily against her or some unimportant noise had stirred her out of a light sleep. She had dressed then, and slipped away, sometimes crossing the path of his cat in the front yard as she stole out to her car hoping the sound of the engine starting wouldn't awaken him.

But this time, somewhat to her shock, the shrill of the telephone tugged her out of a deep dream, and she groped for the phone only to realize there was no bedside stand there, that the sunlight streaming through the window was brighter than morning light in her bedroom.

Beside her a large, dark, hairy man grunted, elbowed her and finally heaved himself to a sitting position and reached for the phone.

"Yeah?" he said in a tone that suggested this had better be good. "Abby?" His bloodshot gaze slid her way. "Uh...yeah. She's here."

Oh, great. Tell the whole world, she thought with

morning disgruntlement, before an icy finger of unease touched her nape. Only her sisters would know
to find her here, in Ben's bed. They didn't call at—
Abby's bleary gaze found the digital clock—
6:30 a.m.

She bunched the pillow behind her and scooted up
in bed. Taking the cordless phone, she mouthed,
"Who?"

"Renee," he whispered.

"Renee?" Abby said into the phone. "Is something wrong?"

"No biggie," her sister said. "I mean, everyone
is okay. But definitely another little incident."

"Incident." Abby didn't feel any too bright yet.
Coffee, she thought. *I need coffee.*

"I have an early morning meeting," her sister
said, voice troubled. "I've already showered and gotten dressed."

Abby glanced involuntarily down at her bare
breasts and quickly pulled the sheet up to cover them.
Her bra, she saw in a fleeting survey, dangled from
the doorknob. Her jeans sat in a heap on the floor,
pleated like an accordion, as if she'd just stepped out
of them. Her panties...God knows where they'd
gone.

She'd have to parade naked to Ben's bathroom,
which seemed far less romantic in the bright light of
morning than it had the night before. *He* looked
somewhat less appealing, too, she saw with a sidelong glance. Scratchy, dark stubble shadowed his
cheeks, and he made another grunting sound as he
moved to sit on the side of the bed. She should have
gone home...

Suddenly Abby realized Renee was talking. "I'm sorry," she interrupted. "Start over. I'm not quite awake yet. You showered, got dressed, then went down to the kitchen to have breakfast."

"I actually went so far as to get a glass of orange juice and a bowl of cereal," her sister said. "That's when I saw it."

"It," Abby repeated.

"Yeah. The newspaper article."

"Something's in the paper about you?"

"No!" Renee said, in clear exasperation. "An old article about Dad. Well, not that old. Headlines after his heart attack. 'Chief Ed Patton Dead At 56.' You remember that one."

"Yeah." She knew she was being a little slow, but she didn't get it.

"Somebody had cut it out, probably a long time ago—I mean, it's really from the newspaper, not a copy or a print from microfilm, and the paper is starting to yellow."

"Uh-huh."

Ben should have looked ridiculous sitting there naked, dark hair standing up in spikes from fingers shoved through it, but he didn't. Intensity radiated from him as he listened to Abby's side of the conversation, his impatience growing with every inane, unrevealing remark she made.

"Only," Renee continued, "they—*he*—blacked out the words 'Ed' and the 'At 56' in the headline. So now it just says 'Chief Patton Dead.' And then he singed the edges of the paper. So they're black and crumbly and I could smell smoke. As if he did it right before I stepped in the kitchen."

"Oh, my God." Abby was climbing out of bed, wildly looking around for her underwear, even as she asked, "Where's Daniel? You're not alone, are you?"

Ben shot to his feet, too. "What?"

"I hope like hell I am," her sister said with quiet force. "Because Daniel's away. I told you. He's trailering some horses down to Scottsdale. The buyer wanted him there. He wasn't very happy about it, but I assured him I'd lock the doors and sleep with my gun under my pillow."

Abby finally found the panties under the skirt of the bed quilt. "You've looked around," she said, scrambling into them and reaching for her jeans.

"Well, of course I have!" Renee said caustically. "What kind of idiot do you think I am? No, I'm alone in the house. What's bugging me is that I can't have been for long."

"Damn it!" Ben exclaimed. "What happened?"

Ignoring him, Abby told her sister, "I'll be there as quick as I can. Don't move. Don't touch anything. You know the drill."

Sounding irritable, Renee said, "I know it better than you do, for Pete's sake! You don't have to come. I can—"

Ben snatched the phone from Abby. "Tell me what happened," he commanded.

Abby used the opportunity to recover her bra from the doorknob and finish dressing. As he listened to her sister, Ben was hopping on one foot trying to insert his leg into his jeans. Once he swore. "Uh-huh," he mumbled a couple of times. "Yeah, hold tight," he said finally, before tossing the phone onto the bed. "Where the hell are you going?" he added when Abby headed for the door.

"The Triple B..."

"Not without me, you aren't. This is my case."

"Actually, technically it's not. The Triple B is inside city limits."

"The hell it is." He let himself be momentarily distracted before scowling at her. "You...will... wait...for...me. Clear?"

Abby quelled her impatience. "If you hurry," she said grumpily. "I don't like Renee being there alone."

"If our friend was going to hurt her, he would have done it already."

"But he threatened her!"

"He sure as hell did." The T-shirt he was yanking over his head muffled Ben's voice. When his head popped out again, he continued. "What I can't figure out is why. Why threats and no action?"

"You *want* him to take action?" she asked incredulously.

"We might have a chance at him if he did. As it is—" he grabbed his car keys and wallet off the dresser "—how are we going to find him? The research we've been doing is certainly very interesting, but nobody is going to stand up and wave a hand and say, 'Hey, look at me! I hate Patton and all his kin. I'm the one.'"

Following him downstairs, Abby said to his back, "We've eliminated some possibilities."

"Look how many are left." He gestured her out the front door and locked it. "And maybe this guy has a grudge from some event that was never filed as a police report. Hell, maybe 'he' is a woman! Your dad couldn't have been celibate all those years after your mother left. Maybe he wronged someone. That could explain why she..." He swallowed the rest of his sentence.

"Hasn't done anything but threaten?" Abby finished, her ire rising. "Because she's a woman, and that means she's all talk and no action?"

He looked at her over the top of her car. "I didn't say that."

She got in behind the wheel and slammed the door with unnecessary force. "You meant it."

Ben opened the passenger door and stuck his head in. "What did you say?"

"Never mind."

"Uh-huh." When she didn't add a word, he added, "I think I'll drive myself. So you don't have to bring me home."

"I could..."

"No, that's okay."

Abby was relieved. She still felt disconcerted to have slept so soundly that she didn't make it home. Without coffee and breakfast, she was grumpy, unable to pretend. She'd mess things up if she didn't have a few minutes to herself to regain her composure.

Besides, she recalled Meg telling her that Ben was a terrible back seat driver.

"It's all I can do to concentrate on driving." Meg had rolled her eyes. "In my peripheral vision, there he is. Fingers twitching, foot stamping the floorboard, head swiveling as he checks and rechecks every lane change I make, every turn... Drives me nuts.''

Abby did *not* feel patient this morning.

Some people would be so unkind as to say that patience wasn't one of her virtues. Ben might have already noticed. If not, she'd just as soon keep it that way.

By the time she parked at the Triple B, Ben's 4x4 turning in right beside her car, Abby thought she'd pulled herself together, metaphorically. She got out and met Ben behind the bumpers.

''By the way, thanks for coming,'' she said, almost meaning it.

His brows rose. ''No problem.''

Renee had the front door open before they could ring the bell. ''You brought your camera,'' she said approvingly, seeing it in Abby's hands. ''Good thought.''

''Did you call Meg?''

''Are you kidding? She's almost due. I'm not going to wake her at the crack of dawn with the latest scare story.''

''Almost due?'' Abby was momentarily distracted. She'd lost track of time. Was Meg really that far along?

''When will Daniel be home?'' Ben asked.

''This afternoon. He's flying home, leaving a couple of the men to drive the rig back.''

They followed Renee into the house, silent now. It was still only 7:00 a.m. In the kitchen, Renee hung back while Ben and Abby gingerly approached the table where the singed newspaper article was set neatly on the place mat, corners squared.

Ben stopped beside her as they studied the setup. A quilted runner in the center of the table held a wooden napkin holder and salt and pepper shakers. Two place mats were on north and west sides of the table, so to speak, not across from each other.

"Do you always sit in the same place?" Ben asked, showing that his thoughts were following the same route as Abby's.

"Yup." Renee sounded tense. "Somehow this guy knew which place was mine."

"Or guessed," Abby suggested quickly. "Odds were fifty-fifty."

Ben shot Abby a glance. "You're probably right," he said slowly. "Unless this is someone you've had to dinner?"

"Then we use the dining room," Renee said. "Or maybe have a buffet set out on this table, in which case the place mats would be put away. I just don't see how anyone but family could know where I sit to eat breakfast."

Ben grunted, as he tended to do when he was thinking hard, Abby had discovered.

"Let me get you a cup of coffee," Renee said. She knew Abby too well. "Ben?"

"Please."

Abby snapped half a dozen photographs before Ben put on latex gloves and lifted the newspaper article to slide it into a plastic sleeve. Except for the headline, nothing had been changed; nothing was written on the back. The headline *was* the point, along with the crisped edges.

"*I'll* be chief on Wednesday." Renee was staring at the article with a mixture of loathing and fear on her face. "Oh, damn…" She swung around suddenly and bolted from the room.

Abby followed. As she'd guessed, her sister was on her knees in front of the toilet in the downstairs bathroom.

"I'm okay," Renee mumbled. "I just haven't had anything to eat, what with…you know. And my stomach's unsettled every morning. Oh, crud. Will you pop some bread in the toaster? I've got to run up and brush my teeth."

Abby backed out of the bathroom. "You're *sure* you're all right?"

"Morning sickness is perfectly normal. Meg went through it. She says Mom told her she did, too." Renee scrambled to her feet and turned on the taps.

"Oh, gee," Abby muttered. "Something else to look forward to."

"Hey. It's not that big a deal." She gargled and spit out the water. "I'm usually okay. As long as I eat first thing." Then she swung around. "Wait a minute. You said 'look forward to.' Does this mean you're breaking your vow to never bring children into the world?"

"I said that when I was about fifteen!" Embarrassed, Abby glanced over her shoulder toward the kitchen. In a low voice she said, "I'm not thinking about getting pregnant tonight, if that's what you mean."

Her sister's grin became wicked. "What about last night?"

Abby swatted her and retreated.

Renee just laughed. "Don't forget the toast."

"She okay?" Ben asked when Abby returned to

the kitchen. "This must have scared the crap out of her."

"Renee doesn't scare that easily." As she grabbed a loaf of bread from the drawer, Abby watched him prowl the kitchen. "It's just morning sickness. She's pregnant, you know."

"So you said." He shook his head. "Ol' Vince Feist is going to have a fit when he finds out that the woman police chief is wearing a maternity uniform."

"Yeah." The thought cheered Abby. "The old guard won't like it, will they?"

"Question is," he said meditatively, "whether any of them hate the idea enough to try to scare her off. Or get violent."

Abby had just pushed down the bread in the toaster. She turned, frowning. "But these threats haven't been aimed at Renee. Until this one."

"Yeah, but this one is the most..." he groped for what he wanted to say "—explicit. You know what I mean? The others were saying, 'I know about your past. And I can get to you.' But they weren't saying, 'Thus-and-so will happen.' Seems to me, this one is."

"Will's bike..."

"He wasn't on it. There was no specific future threat."

"And Daddy's pickup truck..."

"Old history. I'd read that one as, 'This is what I'd have liked to do to him.' The ugly little thing with the doll was an elaborate setup, but seemed to me more a way of letting you all know *he* knows a hell of a lot about your lives. Maybe he was trying to give you the creeps with the idea that Emily's abandonment could have had a different outcome. But was he threatening to hurt Emily? I'm starting to think not.''

''But you do think he's threatening me,'' Renee said from the doorway just as the toast popped up.

''Maybe.'' Ben's big shoulders moved in a shrug. ''Yeah. That's my take. Could be I'm wrong.''

Renee's expression hardened. ''Well, the son of a bitch isn't going to scare me off. I'll admit, I was spooked this morning, but that's all. It passed, just like morning sickness does. I shouldn't have bothered you guys.''

''Don't be ridiculous...'' Abby began.

Ben didn't let her finish. ''How'd he get in?''

Renee snatched a piece of toast and began crunching on it, dry.

''You don't want butter?'' Abby couldn't help asking.

''Nah. This is okay.'' Renee grimaced. ''I found a window unlocked. The family room. I'll show you.'' Her gaze clashed with Ben's. ''And no, I can't swear I didn't miss checking it. I thought I got them all, but I was carrying the cell phone talking to Daniel, and I might have missed it...'' She trailed off. ''I must have.''

Not until Renee had left for her appointment, promising to send a fingerprint crew, did Ben say, ''I don't like it. Would she be that careless?''

Abby fired right up. ''What are you saying? That she's lying? That she threatened herself?''

''Don't be an idiot.'' Glowering at the window in question, he didn't even bother to glance at her. ''I'm just wondering if this guy doesn't have a key to the front door. If this window wasn't unlocked to make us *think* he had to come in through it.''

"A key?'' Abby swallowed some nausea of her own. "You're wondering if he's somebody we know really, really well, aren't you?''

"The thought crossed my mind.'' The grooves in Ben's cheeks deepened. "The trouble is, lifting somebody's keys long enough to get a copy made isn't that tough. Does Renee leave them in her car sometimes, for example?''

Abby opened her mouth to say, *I don't know*. She didn't get a chance.

"What about at work? She's got a different set for her official car. Does she leave her purse sitting in her office all day? Or the keys tossed on her desk?''

"It wouldn't be that hard, would it?'' Abby said hollowly. *She* left hers in the top drawer of her desk sometimes, when she went out in the field. Even in a family of cops, she'd grown up believing Elk Springs was essentially safe.

"Nope. It wouldn't.'' Ben glanced at his watch. "I've got to get moving, too. Can you wait for the fingerprint guy?''

"Yes. Of course.'' Abby tried a smile on for size. "Would you like some breakfast before you go? I could scrounge in Renee's refrigerator.''

"No, I'll stop and get something on the way,'' he said, sounding distracted. "Let me know if you learn anything, will you?''

She followed him to the front door. "Yes, of course.''

"See you tonight?''

"If you want to." Damn it. She sounded timid. A teenage girl hopefully waiting to be asked to dance.

"Huh?" His eyes briefly focused on her. "Yeah. Sure. I'll cook. Seven? Let me know if you get held up."

He didn't kiss her. His thoughts were clearly a mile away. Watching through the tall pane of glass beside the front door—again, like a lovestruck teen—Abby saw that, once in his 4x4, he didn't head toward the ranch gates and town. Rather, he turned left toward the barns. The odds were that nobody had seen anything; if you worked on the Triple B and you saw somebody creeping around the boss's home—especially with the boss away and his wife sleeping there alone—you didn't just shrug and go back to shoveling manure. You called the cops. You gathered a posse of other ranch hands and collared the bastard. But still, it didn't hurt to ask. A car might not have stirred too much alarm, for example.

As Ben had said once, maybe they'd get lucky.

No. Not lucky, Abby told herself. Good. Solid police work cracked cases. *He* would make a mistake; they wouldn't.

Standing in the living room, she saw Ben's Bronco come back up the hill and head out the ranch road toward the Triple B entrance. The red cinder dust hadn't even settled when a white E.S.P.D. van appeared.

She met the evidence tech at the door. "Start with the knob," she said. "Outside—we've had our hands all over the inside. Get the back door, too. And the window latch in here." She led the way.

He had been careful again. Too careful, this time,

because she did learn something: the prints on the window latch and the front doorknob were smudged, in exactly the same way.

"See?" the tech said. "The skin oils are still here, but smeared, probably by someone wearing gloves. Not leather—that would leave its own print. Look at the back door for comparison. I imagine those are Renee's and her husband's prints. We'll compare them, of course."

"He didn't wipe the latch or knob clean."

"Why bother, if he was wearing latex gloves from the beginning?" the young woman asked logically.

The doll and car seat had been wiped clean—but of course he couldn't very well wear gloves when he bought them at a garage sale or secondhand store. The same for the pickup truck—he might have attracted notice if he'd driven the truck all the way from Pendleton wearing a surgeon's latex gloves. He must have stopped for gas, or even at red lights when another driver might have seen his hands on the steering wheel. He wouldn't have wanted to draw attention. He'd had no choice but to scrub anyplace he might have touched.

This time, he hadn't had to.

Yes, she thought, but if he'd wanted to baffle them, he should have wiped all the doorknobs *and* window latches. Then they wouldn't have known how he effected entry.

Maybe he wanted them to know.

Nasty conjecture, Abby decided with a shudder. She preferred to think that he had made a mistake.

BEN WAS IN an exceptionally bad mood that evening, Abby realized within a few minutes of her arrival at his house.

She asked for a tour of his garden and he gave her a flat stare.

"I grow carrots. Potatoes. Green beans. In rows."

"And roses."

"Here." He thrust a pair of clippers at her. "Go cut some for a bouquet. I'm working on dinner."

"How, um, do I know what to cut?"

He shrugged, already turning away. "Take anything you want. Just make sure the stem's long enough."

She hadn't wanted to go out in the yard alone; she'd intended to be agreeable, let him prattle on about his prides and joys among the plants, think he was educating her.

But did she have a choice now? Abby stepped out the back, letting the screen door slam with a bang that scared the cat. It—she—bolted for the detached garage and vanished through a kitty door. The sun was low, but heat still weighted the air. Plants looked dry and dispirited. She supposed Ben hadn't been home enough to water them the way he should be. Porous-looking black hoses wound through the rows and along the fence. Soaker hoses, Abby guessed. Maybe he turned them on at night.

She cut roses, not giving much thought to her selections, adding a few sprays of perennials. Or annuals. She had no idea which was which. Someone at work had grumbled once that hardly anything was perennial with the harsh winters hereabouts.

Back in the kitchen, Ben wordlessly handed her a vase and watched critically—or so she imagined—as she arranged the bouquet. Twice she stabbed her finger on thorns and swallowed curses, sucking the blood away.

"There," she said finally, brightly. "What do you think?"

"Nice."

Piqued, she studied her effort. *She* thought it was darned spectacular, considering that she didn't have any idea what she was doing. Deep pink heavily quartered blooms mingled with white and one single-petalled pale yellow rose. Sprays of tiny white flowers made her think of bridal bouquets.

Annoyed words sat on her tongue, but she suppressed them. Why was it so hard? How many words had she bitten back with Daddy? No, with *Father*. Then, it had seemed easy. She'd never been able to understand why Meg and Renee couldn't just keep their mouths shut.

But she hadn't tried to please anyone in the same way for such a long time; no other man had mattered enough for her to bother. So why, now that she did care enough, did she have to wage an internal battle every time he riled her? Practice should have made perfect. Shouldn't it?

But she swore over the course of the evening that Ben was *trying* to provoke her. Little jabs were interspersed with incendiary political opinions. He even went so far as to wonder aloud whether Vince Feist didn't have a point.

"I have no problem with women cops," Ben said generously, between bites. "You know that. And nothing against Renee, that's for sure. But how the hell is she going to do the job when she's eight months pregnant? Never mind when some squalling kid is waking her up every two hours all night long.''

An acid reply rose to Abby's lips. On the verge of suggesting—rudely—that Renee would do fine, thank you, since women always performed multiple tasks under pressure and with little sleep. But—damn it—he was trying to get a rise out of her, which created a strange feeling of pressure under her breastbone. Not panic—of course not, Ben wouldn't hurt her, he wasn't like her father—but something closely akin. It seemed important that she not give him the satisfaction, that she stay in control, that she coax him from his odd mood.

So instead she affected surprise. ''But you want children, don't you?''

His brows drew together. ''Yeah.''

''Surely *you'll* be woken up by a baby crying, too?''

''Your point?'' Smart man, he sounded wary.

''Just that anyone with a new baby is going to be a little tired at first,'' she pointed out gently. ''What difference does it make whether the parent is the mom or the dad?''

''Tell that to Vince Feist,'' he growled.

''I will, if he ever complains in my hearing about Renee's promotion. Now, come on.'' She touched his hand. ''Let's talk about something else. Movies, maybe. I haven't been to one in ages. I wish they still made musicals. I loved *The Sound of Music.*''

His fork clattered to his plate. ''No. I don't believe it. Not you.''

''What's wrong with that?'' she asked with dignity. Okay, Maria was saccharine, as was some of the music, but Abby had watched the video a million times nonetheless. When she was younger, she'd dreamed that a Maria would come along and transform her father. Later—well, she'd still somehow seen an analogy. An awful man could soften.

Ben took a deep swallow of wine. "I'm beginning to think I don't know you at all." He shook his head.

She literally bit her cheek to keep herself from a hot response. "No, you probably don't," she said quietly. "Isn't that what we're trying to change here?"

He gave her a strange look. "Is it?"

In the end she feigned tiredness and left after he refused her help with the dishes. He didn't seem disappointed; didn't try to persuade her to stay. He did kiss her, his mouth hard and demanding. Part of her wanted to hold back, to punish him for upsetting her, for not letting himself be soothed into a better mood. But she couldn't help herself. She grabbed him fiercely around the neck and kissed him back with a fire as hungry as his.

Maybe I should stay tonight, she thought hazily as he lifted his mouth, but then she saw his face.

His mouth curled insultingly. "At least you're still honest about this. I guess I should be thankful for small favors."

Her eyes stung, her nose burned, and she realized with shock that she was on the verge of tears.

Abby swallowed hard. "I won't even comment. Yes, I will. I don't lie. Remember that, when you think about me tonight."

His voice became gravelly. "Yeah? Ever occur to

you that you're lying to yourself? Think about that, in your lonely bed tonight.''

That weird pressure in her chest increased. *Don't fly off the handle,* her inner voice whispered. *Just leave. He'll get over whatever's wrong with him. Everyone has a bad day. You'll make things worse if you snap back. Fights don't happen if there's only one participant.*

So Abby opened her car door, said, ''Good night, Ben,'' and got in, closing it. *Not* slamming it, as if she were angry, or pouting, or running away.

He watched her back out. Her last view, in the rearview mirror, was him bending his head suddenly and pinching the bridge of his nose. Having second thoughts, she hoped. Realizing what a jerk he'd been.

Just out of sight of his house, Abby had to pull over to the curb, set the hand brake and rest her forehead against the steering wheel, closing her eyes.

She could not fight with Ben.

Renee—sure. Even Meg—Abby had come to believe, deep down inside, that Meg wouldn't pack up and leave again, even if she did get steamed at her little sister.

But Ben wasn't going to stick around to quarrel. What he wanted was a nice wifey and two point five kids. And she was trying. Damn it, she was trying!

Did she do it so badly, Abby wondered unhappily, that he didn't believe in her ''nice''?

No! Don't complicate things, she told herself to suppress that swelling panic in her chest. He was just in a bad mood. It happened to everyone. Forget it.

Tomorrow, they'd be back to normal.

Almost believing herself, Abby released the brake and put the car in gear, pulling back out onto the road.

CHAPTER THIRTEEN

"I'M IN LABOR," Meg said simply. "I can't reach Scott. Can you come?"

Cell phone to her ear, Abby stood in her steel-toed boots on the dry trampled lawn in front of the charred skeleton of a house, burned last night. What had been good furniture lay drunkenly across the yard, shoved through the shattered front window by firefighters.

She almost asked, "Did you try Renee?" But even as she formed the question, she knew it to be foolish. Renee, newly pregnant, shouldn't witness Meg's baby being born.

"How far apart are your contractions?"

"Five minutes."

"Okay. Good. Um…sure. I can come. I guess you don't want Will holding your hand."

"For most things…yeah. But not childbirth. Besides," Meg added, "he's gone fishing with a friend. Contractions started about two minutes after he'd gone out the door."

"Where's Scott?" Abby headed toward her car. This would be no big deal, she told herself, ignoring the flutter in her stomach. She'd been trained to assist in childbirth. In fact, she had even helped deliver a baby girl once, in a winter storm when a nervous dad put the car in a snowbank. This would be in the hospital, with monitors and hovering nurses; all *she* would have to do was play cheerleader.

"Supervising work on the new ski runs that drop down the other side of the ridge at Juanita Butte. Either he forgot to turn on his cell phone, or the battery has gone dead. I don't remember seeing it plugged in last night. He's going to be furious with himself."

"Has somebody gone looking for him?" Abby had reached her car.

"Yeah... Uh, Abby?" Meg's voice changed. "Hold on. Another contraction's coming on."

Abby heard noises, like an air decompressor. Her pulse leaped. "Are you all right?"

"Just—" huff "—a—" huff "—minute."

The calm, professional cop and former firefighter flung her clipboard and camera into the car and raced around to the driver's side. "Oh, my God. They're less than five minutes apart, aren't they? The baby's coming. Meg, hold on! I'm on my way! I promise!"

Puff, puff, puff.

Abby reached for the seat belt, then remembered she needed car keys. Bending over, she scrabbled on the floor for them. The phone was wedged between her ear and shoulder.

"Meg? Are you there? Is something wrong?" She swore. Where were the blasted keys? She *always* dropped them in the exact same spot. "Meg? Say something, damn it!"

The long sigh in her ear sounded like the ones heard around the Thanksgiving dinner table when stomachs began to fill, when satisfaction and relaxation reach a peak.

Abby found the keys and slowly straightened, transfixed.

"I'm fine," Meg said in an astonishingly normal voice, except for a rich undertone that suggested she was...happy. No—weak word. Fulfilled.

Could anyone *enjoy* childbirth?

Abby gave her head a quick shake. Live and learn. "I'm on my way." She fumbled with the keys, finally stabbing the right one into the ignition. In an instant, she understood why the fathers-to-be always looked so scared and excited all at the same time.

Gunning away from the curb with barely a glance over her shoulder, she asked, "What about Emily?"

"Day care."

Meg had another contraction just before Abby slammed to a stop in front of her sister's house. A quick check of her watch told her they were only four-and-a-half minutes apart now.

She used her key to Meg's front door and burst in. "Where are you?"

Meg heaved into sight in the living room doorway, a still slender fine-boned woman with this enormous belly thrusting out. "Here. I took a shower. I'm all set."

Her hair was shiny and clean, her cheeks pink, her hands resting protectively on her belly.

"Suitcase?"

"Right by your feet."

"What?" Abby looked down. She'd have tripped over it if she'd taken another step. "Oh. Um...let's hurry and get you in the car before the next one hits."

"Let's do," her sister said dryly.

They barely made it; Meg waddled about as fast as an old lady drove on the freeway. "No seat belt," she said urgently, waving Abby away when she reached for it. "My stomach's...tender."

"Yeah. Okay." Abby went back for the suitcase, locking up behind her. When she reached the car, Meg was puffing rhythmically again, her nostrils flared and the cords on her neck standing out.

Oh, Lord. Abby fell in behind the steering wheel and threw the car in gear. "You're doing great," she said inanely. "Just hold on. We'll be there really, really fast."

On the way down the mountain loop highway, she threatened speed limits, grateful for dry summer roads. She spared a thought for that poor father who'd hit the snowbank, and wished she could apologize for the rolled eyes behind his back.

When she swore at a red light, Meg touched her hand. "It's all right, Abby. I'm fine. The baby will wait until we get to the hospital." Her voice turned rueful. "I just hope he waits for his daddy."

"Scott would be so disappointed!"

Abby pulled up in front of the Emergency Room entrance. They had to wait through another contraction before the nurses were able to help Meg out and into a wheelchair. Abby parked the car and came back to find Meg had already been sent up to a birthing room.

"We were able to check in ahead of time," Meg explained when Abby caught up with her in the pretty room papered with flowers. Her eyes widened. "Oh!" she gasped, snatching Abby's hand and gripping with painful strength. "Oh! They're getting…harder." She let out a little cry. "Fast."

"You know your breathing. Come on. Do it," Abby ordered, her gaze holding her sister's. "One, two, three, four. That's it. One, two, three, four."

She was helping Meg disrobe and put on a hospital gown when the next contraction came. She gazed in fascination at her sister's hugely swollen belly, rigid as the muscles squeezed.

"Touch it," Meg whispered.

Hesitantly, Abby stretched out her hand and laid it over the crown of Meg's belly. She jerked in surprise at how hard it was, as if just beneath the skin was steel. As the contraction passed, some of the rigidity left Meg's body, and Abby felt a sudden bob, like a fish surfacing in a trout stream. She'd felt the baby move inside Meg before, but it still astonished her. A smile dawned as she looked up.

Meg nodded, a grin tugging her mouth, too. "Yup. That's him."

"It's so…weird." Reluctantly, Abby pulled her hand back and smoothed down the hospital gown. As she tied the ribbons behind Meg's neck, a nurse began strapping on a fetal monitor.

The sight of the baby's heartbeats skittering across the screen moved Abby unexpectedly. "It's so fast!" she exclaimed.

She felt immediately foolish; of course a baby's heart beat faster than an adult's, she knew that.

But the nurse said seriously, "Labor puts stress on the baby. See? A contraction's starting, and the heartbeat speeds up."

Abby grabbed Meg's hand again and endured the

powerful grip, gazing into her sister's eyes as she commanded her over and over to breathe, to concentrate on the pattern, on each puff, to ride the waves of pain and stay above them.

Tingles ran from their handclasp up her arm; she imagined that they had formed a sort of umbilical cord, through which Meg shared her pain and Abby answered with comfort and strength.

While the doctor checked to see how dilated Meg was, Abby stepped out of the room. Otherwise, the sisters talked in between contractions, of everything and nothing. The decorating of the nursery, how Emily would react to a new sister or brother, Renee's pregnancy...

The minutes between shrank. Nurses and the doctor came and went. Abby wiped Meg's face with a cool wet washcloth, helped her sit up and take a mouthful of ice chips.

"I can't believe I'm doing this again," Meg murmured. "So many years..."

"I can't believe you were alone last time."

Meg gripped her hand, and for a moment Abby thought another contraction had come too soon. But, no—Meg's gaze compelled her. "I'm sorry. I wish I hadn't had to leave you. It was the worst thing I could have done to you, wasn't it?"

"I—I survived." Her standard line, although her voice shook this time.

"Surviving's not enough." Still Meg stared at her with that odd, fierce expression. "Live, Abby. Take chances. People *can* be trusted. You must believe that."

"I do." Her tongue touched her lips. "Renee...Renee was always there."

Once she would have added, *Daddy was always there.* Now she knew better.

"I love you," Meg whispered. "I always did."

"I know." Absurdly, Abby whispered, too, as if they were exchanging confidences.

"Oh-hh." Meg threw back her head.

Abby stole a glance at the monitor. Another contraction mounted and she encouraged her sister. "That's it. You're doing wonderfully. Breathe."

Meg let out a strangled scream.

"Damn it, breathe!"

Gaze fastened desperately on Abby's face, Meg resumed the rhythm of cheek-rounding puffs.

Just then, out in the hall, Scott roared, *"Meggie? Meg, where are you?"*

"In here, sir..." a nurse tried to direct him.

He burst into the birthing room and brushed Abby aside, squeezing both of his wife's hands in his big ones. "Meg! The goddamn phone was dead and I didn't know it. I'll never forgive myself."

As the latest contraction passed, Meg's exhaustion sounded in her voice along with a trace of amusement. "You're in time. *I'll* forgive you, and that's what counts."

He looked up at Abby, face haggard. "I don't deserve your sister."

Abby gave a weak chuckle. "I don't know. This has been kinda fun. Sisterly bonding and all that. I'll forgive you, too."

A moan came from Meg's parted lips.

Her husband groaned and focused his intensity on

her. "You know the drill, Meggie. Come on. Stick with it. That's it. One, two, three, four."

Forgotten, seemingly invisible but not minding, Abby retreated to the corner by the window and watched. Meg had responded to her, but not the way she did to her husband. His voice was rough but gentle, his expression tender; their gazes never parted. Now the contractions were on top of each other, like a symphony, the music rising from a whisper to a powerful rich crescendo, then sinking again to a murmur before gathering power yet again.

This was nothing like that terrified mother lying in the back seat of the car, with the cold air pouring over her, Abby and the other firefighter taking turns guiding the slippery squalling infant into the world. This was well-orchestrated, a child coming into the world as he was meant to come, his mother pushing with wild cries and his father waiting, gowned, beside the doctor to receive the baby when he emerged.

"It's a boy," the doctor declared, holding up the kicking, screaming baby slick with blood and mucus.

The nurses cleaned, weighed and swaddled him while Scott held Meg's hand again. Finally, Matthew Jerome McNeil was laid at his mother's breast, where she guided him to a nipple.

Abby was unashamedly crying as she watched not only her sister, but Scott, who had lost his only child from his first marriage at less than six months from SIDS. His grin lit the room, but his cheeks were wet, and she knew he saw his first son in this one.

"Abby." Meg's glowing smile drew her sister. "Come see him."

Any rational person would have said he was ugly

as sin. Abby discovered she wasn't rational any more than the fond parents. Matthew's eyes might be screwed shut, his mouth latched about his mother's breast, his few thatches of copper hair damp and his face beet red, but she thought he was beautiful and said so.

"He's going to be as handsome as his daddy."

Scott's dazed smile, full of glory and grief at once, became tempered with humor. "And here I never knew you felt that way."

"Don't let it go to your head," she advised. "I'm being nice for Meg's sake."

Meg's tender gaze returned to her son. "But he is the handsomest—well, one of the handsomest—baby boys ever born, right?"

"You betcha." Abby thought of seventeen-year-old Will, six feet plus, self-assured, a boy rapidly becoming a man, one who turned all the girls' heads. "I can hardly wait until Will sees him."

The nurses were ready to transfer Meg to another room and Matthew temporarily to the nursery, so Abby said her goodbyes. She kissed Meg's cheek and they hugged each other with such fervor Meg's grip hurt. Abby took one last lingering look at their crinkled red-faced baby boy, eight pounds eleven ounces. Scott engulfed her in an embrace nearly as heartfelt as Meg's, and then Abby left.

The hospital corridors seemed to go on forever, stark white and surreal. Abby felt curiously alone, although she passed visitors and nurses, caught glimpses into rooms where families hovered at bedsides. She didn't want to be by herself.

Ben. She would call Ben. Was he at work…?

She was vaguely shocked to discover that the entire day had passed. Her watch told her it was 7:52 in the evening. Ben would be at home. She would simply go over there. He wouldn't mind.

Her steps grew quicker, until she was almost running by the time the glass entrance doors glided open and then shut behind her.

HER MOOD WAS STRANGE, Ben thought from the beginning; she stepped across his doorstep with a mixture of shyness and eagerness he didn't remember. She came into his arms of her own accord, her kiss quick and fervent.

"Meg had her baby! A boy. Matthew Jerome McNeil. He's a redhead like his dad."

"A baby." For some reason, Ben reeled at the idea. He was getting to an age where he'd been thinking that he would like to have a son or daughter to wake him at night, to solemnly watch him shave come morning, to demand to be pushed in the swing set he would build in the backyard. His own inchoate hunger made it both easier and harder to imagine Detective Meg Patton holding a newborn.

Of course he'd seen Meg pregnant... But still. A baby.

"I saw the whole thing." Abby squeezed his hands, her cheeks flushed with excitement. "Scott was out of touch for a while. I got to hold her hand. It was scary but awesome. You know? I'd seen a baby born once, but it was different. More rushed, everyone frantic. But this!"

He gently shut the front door and steered Abby into the living room. "Did Meg scream?"

"What?" Abby's eyes briefly focused on him. "Scream? Oh...I guess. But not the way you mean. Not like in a horror movie. More...like the grunt an athlete makes. Just ripped out of her by the effort."

Ben sat at one end of the couch. "Did Scott make it in time?"

Abby's smile dawned, sweet and funny. "You should have heard him coming! Bellowing, 'Meggie!' as he tore down the hall. And the way he rushed in, as if he couldn't stand not being there..."

"A man wants to see his son born."

"He had another son once, you know." She had briefly alighted next to him, but now she sprang to her feet and began to move restlessly, touching the back of the couch, peering out the window, tracing the spines of the books in a case. "Nate. That was his name. He died of Sudden Infant Death Syndrome."

"No." *God.* What would it be like? Bringing that baby into the world, seeing those wondering eyes, the trust, holding him, rocking him, and then one day to find him dead... "No, I didn't know." Shocked, Ben shook his head. "My God."

"It would be the worst thing in the world. I could see it in his eyes today. He'll treasure every minute with Matthew, and be afraid every minute, too."

"I suspect all parents feel that way, to a lesser extent."

"Maybe." She looked at him suddenly, and he was stunned to realize that her eyes brimmed with unshed tears. "I felt so close to Meg."

"I'm glad." Ben cleared his throat, not knowing what else to say.

But apparently it was enough, because Abby rushed to him and tumbled onto his lap. "Kiss me," she said, her voice thick with those tears she would never acknowledge.

Ben pushed his fingers beneath her hair to cup the back of her head. One tug, and their mouths met. Singed by the sweet idea of a man seeing his son born, Ben kissed Abby as if they were already in bed, as if she lay open beneath him.

He tasted salt; groaned; licked it from her cheeks.

"I need you," she whispered.

The words were ones he'd never expected to hear from Abby Patton, who took on the world with such panache and defiance.

He told her he loved her, but she didn't seem to hear. He nipped at her lush mouth, ran the pads of his thumbs over her damp cheeks, gazed into eyes so blue the sight made him dizzy.

They made love right there on the couch, both half dressed. She straddled him, her head thrown back, her eyes closed. Her lashes were damp, shimmery. Ben kissed her white throat, buried his face in the silken fall of honey-gold hair. He groaned and buried himself in her, gripping her hips as he helped her rise and fall, as he drove upward into her.

"Yes! That's it, sweetheart," he coaxed. "You feel so good. I love you. *I love you, Abby Patton.*"

She shuddered, her core rippling with the flex of tiny muscles. He was still talking, incoherently, when he climaxed.

They ended up tumbled sideways on the couch, wrapped together, legs tangled and arms holding tight. Her face was pressed into the crook of his neck where her warm breath tickled him; he felt as much as heard a small murmur from her.

I love you. Had she said it?

He kissed the top of her head. "What?"

She mumbled something and burrowed into him.

"Meg having the baby got to you, huh?"

Abby stirred. "Got to me?"

He rolled to a more comfortable position, sweeping her with him. In the process he saw her face, so damned beautiful he had a moment of purely male exultation—the hell with it being shallow to revel in appearances alone. Abby's delicate high cheekbones, dainty chin, pouty mouth and high curved forehead were brought alive by those huge blue eyes. She was every teenage boy's wet dream. Only his had come true.

"Yeah." He slid his hand inside her open bra and cupped the smooth soft flesh of her breast. "Isn't that what got us hot today? The idea of making a baby?"

She sounded—odd. "I use birth control. I told you that."

Her nipple peaked against his palm, but he took his hand away and tenderly brushed hair back from her face. "The *idea,* I said. The elemental notion of fertility is an aphrodisiac."

For a moment Abby didn't answer. When she did, she spoke lightly, as if humoring him. "If you say so."

He frowned. "Come on. Isn't that why you came over here?"

"For sex?" She moved a few inches away. "Of course not! I asked for a kiss. That's all."

Ben swore and sat up, forcing her to do the same. Shoving his hand through his hair, he said, "You told me you needed me."

Her eyes were wide and curiously opaque. "Do you like that idea?" Her tone was almost—flirtatious. As if this conversation wasn't serious. "It's a guy thing, isn't it?"

His jaw clenched and he grabbed for his jeans. "Do I want a woman clinging to me?" he said between gritted teeth. "No. What I like is for you to tell me what you feel. And not to pretend you don't feel it."

"I need you." She batted her eyes at him. "This was fun. Let's not spoil it by quarreling."

Ben stared at her for a moment with incredulity. "I need you," she said, and *she didn't mean it.* Goddamn it, she didn't mean it. She was saying it just to pacify him.

He had fallen in love with a woman who was gun-shy but honest. A woman who taunted and teased and snapped, but who sometimes, in a small husky voice, admitted to feelings that ran deep and true.

Where had that woman gone? When had she turned into this kittenish beauty-pageant princess who was sweetly eager to smile acquiescence, but who didn't seem able to feel real emotion?

To give himself a second, he yanked on his jeans, then his T-shirt. Looming above her, Ben looked down at pretty Abby Patton, sitting brazenly on his couch wearing panties again, her tiny lace bra fastened, but her shirt hanging open and her long bare legs tucked under her. She offered him a tentative smile and patted the seat cushion next to her.

"You didn't tell me about your day."

She was like a caricature from the 1950s: the good little wife who dressed up when her husband was due home, and who would never dream of burdening him with her disappointments or household triumphs. His day was what mattered.

Frustration and anger roughened his voice. "But you won't tell me any more about yours, will you?"

She looked wary. "What do you mean? What do you want to know?"

He put his hands in his pockets and stared down at her. "You said you felt close to Meg. Didn't you before?"

Abby bowed her head, hiding her expression. "It's just that she was gone for so many years. We talked about things today. Nothing important. It was... nice."

"Nice," he repeated.

"Don't say it that way!" Her chin shot up, and for a second he saw a flash of the old Abby.

"*Nice,*" he goaded. "That's the best you can come up with? A life-affirming moment shared with your sister, and you think it's *nice?*"

Anger kindled in her eyes. Her nostrils flared; they stared at each other for a charged, combative moment. And then he saw her stamp out the anger as if it were a brush fire that couldn't be allowed to take hold. She took a slow breath, then another; her tongue touched her lips; she closed her eyes for an instant.

When she looked at him again, he saw...nothing. Pretty blue eyes. Any spark was dead.

"I think," she said, putting her feet on the floor and sitting up straight, "that I'll get dressed and go home. You're obviously not in the mood for company." She reached for her pants.

"You're right," Ben said deliberately. "I'm not in the mood for company. And that's all you're willing to be, isn't it? A stranger sharing my bed and my dinner table."

Her voice caught. "I thought we were more than strangers."

His gut burned. "I did, too."

Hurt blazed on her face, but she doused it, too. Another unacceptable emotion. "I think this was a bad idea from the start."

No! Never! he cried inside. "Probably," he agreed coldly.

Abby pulled on her pants, shoved her feet, sockless, into her shoes and faced him. Head high, eyes dry, she said, "Goodbye, Ben. I'm sorry I couldn't be what you wanted me to be."

"But that's what you never got, isn't it?" He turned, talking to her back as she walked out of his life. *Don't leave.* "I didn't want you to be anything but yourself."

She stopped partway to the door, faced him with a twisted smile. "But this *is* me."

He shook his head. "No. I don't think so."

The hurt was there again; denied again. "You're wrong," she whispered, and the tears were in her voice this time.

Before he could say another word, she was hurrying to the door. He heard it open and quietly shut. Abby was gone.

The pain in his gut was either a bleeding ulcer or a broken heart. Either way, it was untreatable.

CHAPTER FOURTEEN

MEG AND BABY MATTHEW were home by the next day. Gifts in hand, Abby and Renee visited together, both in uniform, both solemn and on their best manners.

Perched on the edge of the couch, forcing a smile as she watched Emily opening the present Renee had brought her, Abby felt stiff, artificial.

Company. That's all you're willing to be, isn't it? A stranger.

Did her sisters feel that way, too? Or were they the only people in the world who really knew her?

Did they *like* her? Abby had wondered sometimes. Love was one thing; enjoying someone's company was another.

Despising herself for her insecurity—her self-centeredness—Abby tried hard to appear cheerful until she and Renee walked out together after the visit. Around the shingled house, ponderosa pine stretched tall, the manzanita and Oregon grape along the path and driveway dry and dusty at this time of year. Pine needles crunched underfoot, the smell pungent, the August sun hot.

Time to tell Renee about Ben.

And then she sounded so blithe, so uncaring, she

despised herself all over again. How could her voice *not* reflect her anguish and turmoil?

"Ben and I seem to have parted ways."

"You've broken up with Ben?" Renee's tone said, *What kind of idiot are you?*

How many times had Abby heard that same tone, the one that always implied she couldn't do anything right. She'd been able to do only one thing better than her sisters: she'd been able to soothe the roaring beast, to fool him into thinking he was getting his way. *She* had been able to handle Daddy, as neither Meg nor Renee could.

So why, when it mattered even more, couldn't she handle Ben?

Pain seared, as it did each time she thought, *Ben,* and wondered, baffled, what she had done wrong.

"Actually, *he* ditched me." She still sounded— almost—as though she didn't care. She stopped by her car, leaning casually against the fender. "Amazing, isn't it? Apparently I've gotten my just dues back."

Renee laid a hand on her arm. "I'm sorry. Do you want to tell me what happened?"

"You always know what I've done wrong." The words just came, sharp, bitter, adolescent. "Why don't you tell *me?*"

Renee's mouth literally dropped open. "What do you mean?"

A lump swelled in Abby's throat. "You like to play mommy. Here's your chance."

Her sister's green-gold eyes were stricken. "You think I criticize too much."

"Yes." Oh, God. She was going to cry. "No. I don't know."

"You do."

"No…"

"I meant well," her sister said softly.

"I know you did. Do. I needed you to be mom." There, she had said what she had always secretly known. "I just…wished I didn't. But I don't feel that way anymore."

"Oh, Abby." Renee's eyes welled with tears. "I'll quit nagging. Do I still? I must. I promise, I'll quit. You're a big girl."

"You can nag if you want." Abby's vision misted. "I need you to care."

"Oh, honey." Renee held out her arms and the two sisters embraced, tears pressed hot and damp between their cheeks. They blubbered, as Abby couldn't remember doing since Meg had left.

Suddenly Renee said in a rush, "I resented you, too. Didn't you know that? I was always so afraid you knew that I'd let you down. None of it was your fault. But I was a kid, and I had to be mom to you, and sometimes I had to give things up, or get in between you and Dad, and I *hated* it."

"No." Abby pulled back a little and sniffed. "No. I never guessed. Of course you resented me, too! I never thought… But it wasn't fair to you. Or to Meg in the first place."

"Maybe not." Renee looked awful, eyes puffy, nose dripping. "Wait. Let me get a tissue out of the car."

She came back in a moment and handed Abby a bunch. They blew noses and smiled shyly at each other, as if they were two acquaintances who had taken a giant step into intimacy.

That's all you're willing to be, isn't it? A stranger. Could she change that?

Renee said, "I wonder if Meg's going to wonder why we haven't left."

"She's probably asleep by now."

Renee looked squarely at her. "A minute ago, we were talking about whether Mom and Dad were fair to us, and of course they weren't. Let's face it, neither of them really thought about us at all. But the thing is, now I don't regret what seemed a burden then. The three of us *had* to depend on each other, and sure it caused resentment at the time, but look at us now. We care more about each other than most sisters or brothers ever do. Before Daniel, you were the only person in the world I was sure I could count on. We've always had that."

Miserably, Abby said, "But it was always the easiest for me. I didn't have to take any responsibility! I was always the baby."

Her sister stared incredulously. "Easiest? You thought that? And here I always thought *you* were the one hardest hit. Meg and I were more grown up when Mom left. And I was a teenager when Meg went, too. But you were just a kid. I don't think you ever understood, not the way I did. I've sometimes thought—"

"Thought what?"

Renee made a face. "Oh, the obvious, I guess. That you seem to have trouble making close friends, or falling in love. And no wonder. Only, then Ben came along, and I had the impression…'' She trailed off again.

Abby tried to smile and knew her effort was a wretched failure. ''That I'd fallen madly in love and would soon be prancing down the aisle all swathed in white?''

''Something like that.''

''Yeah, well, you know the funny part? I was starting to think maybe I would. Prance down the aisle, that is.'' Oh, God, this was hard to say. The lump rose in her throat again, making her voice sound soggy. ''I—I tried. To make him happy, I mean.'' Oh, crap. She was crying again, just like that. ''The harder I tried, the worse things got. And I don't know why!'' The last came out as a wail.

Renee held her again; she blubbered again. They must look ridiculous, Abby thought with the one sane part of her mind. Two women in uniform standing in the driveway in the hot midday sun crying. Thank God the men who would soon be calling Renee ''Chief'' couldn't see them. Or the police officers and firefighters Abby had to deal with, for that matter!

Eventually Renee suggested they sit in her car and talk. ''Tell me about it,'' she said. ''How did you *try* to make Ben happy?''

The police radio crackled, voices coming through in bursts; both women ignored it.

''I figured,'' Abby said unhappily, staring down at her hands on her lap, ''that I'd be good at keeping everything smooth if I tried. I could with Dad. You remember.''

"Yeah, I remember." Renee sounded wry. "We called you our 'peacekeeper.'"

Abby puzzled over her recollections. "Ben seemed to *want* me to be mad. I don't understand! Why would he try to annoy me?"

"I don't know." Renee frowned. "But what I don't understand is why you had to keep everything smooth in the first place. Were you guys fighting? Or does Ben have a temper you didn't happen to mention to us?"

"A temper?" Abby tried to laugh. "I would have said no, until this week. He's been pretty grumpy."

The creases in Renee's forehead deepened. "Then what were you smoothing over?"

Abby turned her confusion on her sister. "The usual stuff. You know. Nothing big. I just…headed off subjects I knew would lead to trouble. I mean, I can be hard to get along with. I was trying to be *nice!*" Somehow, she found her voice rising to a wail again.

"But, Abby, you *are* nice." Renee took her hand. "You're *not* hard to get along with. You're funny, and smart, and you stand up for yourself. What's wrong with that?"

Dumb question. "Jeez, Renee. You know better than that. Men don't like women who stand up for themselves."

"Daniel does."

"He's one of a kind."

"Scott sure as heck does."

"Okay, two of a kind."

"Maybe Ben's three," her sister said quietly. "If

he's not—why would you bother trying to please him?''

"Because…" *I love him.* Her breath rushed out. How had it happened, something so foolish? She grappled with the question in stunned silence. He was a cop, and she'd sworn never to date one. He wanted children, and she didn't. Had thought she didn't, she corrected herself, disconcerted anew; watching Matthew Jerome come into the world had shifted something inside her, so that pieces seemed to fit in a new way that was different but just as whole.

"Because?" Renee prodded.

"Because I'm an idiot," Abby moaned, burying her face in her hands.

"Ah." A smile—an insufferable, sisterly smile—sounded in Renee's voice. "I thought so."

Abby wanted to resent that tone, the smug certainty that big sister knew best. She couldn't.

Instead, she raised a tear-drenched face. "What do I *do?*"

Renee's smile faded. "I can't help you there, kiddo. Only you know what you said and did, and what Ben said and did. Only you can figure out how to fix what went wrong. I have just one suggestion."

"What's that?"

"Don't be the peacekeeper. It was too hard. You don't want to live that way, not forever."

No. She'd hated the burden of responsibility. She had chosen not to fall in love so she never had to bear it again.

Abby swallowed. "You're right. I don't."

"Figure out what went wrong," Renee repeated. "If Ben's worth a lifetime, you can fix it."

Abby gave a hiccuping sigh. "Oh, thanks," she said sarcastically.

"Hey." The—almost—Chief of Police elbowed her. "At least I have faith. What more do you want?"

"A strategy!"

"Sweetie," her sister said gently, "the word 'strategy' implies...some kind of manipulation. Forget it."

"That's two suggestions."

"So it is." Renee smiled crookedly. "Hey, keep talking and I might come up with half a dozen more."

Abby heaved another sigh. "Forget it. You're right. I'm on my own."

"No." This time Renee's expression was deadly serious and the grip of her hand firm. "Never on your own. You've always got us. Meg and me. Don't forget that."

"You're getting mushy on me."

"Yup."

Abby had to blink away tears. "Oh, for Pete's sake!"

"One for all..." her sister prompted.

Along with her mother's face, she'd forgotten their solemn childhood vows. Slowly, tentatively, she finished what Renee had begun, "And all for one."

"So, even if you did something stupid..."

"Like fall in love."

"*Yes!*" her sister crowed. "I can hardly wait to tell Meg. You said it!"

"Oh, God, I did, didn't I?" She reached for the door handle, feeling a sudden need to flee, harshness entering her voice. "Well, forget you ever heard it."

"Abby?"

"Listen…thanks." She climbed out, bent over to see Renee's face. "I'll think about what you said. But some things can't be fixed. And this one…I don't know." She shrugged uncomfortably. "He said he loves me, too, but does he really know who I am? I'm not even sure I do. I don't know," Abby said again. "I just…have to think. So don't tell Meg anything. Please. And…well, I'll see you later, okay?"

Abby didn't wait for a response. Instead she slammed the door and hurried to her own car.

Love… She had always believed she wouldn't be good at it. Nothing that had happened changed her mind. She'd fallen in love—and he apparently didn't want her, not warts and all. *Her* wart was much too big and ugly.

Right now, she felt terribly alone, however Renee had tried to comfort her; Renee had Daniel, Meg had Scott and Emily and Will and now Matthew, but she—Abby—had no one.

Well, she'd lived without Ben Shea before, and she could again.

Because, in Abby's experience, miracles didn't happen. Ben was worth a lifetime, but he obviously didn't think she was.

Sometimes—too often—lives were shattered and they couldn't be fixed. She was only twenty-seven years old, and thanks to her job she'd seen plenty of 'em.

Her own was a minor casualty.

BEN PHONED ABBY, knowing he sounded like some-one who didn't give a damn. Pride was an ugly thing, he thought wryly.

"With the swearing-in ceremony coming, we'd better talk about extra security," he said. "We're probably worrying about nothing, but I'd rather be safe than sorry."

"Damn right," she agreed promptly, tartly. "This is my sister we're talking about."

As coolly and politely as two police officers from different jurisdictions acting as liaisons on a joint project, they discussed who to bring in on the prob-lem and set a time and place.

Then Ben tried to think of an excuse to keep Abby on the line, and came up short.

"Tomorrow, then," he said, and heard a click as she hung up.

He sat there in his office staring at the scrawled note he'd made on his calendar for the meeting to be held at the E.S.P.D. station. Had she sounded natural, as if she wasn't bothered by talking to him? Or had her voice been stiff, strained? Like some goddamned love-struck teenager, he analyzed every word, every nuance, and came up just as short. He had not the least idea in the world whether she'd been con-strained by pride, too, or whether she just didn't care.

Ben muttered a profanity. What the hell difference did it make, anyway? He was the one who'd said, "Enough." She'd been playing games with him, and if there was one thing he couldn't put up with, that was it.

If he just didn't have this uneasy feeling that what-ever was going on with Abby was more complicated than he'd guessed in his frustration. She'd been hurt there, at the end. And he'd seen her enough times struggling with herself.

Ben groaned and leaned back in his office chair, clasping his hands behind his head. Her father had been abusive, he'd known that. Ben swore again. She wasn't *afraid* of him, was she?

He couldn't believe that. She'd never flinched; he'd never seen that kind of fear in her eyes.

What, then?

He had no more idea today than he'd had the other day. No more idea whether he'd done the right thing, or been a fool. He hadn't meant to break off with her. Even in the heat of the moment, he hadn't meant what he was saying. He'd figured—what—that she'd say, *Oh, gosh, Ben, I'm sorry. I'll go back to being my regular self.*

How did he know what her "regular self" was?

One thing a night of lonely brooding had told him: she *wasn't* like his mother. Abby had gotten fakey, all right; sweet when he could see that she wanted to give him hell. But his mother's sweetest smiles were invariably followed by the sting of a whiplash.

He could hear her, clear as day. His father excited about something he'd been asked to do at an Elks Club meeting, and his mother patting his dad's arm and murmuring in that low, deceptively gentle voice, *Now, Hugh, you remember what happened the last time you tried to take on a project like this. You felt so bad letting other people down. Remember? I know you don't want to put yourself in that position again.* She could demolish Dad's self-esteem with a few well-chosen words.

No. That wasn't Abby. Hell, if anything she'd been trying to build him up. She'd started refusing to criticize, argue, or in any way be difficult. He liked being kept on his toes. He didn't want a wife who acquiesced in his every wish and opinion.

Wife.

"Crap," he said out loud, and stormed to his feet. Enough. He'd see her tomorrow. What would be, would be.

Think about something else, Ben ordered himself. *Do your damn job.*

He needed to do interviews in the neighborhood where, during a robbery, an elderly man had been tied, beaten and left after the unknown assailant made several trips to carry out the TV, VCR, microwave and the old guy's long deceased wife's jewelry. The victim had been lucky, because a neighbor checked on him regularly and discovered him within twenty-four hours.

Ben stalked through the station, ignoring the chaos of booking and the line of people waiting to talk to the desk sergeant. Yeah, he had better, more important things to do than obsess about a woman.

If she loved him, she'd tell him what was going on with her. If she didn't—well, he was better out of it now, that was for damn sure.

Too bad he didn't quite believe that.

GROTESQUE DREAMS kept Abby tossing. A hotel was burning, and suited up she fought her way through the flames, breaking down the doors of room after room. In every single one, the beds were empty, the bathrooms empty. Not until she dropped to her knees and lifted the bedspread did she see them, huddled under there. At first they were dolls, like the one in the car seat. Plastic with jointed limbs and pink dresses. But as she battered down door after door, not bothering after a while to look anywhere but under the beds, the dolls got more and more lifelike, until they were children. Dead, waxy, staring. She felt tears on her cheeks and knew in that weird way one did in a dream that she was sleeping and she was crying, that her pillow would be wet.

The smoke was so thick she could hardly see; the brass numbers on the hotel room doors began to look alike and she worried she'd missed a room, or was going into the same one over and over, and that was why the children also looked so much alike. Her oxygen must be getting low; she should find her way out.

But what if someone was alive in one of these rooms?

Sirens screamed, muffled by walls and smoke and her headgear.

No. The dream began to disintegrate, although she could fairly taste the smoke, acrid on her tongue. The ringing continued. Her alarm clock—she batted at it, but the sirens wailed on. No, not sirens. She was awakening. Telephone. It was her telephone.

But something was wrong. Her eyes stung, and she coughed as she groped for the telephone. The room seemed too dark. Her dream was bleeding into her reality, until she wasn't sure which she was living.

"Hello?"

The silence in her ear was absolute.

"Who—?" She began to retch.

Click.

She was awake suddenly, and knew her unit was on fire. No flames that she could see, only smoke. She couldn't see as far as the bedroom door, which she had left open. Usually the night-light in the hall touched the night with a golden glow. Not now.

In fact—terror spurted in her—she didn't know which way the bedroom door was. Tears streamed down her face now, and she couldn't breathe. She didn't know where anything was. She had dropped the telephone.

She rolled off her bed, stumbled to her feet and bumped something. A crash included the tinkle of breaking glass. Her lamp. Oh, God. She had to get out. She spun in place. Which way?

Anger came to her rescue. The son of a bitch wasn't going to kill her. She knew fire, by God. She'd get out of this.

Think!

She dropped to her hands and knees, finding cooler air that she could breathe. Barely.

Okay. She reached out, found the bed. The child in her wanted to creep under it to safety. The woman knew she'd find none there. She had a flash in which she saw those children, dead from smoke inhalation. She would look like them if she didn't escape. Soon.

Crawling, she followed the bed, then the cedar chest that sat at its foot. Orienting herself in the darkness, she set off toward the door. Hit a wall, groped to the right, then the left. Ah! There it was. Closed. She never closed it.

She flattened her hand against the wood and felt

the roaring heat through it. *Block the crack at the bottom,* she told herself.

Back to the bed. Abby yanked the spread off the bed and returned to shove it against the door. Then, crawling fast, she found the bed again. Okay, the window was *this* way. It should be a straight line. The blinds were closed, she wouldn't be able to see light from street lamps even if the smoke wasn't so thick.

Her head bumped—*hard*—into something. Crying, she collapsed to the floor, oh, so tempted to give up. She could sleep. Someone would spot the fire and call 9-1-1. Firefighters would crash through her window to the rescue. She didn't have to do everything herself.

A stern voice in her head said, *No, but you do have to do this.* Her confusion was growing, her exhaustion, her dizziness. She'd die soon, if she didn't get out.

She'd never see Ben again.

Abby managed to get to her hands and knees again. She'd hit her head on the dresser. The window was just to the right. She felt her way up the wall until her fingers found the slatted blinds. No time to find the cord—she rose inside them, with the bottom rail bumping down her back. Eyes closed, she envisioned the lock, found it, turned it, pushed open the window and hung out.

Her bedroom was second story. Shaking, sucking in fresh air, she squeezed into the opening and teetered on the sill. Stay here? She could breathe. If she screamed...

A small rattle came from her throat. Abby tried

again and produced a croak. She turned her head and saw with horror that flames were licking around the door.

Okay. She couldn't wait. Still squatting, she rotated until she was facing the room again, then gripped the sill with her fingers and swung her body outside like a gymnast hanging from a bar. Her bare feet bumped against the shingled side of the condo. Abby's fingers trembled; she closed her eyes, prayed, braced her feet against the wall and jumped into the darkness.

CHAPTER FIFTEEN

BEN'S PHONE RANG, yanking him out of a deep sleep at 3:20 a.m. A small croaky voice whispered, "Ben?"

He struggled up on one elbow. What the hell? "Who is this?"

"It's…it's me. Abby."

"Abby?" Alarm shredded the remnants of sleep. Ben swung his legs out of bed. "What's wrong?"

"Fire." He heard her fight to get every word out. "My place…burned."

Ben swore. "You're hurt. Goddamn it. I should have expected this. Where are you?"

"No," she whispered. "Not hurt. I'm outside. They're putting it out. Can you come?"

"Close your eyes, take a deep breath and I'll be there." He tossed the phone aside and yanked on yesterday's jeans without underwear. Shoving his feet into canvas shoes, he pulled a sweatshirt over his head, grabbed his semiautomatic still in a shoulder harness and took the stairs two at a time. Keys were in the basket with his wallet and change.

He slapped the light on top of his car and hit the corner so fast, he smelled burning rubber. Traffic was sparse and he ran red lights and stop signs. A ten-minute drive took four.

A floodlight exposed in raw detail the blackened yawning opening where Abby's condo had been. The fire was out, Ben saw; water still arced from hoses and yellow-suited firefighters were shouting orders and crawling all over the place.

He slammed to a stop right behind one of the two big fire trucks and leaped out.

"Sir, this is a restricted area..." one of the firemen began.

Ben flashed his badge. "Where is she?"

The man nodded to the other side of the truck. "Right there, Officer. She called you?"

He didn't answer. Rounding the truck, stepping over a thick hose, he saw her sitting forlornly on the running board. Wrapped in a blanket, she was staring at the ruin of her home with the blank dirty face of shock.

"Abby."

Her head turned slowly; she lifted her gaze as though it was a physical effort. "Ben?"

He lifted her into his arms as if she were a child, guilt and relief playing a duet in his head and heart. "God. I'm so sorry. I should have been here."

She burst into tears.

Swearing, Ben held her tight, head bent and murmuring comforting nonsense as she sobbed against his shoulder.

"I'm sorry," she kept trying to say.

"Cry," he said, voice thick. "Don't be sorry."

She cried herself into such a limp state he knew she'd collapse if he let her go.

When she had been quiet for a minute, Ben asked, "Have the EMTs taken a look at you?"

Abby sniffed. "I'm fine."

"I want you checked out at the hospital."

"I—I should call Renee."

"I'll call her," he said firmly. "From the hospi-tal."

Against her husky, whispered protests he carried her to his Bronco and settled her into the passenger seat. He went back and briefly conferred with the fire lieutenant and an EMT who agreed fully that Abby belonged at the hospital.

"She absolutely refused to be transported," she said. "Stubborn woman."

Ben grunted. "You could say that." He looked at the lieutenant. "Arson?"

"Between you and me? Damn right. Look at that smoke."

Ben looked at the oily black tendrils.

"Kerosene is my guess. Place went up like a Fourth of July rocket. Patton is lucky. I don't know how she got out in time."

Ben gave him a light slap on the back. "Thanks. We'll be in touch."

During the drive to the hospital, Abby sat quietly, only once trying to smile when he touched her cheek.

After an exam, the doctor wanted to keep her for observation. Ben walked beside the gurney and went in as soon as orderlies had her settled into a room.

Abby clung to Ben's hand, even as she whispered, "You can go home. I called because" she swal-lowed "—I thought you should know. About the fire."

He held her gaze. "You know I'd want you to call anyway."

Her eyes swam with tears and she gave a small nod.

Ben swore and gathered her back into his arms. He sat on the edge of the narrow bed and kissed the top of her head, running his hands over her tangled blond hair.

"This time—" he vowed, "our friend made a mistake. He shouldn't have gone after you."

"I think—" she tilted her head back, expression startled, as if she were just remembering "—that he also saved me. Somebody...somebody called." Her voice was so small and rusty, so weary, it twisted his gut. "The phone rang. I wouldn't have gotten out if it hadn't. He must have disabled the smoke alarm. I was asleep, and dreaming of smoke. And breathing it. That's how people die, you know."

His arms tightened as fear gusted through him. "Yeah," he said, voice raw. "I know."

"But when I picked up the phone..." She was thinking it through even as she talked. "Nobody answered. I said 'hello,' and whoever it was hung up."

"As if he was satisfied because he knew you were awake."

Now her gaze clung to his as desperately as her hand did to his. "It might have been a wrong number."

"But you don't think so."

She shook her head slowly, her sooty hair swinging to veil her face.

"Me, either."

"He didn't really want me to die."

"Or else," Ben growled, rage gnawing at his

belly, "he wanted to be damn sure you were awake to know what was happening to you."

"The way...the way it happened to him. Or to someone he loved."

Ben had a sudden image of a child—a boy—hiding in terror while smoke filled the house, seeping around doors and through floorboards, the crackling growing into a horrific roar. The boy knew someone else was dead. Perhaps everyone else.

"Yeah," Ben said gruffly. "I think that's the way it happened."

"But who?" Her eyes were frightened but also glassy with tiredness and the drugs she'd been given. "And what next?" she croaked.

"We'll worry about it tomorrow." Tenderly, Ben laid her back against the pillow and smoothed her hair from her face. "You're all right. That's what matters."

Her eyes were drifting closed. "Survivor..." she murmured.

"What?"

But she was too far gone to hear him.

The window bed was empty, white sheets and blanket pulled taut. The heavy curtain that could divide the room was shoved back, so that he could see the dark rectangles of windows. Ben pushed the door almost closed, so only a band of light reached in. He quietly carried a chair from beneath the window and set it right beside the bed, where he could touch Abby if nightmares made her restless.

Then he sat and watched her sleep, her lips parted, her eyelids fluttering. A nurse had helped her wash her face, and now her skin was like porcelain, fine-textured and pale. He remembered her description of the children she had found dead of smoke inhalation and shuddered. She wouldn't have looked so very different when they found her—unless the flames had caught her.

Night waned; the soft whisper of footsteps passed in the hall from time to time, and once a nurse peeked in, smiled and left again. The sky became purple and finally peach and life began to stir in the hospital. Ben stood up once to close the curtains, then resumed his seat beside Abby.

She had called him rather than one of her sisters. That must mean something. He had to believe it did.

He'd almost lost her. He could have woken up this morning like always, maybe even gone into work, before a phone call from Meg or Renee ripped open his world.

Now he knew: he'd been a goddamned fool. Abby had been wary of falling in love. Her father had been a monster.

Ben made a sound in his throat. He'd known none of it was easy for her, and what had he done? Demanded instant intimacy, promises she wasn't ready for, truths she couldn't yet share. They'd have come in time if he'd been patient.

Patient. He could wait for a cat, but not for the woman he loved. "A fool" was putting it kindly.

Voices were murmuring out in the hall now. Pale light seeped around the curtains. Ben gazed hungrily at Abby's still face.

How close he'd come to never having a chance to repair the damage he'd inflicted. She could have died believing he didn't love her enough to give her the time she'd begged for.

But she had lived, and he had learned.

"I love you," he whispered. Finally he stood, stretched, and backed away.

Time to call her sisters, before they got a hell of a scare by hearing from some other source.

ABBY HAD INSISTED that her voice was only a bit hoarse, her throat a little sore, that she was fine. She was determined to make the meeting.

Truthfully, she felt shaky and kept wanting to burst into tears, which annoyed her no end. She, Abby Patton, *didn't cry*. Now here she was, afraid to let Ben out of her sight, getting weepy at the mere sight of Renee, who brought her some clothes.

They hugged, and Abby, determined not to cry yet again, made a joke out of being left homeless. Ben waited patiently, his intense gaze seldom leaving her. She felt his presence, even when he stepped out into the hall so that she could get dressed in the jeans and T-shirt Renee had bought on the way.

When Ben came back into the room, Abby looked at him. "Have you been by my place this morning?"

He looked wary. "Yeah."

"Is there anything left?"

A muscle twitched in his cheek. "No. I'm sorry. It's...pretty well gutted."

She nodded and bowed her head, pressing her lips together. *Things* had never been that important to her. Or so she'd told herself. But now Abby found that her mind boggled at the idea of having absolutely nothing. She couldn't seem to grasp the fact that every single thing she owned was gone. Her clothes, jewelry, dishes, artwork. Furniture. She didn't have a hairbrush or cosmetics or a checkbook.

But what she hated most to think about were her bottles. She closed her eyes and saw them blackening, cracking, melting. Sunlight falling through the jeweled glass in her kitchen window. The amber of her first treasure. Somehow, secretly, she had always believed it brought her luck. And now it was gone, shattered or melted in the furnace of an arson fire.

She'd survive this, too, Abby told herself. By tomorrow she wouldn't have to fight to keep these ridiculous tears from leaking out. She would replace her checkbook and wallet and credit cards...

"My car?" It suddenly occurred to her.

Ben shook his head. "The garage went, too."

Insurance would pay for everything. She could create a new home, one this time that held more life, more of herself. She hadn't lost much that was important.

So why was her grief so overwhelming?

"I'm taking today off," Renee was saying. "After the meeting, we'll go shopping. At least get you some more clothes and necessities. You can come home with me..."

"No." Ben dropped the one word like a rock. "We don't want you two in the same house. She'll come home with me."

"*She?*" Abby held up a hand and waved it. "Hey. I'm here. You can talk to me. What if I'd rather go with Renee?"

"I'd tell you not to be an idiot." His implacable

gray eyes met hers. "I have a spare room. You already have a toothbrush in my bathroom."

She *wanted* to go home with him. She didn't want to sleep in his spare room, but she would. That's all he was offering; all she was sure enough to accept. Nothing had changed, just because some fruitcake had burned down her condo.

"For tonight," she agreed finally.

She rode with Renee over to the modern Elk Springs Public Safety Building, which housed the police station and city jail. In the conference room, a dozen law enforcement officers from the county sheriff's office, the city police department and the Federal Bureau of Investigation gathered. Abby smiled and nodded for five minutes while they all told her individually how angry they were about the assault on her the night before.

Only Jack Murray's brief words, the grip of his hand on her shoulder, seemed to move her out of the remote place she occupied. He was—could be—a friend, she realized. She saw genuine anger in his eyes, which moved her almost to tears again. They could care about each other without feeling romantic love. She could let him be part of the family.

Abby stole a glance at Ben, who was watching closely. This time her smile was real, although she had to blink away moisture in her eyes and blow her nose firmly.

Finally, they got down to business.

"We could call the whole thing off," Renee suggested from her place at the head of the table. "Do the swearing-in privately. Or later."

"Do we want to give him that satisfaction?" Ben asked, tapping a pencil on the table.

"Would it be satisfaction?" someone else ventured. "He may *want* the ceremony to take place. This kind of public affair puts Chief Patton in a vulnerable spot."

"Vulnerable isn't what he's looking for," Renee interjected. "For God's sake, the other day he walked right into my *house* while I was taking a shower. If he'd wanted to hurt me or kill me, why not then?"

"Because he wants to do it publicly," Jack Murray said from his seat at the foot of the table. "This has got to be some kind of symbol for him. Chief Patton. Déjà vu."

"Yeah. That's what I think, too," Renee agreed. "And no, I don't want to give him the satisfaction. I say we use this chance to flush him out."

"Now we're talking." The federal agent hitched himself forward in his seat, his grin feral. "Let's get down to business. How are we going to protect Renee?"

They drew charts, figured out where to place uniformed and undercover officers. Planned for two sharpshooters on rooftops.

"Bulletproof vest, of course," Ben said, ignoring Renee's grimace.

"That's a little obvious, don't you think?" she muttered.

Ben raised his eyebrows. "Vanity, vanity."

Contributing for the first time, Abby said, "Wear one, Renee."

Her sister sighed and conceded.

When the discussion petered out, Renee looked around. "Okay, everybody. I'll see you tomorrow. Stay on your toes." She grinned wryly. "Please."

Laughing, everyone but Jack, Ben, and the sisters left.

"Okay," Ben said the minute the door shut behind the FBI agent. "We've got one day. We've done plenty of research. Leads, anyone?"

Head shakes all around. Abby told about David Price's disappearing paperwork trail. Renee had a couple of similar stories.

"People change names, move to New York..." Renee shook her head. "We could find them all, with enough time. But that's something we've run out of."

"Anybody have a gut feeling?" Ben asked.

Renee shook her head. "Not me."

Jack pulled out some notes. "Here's a couple Meg wished she could have followed up on more thoroughly."

They agreed on the three or four likeliest candidates.

"For what good that does," Abby said, wrinkling her nose.

Jack stood. "It gives us an idea what to look for in the crowd. You've pretty well eliminated the women, for example. My money's on this Price or Yeager or..." He glanced down at his notes, "Bill Drake."

"Why not this Smith guy?" Renee challenged, shuffling her own pile of papers. "He's the one who was so disfigured in a fire he thought ol' Pops should have prevented. If anyone has reason to be really, really angry, it's him.''

"Too old," Jack said succinctly. "He reached adulthood during your father's reign as chief. If he hated him that much, why not go for revenge then? Why wait?"

"As someone pointed out," Renee argued, "this is not exactly rational behavior to begin with."

"Yeah, but that doesn't mean not logical," Ben put in. "I agree with the sheriff. The guys in their early twenties missed out on a chance to pay back your dad. They've been nursing their grievances a long time, and now that they've reached an age of…" He hesitated, seeming to search for a word.

"Power," Abby contributed.

They all gave her startled looks, as if they'd forgotten she was present.

"Right," Ben said after a pause. "These guys are *capable* of taking revenge now, only Patton's gone. But, hey, his daughter is standing in for him. Hell, on some level, all *three* daughters are—they're cops, aren't they? It makes a twisted kind of sense. But some dude who's in his forties or fifties? Why would he have waited? Tell me that."

"Because he was in prison," Renee suggested.

"Maybe," Ben conceded. "But we haven't found a good possibility who fits that profile. So let's go with the likeliest—we're watching for a white male, twenty to, say, thirty years old on the outside. And somehow, some way, he's going to use fire as a weapon."

"I agree," Jack said in turn.

They briefly tossed around ideas on methods: a

bomb, a flamethrower, a splash of gasoline and a match.

"His methods so far haven't been sophisticated," Abby said. "Where the heck do you buy a flamethrower?"

"These days, you can build anything from directions on the Internet." Jack sighed. "Abby, get some rest. Renee, you, too. Big day tomorrow."

Renee plucked Abby away to go shopping, despite Ben's clear reluctance. "Scout's honor," Renee said, lifting one hand, "I'll deliver her to your doorstep when we're done. Safe and sound."

Some men wouldn't have backed off. Letting two women who were being stalked by a nutcase go off on their own... Male genes rebelled.

To his credit, Ben scowled but nodded abruptly. "Okay. You're carrying your piece?"

"I am."

"I'll walk you out."

In the lot behind the public safety building, he insisted on looking over Renee's car, even scooting beneath the chassis on his back.

"All right," he conceded, standing and dusting himself off.

"We have permission to go?" Renee asked.

Ben grinned crookedly. "I doubt our boy is going to be loitering at the mall. Go in peace."

"He is seriously cute," Renee informed Abby once they were under way. "If I weren't married..."

"But you are. *And* pregnant."

"So I am." Renee looked especially innocent. "Point is, he'd make a fine brother-in-law."

Abby couldn't think about Ben; not now. Abruptly she said, "Can we start at the bank?"

Renee gave her a sidelong glance. "Sure," she said agreeably.

The banker promised new bank and credit cards with all possible dispatch. Abby left the branch with checks—not personalized, of course—clutched in her hand.

Using Renee's cell phone, Abby called her insurance agent, who'd already inspected the damage and was cutting a check.

"It'll be ready tomorrow," he said. "The condominium association is eager to talk to you about rebuilding. The unit beside yours sustained damage, too, of course. We're also covering theirs."

"Yes. Of course I'll rebuild." But did she want to live there? Right now she felt the need for a fresh start. She could sell the condo once it was done. Or change the design or interior so that she didn't feel as if she were living in exactly the same place somehow magically restored without the nicks in the windowsills or the bent blind or the holes in walls where pictures had hung.

At the very least, she needed it to *look* different. But that would involve so many decisions.

Already she felt overwhelmed. She'd lost so much. It was hard to know where to start.

Renee had no such doubts. "Clothes. Undies. Makeup. Hairbrush. You'll feel better once you have the important things. I promise."

Abby stopped first to order a new uniform, bought steel-reinforced boots for work, then went hog-wild at the mall, buying recklessly.

As promised, Renee walked Abby into Ben's house, both women carrying bags full of her purchases.

"Good God," Ben said, setting down the spoon he'd been using to stir a sauce bubbling gently on the kitchen stove. "You two didn't waste any time."

Unfazed, Renee smiled cheerily. "This is only a few outfits. The rest we're leaving in my trunk. Since I imagine Abby will be staying with me for a while. Once tomorrow is over with."

"If the guy makes his move tomorrow." Ben frowned. "We've been making assumptions. What if we're wrong?"

"We're not wrong." Abby's voice still sounded odd, small and husky. "Especially since he failed to kill me. Or chickened out. No, he's got to live up to his threats tomorrow, for his own self-esteem."

"I think you're right." Ben rubbed the back of his neck, his alert gaze moving to Abby's sister. "You okay with this?"

"I want it over with." The tension Renee had to be feeling finally surfaced. Her smile was gone, her voice taut. "Yeah. I'm okay."

"Then we'll see you in the morning." Ben nodded toward the stove. "Unless you want to stay for dinner?"

"Thanks, but Daniel's expecting me."

Leaving Abby, Ben escorted Renee out. Through the window over the sink Abby observed the way he scanned the street, walking on the balls of his feet, hovering so close to Renee, Abby might have been jealous under other circumstances. Then he kissed Renee's cheek and opened the car door for her.

When he came back into the kitchen, Abby leaned back against the counter. "Thanks. I'm...scared for her."

A big graceful man, shoulder holster worn over his T-shirt, he walked toward her. Looming. Crowding her. His voice was gritty. "It's you I'm scared for."

Her gaze lifted, found the burning intensity in his eyes. "Last night..." She was unable to finish.

"You shouldn't have been alone."

"I don't need a keeper," she whispered. "I need..."

"What?" He wasn't more than inches from her.

Cowardice gripped her, and she closed her eyes. "I don't know yet." She tried to smile. "I guess I'm a late bloomer."

His rough voice gentled. "Take your time. I never should have tried to hurry you."

Those blasted tears she'd fought off all day burned in her eyes again. "I—I'm going to put my stuff away. If that's okay."

"Yeah." After a moment Ben stepped back, releasing the invisible tension that had held her captive. "I'll call you when dinner's ready."

Abby nodded and passed him.

"Wait," he said, behind her. "I was going to save this for dinner, but maybe now's the moment."

She turned in surprise.

"A present." Ben cleared his throat. "Nothing much. Just... Something to help you look ahead."

He sounded so uncertain. But her gaze was fixed on the small wrapped box he handed her. She knew what was in it.

She undid the bow with painstaking care, ignoring his impatient fidgeting. She unwrapped the paper as if a tear would mean the loss of an eternal truth. Setting the white box on the counter, she lifted the lid and reached in. Crumpled tissue fell to the floor as Abby lifted out a fat amethyst bottle with a delicate fluted lip.

"I couldn't find an amber one." He was watching her. "But I thought this would get you started."

Cradling it in her hands, Abby lifted the bottle so that light from the window awakened a smouldering glow. Her mouth worked; she couldn't seem to say anything.

"You don't hate it, do you?"

Breath scraped from her throat. "Oh, Ben." With loving hands she set the bottle on the counter, only then turning so that he could see her wet cheeks and the fear and need she tried so hard to hide. Through a blur, she looked at him, almost believing he could provide the answer. "Everything is gone. Why does it keep happening?"

He tried to gather her into his arms. "Things don't matter that much."

Abby held him off, shaking her head violently. "Not things. It's...everyone I love. They always leave me. Why? I don't understand."

"Oh, God, Abby." He framed her face with his hands, made her look at him. "*It's not you.* You've got to believe that." The compassion in his eyes was deep enough to drown in. "It's not you," he repeated more softly.

"No." Abby took another shuddering breath. "I know that. I think I do. But sometimes I feel like I did when Mom left. And then Meg, too..." She searched for answers on his lean face. "And Dad... I tried so hard, and he never did love me. Not really. Why?"

How could Ben answer, when she'd spent a life-time wondering, blaming herself? But she couldn't stop herself; the fire had destroyed more than the tangible bits and pieces of her life. It had also de-molished the walls she'd built to hold in her pain and questions. She had to ask; had to find out if anyone else understood what she never would.

"Your father couldn't love you. Maybe he was incapable of love." Ben kissed her forehead, then rested his chin on top of her head. "And your mother was an abused woman."

"I know that." She rested her forehead against his chest and heard the steady powerful beat of his heart. "I know that," Abby whispered again. "It just...all hit me today. People might leave me, but *things* don't do that. Do they? Only...only mine are all gone now."

"Oh, God, I'm sorry." His hands were massaging her back, her neck, a caress that moved her not to sexual desire but to tears again.

Like a child, she cried, "How can I wish for any-thing again?"

Above her, he was silent for a moment. "Without your bottle? Maybe—" his voice was gruff against her hair "—you don't need a genie anymore."

"I do!" Abby bumped her head against his chest, as if she were trying to batter her way through it. "I do!"

"No. You just haven't realized it yet."

"You're wrong!" She was lost, washed away on a river of memories and grief.

"Cry," Ben murmured. "Say goodbye. It's time."

He held her, there in the kitchen, rocked her, dried her tears, and finally carried her to bed.

But not to his. Instead he sat beside her in the spare room until she fell asleep on the last despairing realization that she had lost yet another loved one.

This time, no one could deny that she had driven him away.

CHAPTER SIXTEEN

"YOU SHOULD HAVE gotten me up sooner." Still looking fragile, Abby was bare-footed and wore a nightshirt covered with puffy sheep. Her toes curled on the cold wood floor. Shoving the mass of hair back from her face, she stared accusingly at him. "I should be *doing* something!"

"What?" Ben asked practically. Just the sight of her, in *his* house, awakened that same primal satisfaction he'd felt at having her toothbrush stored in the niche beside his. *His woman, where she should be.*

But for how long?

He pulled out a chair. "Here. Sit down. What do you want for breakfast?"

"I don't need breakfast." Her expression was mulish. "They're already setting up for the swearing-in. I should be checking it out. Or making phone calls. The guy has to live around here. We ought to be able to find him."

Now she was starting to tick him off. When was the last time she'd had a decent meal?

"Eat." Ben whacked a box of cold cereal in front of her. "Slice a banana onto that."

"I'm not hungry."

"If you don't take care of yourself, you can't help your sister."

Abby held his stare for another minute, then plopped down on the chair with the gangly grace and irritated sigh of a rebellious teenager.

"Other people are on site. You know that." He waited for her reluctant nod. "You and I need to put our minds to figuring out what we've missed."

Expression arrested, she looked up in the act of pouring cereal. "What makes you think we've missed anything?"

"Nobody is invisible. The guy just waltzed right into Meg's place, Renee's, yours... Why didn't anybody see him?"

She pushed out her lip and looked thoughtful. "He torched my condo in the middle of the night. Not many people are out and about."

Ben sat, too, legs stretched out, warming his hands on a mug of coffee. "Granted."

"Neighbors can't see Meg's. She and Scott don't have an alarm system."

He grunted. "She's a cop. It takes balls to break into a cop's house. Walk right into her bedroom, maybe finger her bras. Especially if she was lying there five feet away, asleep. Even if she wasn't there... What if she'd only gone to a neighbor's? Or realized she'd forgotten something and come right back?"

Abby had picked up the milk, but not poured. She was frowning. "So, the guy took risks. That's consistent with his profile. He's obsessed with revenge. Carrying it out is what counts to him, not his safety."

"But he wants to carry it out." Ben leaned forward to make his point, elbows on the table. "He doesn't want to screw up and get caught."

"What are you getting at?"

"Eat," he said.

She poured the milk and obediently ate a spoonful.

"It's the two incidents out at the Triple B that bother me. Tell me how this guy got on and off the ranch without being seen."

"A pickup, coming and going…" She wolfed another bite.

"Would have been noticed."

Abby swallowed and said slowly, "Unless it belonged to someone who goes out there regularly. For an acceptable reason."

"Or—" Ben felt stupid for not confronting his niggling uneasiness sooner "—it's someone who is already there."

"You mean… Someone who works there." Abby set down the spoon, her mind working in concert with his, her focus as sharp. "Oh, God. Daniel employs…I don't know. Ten, twelve young guys? And a few women. Lee's the only one over thirty."

"Barnard must check references."

"But the guy may not have a criminal history," Abby said. "Probably doesn't, in fact. Daniel had no reason to ask how a new hiree felt about Ed Patton."

Ben leaped to his feet and began pacing. "If you hated the Pattons, the Triple B might have seemed like a dandy place to get a job. Keep an eye on Renee, and through her, you and now Meg."

"That would explain how he knew which place at the table was Renee's. He probably brought a message to Daniel when they were eating breakfast or lunch.''

Ben slapped the table. "It makes sense! Finally.''

Abby quit eating. "Yeah, but...the names would have showed up on DMV records. I imagine driving is part of the job. They're always transporting horses and steers.''

"Names are easily changed.''

"Oh, God,'' Abby said again. She leaped to her feet and raced from the room. "Let me grab my notes.''

She spread a sheaf of papers on the table. They bent over them together, Ben trying to ignore the faint lemony scent from her hair and the creamy curve of her cheek. He glanced down and was unable to tear his gaze from her narrow feet and slender calves. He'd tucked her into bed still wearing her shirt, bra and underwear. She'd gotten up during the night and put the long T-shirt on. Did she wear panties beneath a nightgown?

If he looked at her, and she looked at him, their mouths would meet...

Abby was murmuring names as she ran her finger down one sheet. The creases between her brows were cute, Ben thought.

Damn it, he was getting aroused. Lousy timing. He made himself examine Abby's notes.

One name leaped out at him as if she'd written it in fluorescent ink. He stabbed it with his index finger. "Who's this?''

"Huh?'' She peered down. "You remember David Price. The boy whose dad killed his mom and sister, then burned their house down.''

"He's the one you knew."

"I knew his sister," Abby corrected him.

"Yeah, yeah," Ben said impatiently. "I couldn't find him, so I dumped the lead on you."

"And I told you, his foster family moved to California, taking him with them. Then they moved again and decided they didn't want to take him. So he went through a bunch of foster homes. The Cronins were his last. He was with them a couple of years."

"Cronin." Ben swore. "Do you know his middle name?"

Abby leafed through pages. "Yeah, somewhere here I have a copy of court papers... Here. David James Price."

"David James Cronin. *Jim Cronin.*" He shook his head in disbelief. If he hadn't dumped this investigation on Abby, they'd have nailed the guy a week ago. Before he almost killed her.

She was waiting in exasperation. "What?"

"Jim Cronin works at the Triple B. Young guy, says he's been there about a year."

Her mind was working feverishly. "Yeah, I know who he is. I ride there sometimes, you know."

"He's the one who showed me the garage where Renee's mother-in-law keeps her car."

"He showed you himself..." Abby snapped her mouth shut. "Let me get dressed. No. I'll call Renee first..."

"I'll call Renee."

She wasn't home; he got only an answering machine. When Abby reappeared, wearing jeans, running shoes and a plain white T-shirt, he shook his head in answer to her look of inquiry. "Not home."

"Daniel was going with her." Abby's voice was threaded with tension. "We've still got an hour and a half."

"Let's get out there."

Ben drove fast. They scarcely talked. Beside him, Abby leaned forward as if to hurry him. Twice she tried Renee's cell phone only to find it busy.

"We can alert Murray," Ben said the second time she groaned in frustration and pushed End on the phone.

She glanced at her watch. "We'll be there in a minute. Let's see if he's around first. What if we're wrong?"

"I don't think we're wrong."

"Yes, but what if…?"

He fishtailed onto the cinder ranch road and stepped on the gas. In the rearview mirror he saw the huge plume of red dust his Bronco was outracing.

In front of one of the barns, he slammed to a stop and yanked on the emergency brake. Abby was already out her side.

"You're not armed," Ben said brusquely. "Don't get ahead of me."

She was almost dancing in her impatience. "Well, then, don't dawdle."

Lee LaRoche emerged from the shadows of the barn. "Detective." He sounded surprised. "Abby. Are you looking for your sister? She left two hours ago. Daniel's with her…"

They told him what they'd come for, saw him chew it over.

"Goddamn." He took his Stetson off and slapped it against his thigh. "Cronin. You're sure?"

"We can't be until we find him," Ben said.

"He's off today. He left first thing this morning, even before the Barnards."

"This Cronin's usual day?"

"Yeah, this last month or two. He switched to midweek—" LaRoche stopped.

"Because he knew he needed today," Abby said.

Ben took the information on Cronin's pickup and he and Abby leaped back in his vehicle. As he jammed it into reverse to turn around, she said, "I'm calling Jack."

"Do it."

Ben heard her describe Jim Cronin, then pause to listen to a question.

"LaRoche didn't see him," Abby said, "just his pickup pulling out. He thinks Cronin would have been noticed if he'd worn anything but his usual jeans, brown suede boots and maybe a dressy Western shirt."

She listened again. "Remember—brown hair, hazel eyes, five foot ten inches, stocky build. Don't let him near Renee." Abby ended the call. "Ben… hurry. I'll feel better to be there."

They raced along the cinder ranch road. Brooding about his stupidity, Ben slapped his hand on the wheel in a burst of frustration. "We should have checked out ranch employees more thoroughly at the beginning. It's so obvious! How did I miss him?"

"How did we all?" Abby touched his arm. "Don't beat yourself up, Ben. Just…hurry."

He barely paused when he reached the Triple B

arch, swinging out onto the main road and accelerating so that the Bronco rocked. His stomach was on fire. If that bastard got to Abby's sister, Ben would never forgive himself.

He stole a glance at Abby, gripping the edge of her seat and staring ahead as if she could will them to arrive in front of the public safety building where the ceremony was to take place. She wouldn't forgive him.

No, she wouldn't forgive *herself*. And she'd spent a lifetime blaming herself for everybody else's failings. His jaw tightened. He would not let some crazy son of a bitch rob her of whatever confidence in herself Abby still possessed.

"I wanted you to love me."

Cronin wouldn't make his move until he had an audience in place, Ben figured. They had time…

Abby's words sank in. Ben whipped his head around so fast his neck popped. "What?"

"Before, when you said all I was willing to be was company. A stranger." She didn't look at him, the small croaky voice matter-of-fact. "I just want you to know. I was trying to be nice and…and please you. Not shut you out."

"Please me," he repeated incredulously. "Did you think I *wasn't* pleased before?"

"No." She sounded unhappy. "It was ridiculous of me, wasn't it? So…Victorian."

The sparse desert country was giving way to modern homes and artificially green lawns. Ben slowed down.

"What were you thinking?" he demanded. This

had to be a nightmare. She'd been trying to *please* him?

"It was my father...oh, it's complicated."

"I'm listening." Even to his own ears, he sounded grim.

Not looking at him, Abby began talking, so fast the words tumbled over each other. "Renee said I was the peacekeeper in our house. I'd chat through dinner—you know. Jump in before Daddy could get mad about something, or Renee could bait him, or any subject would come up that set him off. I used to think I worked so hard because I hated it when he was angry. Now I know I was trying to pretend we were like other people." She took an audible breath. "Or maybe I was trying to make him love me. I don't know."

Traffic was getting heavier; Ben switched on his lights and watched distantly as cars scattered out of the way. Rage tightened in his stomach; he was beginning to understand how someone could spend a lifetime plotting revenge on Chief Ed Patton. Too bad the bastard was dead.

Ben had to fight to keep his voice level. "You were afraid of me?"

"*Afraid?* Don't be ridiculous." She scowled at the windshield, finally sighing. "No, it was never you. It was me. I don't know *how* to make anyone happy. I was...well, trying the only way that ever, kind of, worked for me. Only I didn't know I was doing it."

Taking a corner with a squeal of tires, he asked, "It didn't occur to you that I'd fallen in love with an argumentative, passionate woman? That *she* made me happy? That I'd notice the three-sixty?"

Abby jerked her shoulders. "You talked about… about getting married, and having children, and the garden and house, and…I thought I couldn't possibly be the kind of woman you wanted."

He risked taking a hand off the wheel and reached out to massage the back of her neck, feeling the fragility and quivering tension. "You are exactly the kind of woman I want." He waited until she lifted her head and looked at him before he added roughly, "You *are* the woman I want."

Only when she finally looked at him did he realize how unhappy she'd been. For an instant, hope lit her eyes like sunlight did the brilliant glass bottles she'd loved. But then she squeezed her eyes shut and shook her head hard. "No. Don't say that. Not yet. You…you can't know. I'm difficult."

"You're…" He squealed around another corner and had to slam on the brakes. Traffic had come to a standstill; ahead, a patrol officer was waving urgently at a car that was trying to take a forbidden turn. "*Damn*. Look at the traffic."

"We're almost there. Oh, no. Remember, the street is shut off. Park," Abby said urgently. "We've got to find him."

Ben hit the siren and managed to edge out of the line of traffic and down a cross-street. Still no parking; he pulled onto the sidewalk, wheels on someone's lawn, and killed the siren, lights and engine.

He and Abby leaped out and sprinted the half block toward the public safety building. Ben grabbed the first cop they found. Showing his badge, he said, "Anybody find Cronin?"

The patrolman gave him a wild look. "Every man here has brown hair and is in his mid-twenties!"

Shoving through the crowd, Ben and Abby finally found Jack Murray with Renee just inside the glass doors of the city building.

"Nothing," Murray said, on seeing them. "The SOB could be wearing a dress and standing right up front!" He swung around and glowered at Renee. "We can't go on with the ceremony."

"Yes, we can." She was all steel. "He's not going to win."

"He wouldn't be winning. That's not what he wants."

Her jaw tightened in a distinctly unfeminine way. "We have to flush him out. This is our chance."

Jack Murray muttered a profanity. His eyes met Ben's. "All right. Let's find the bastard." He handed Abby and Ben walkie-talkies. "If you see anything—anything—check in. Got it?"

Nods all around.

"You two take the north end. We haven't gotten there yet."

"Where's Daniel?" Abby asked.

"Casing the crowd." Renee sounded tense but calm. "He's the likeliest to spot Cronin."

Perhaps two hundred people milled in a semicircle around the front entrance of the public safety building, where the ceremony was to take place. A clown was handing out helium balloons to children. Ben took a hard look at him, but even taking into account the gaudy red wig the guy was six foot two or three inches tall and skinny, to boot.

They met up with Daniel Barnard, who shook his

head and kept moving, gaze never ceasing its sweep through the mob. He looked a hell of a lot more rattled than his wife did. Ben didn't blame him. He kept thinking about Abby, huddled there on the running board of the fire truck watching her home burn, her face sooty, her eyes blank with shock.

The Patton women were too gutsy to feel the fear they should. Their men had to be scared for them.

Two o'clock ticked near. They reached the outskirts of the crowd and Ben glanced back. "Cronin must have a motorcycle," he said suddenly. "Let's get the sidewalk blocked with patrol cars so he can't come out of nowhere and be on top of her."

Abby stared up the street. "If he's thinking something like that, he won't be here yet. We need to spread our search."

They gave orders and left them being carried out as, running, they covered one block, then the next. Abby stopped so fast, Ben cannoned into her.

"That's him, isn't it?" she murmured.

It was too easy; Ben didn't like easy. But the blue pickup truck ahead had a dent in the left front fender, per the description. The gate was down, and a motorcycle lay on its side in the back. A man in blue jeans, a brown Western-style shirt and cowboy boots stood beside the pickup, facing it, hands gripping the sides of the bed. His arms were braced and his head hung low, as if he were steeling himself for something.

Like killing a woman who'd never hurt him.

Abby walked slowly forward. Ben grabbed her arm and yanked her behind him. He pulled his gun. "I'm a police officer. Hands up!" he yelled.

The young man jerked around and crouched.

"I'll shoot!" Ben advanced, keeping a car and the street between Cronin and him. "Get your hands up! Now."

Cronin straightened, holding a gas can that Ben hadn't seen by his feet. Staring straight at Ben, he lifted it and poured a clear liquid over his head. It soaked his hair, ran over his shoulders and pooled on the street. "Shoot me," he challenged.

Ben swore. "He's crazy. Goddamn it, he's really crazy."

Jim Cronin had something else in his hand now.

Abby straightened from where she'd ducked behind the car. "A lighter! Oh, my God, he's got a cigarette lighter!"

"Don't do this." Ben tried to keep his voice level, easy. "You don't want to die this way. Put that lighter down. Come on. Just kick it to me."

"Why should I?" Even from this distance, the man reeked of despair as much as gasoline.

"You can get help."

"Help?" He laughed bitterly. "The only way you can help is to pull that trigger."

Ben didn't let the barrel waver. "You don't want to kill yourself."

"No. I want to kill her." Cronin's gaze briefly flicked to Abby, her head just visible to him where she crouched beside Ben, murmuring into the walkie-talkie. "I want to kill her sisters."

"You've had your chances." Keep him talking, Ben figured. Let him vent. "Why didn't you?"

"Apparently I don't have my old man's balls."

His face contorted. "I thought I did. I wanted them to die. I've hated the Pattons my whole life."

"Because of Ed Patton."

"Do you know what he did?" Now Cronin sounded eerily calm. He let the gas can drop to the street with a clang that made Ben wince. If it struck a spark… But thank God it didn't, only tipping onto its side so that gasoline trickled out.

The whole while, the young cowboy held out the lighter with his thumb poised to flick, as if the damn thing was a weapon.

Hell, with the quantity of gasoline vapor in the air the lighter was a weapon—a detonator.

"Yeah. I know what he did," Ben soothed. "He as good as killed your mother and sister."

"He rooted my dad on. 'Do it,' he said. 'Why not? You want to kill your whole family? Go ahead.' And then he laughed and told Dad he didn't have the guts." Cronin's tormented gaze stayed focused on Abby. "I have suffered my whole life because of a Patton. I came back to town to kill him, but he was already dead."

Abby set down the walkie-talkie and stood up, stepping away from Ben. "So you decided to hurt his daughters, instead."

"That's right. Why not?" He mimicked her father, his tone corroded by the bitterness that had eaten him alive for over fifteen years. "Look at you. All cops just like your daddy. You don't deserve to live."

Her jaw squared and her voice rang with pity and anger at the same time as she stepped out from behind the car despite Ben's lunge for her. "Well, let me tell you a little secret," she said. "You weren't the only one who suffered. That night, when your mom and sister died, you crawled under the bed, didn't you? I know, because I hid under the bed plenty of times. I was scared of him. He hit us, his own children. We had broken bones and black eyes and we had to lie when he took us to the Emergency Room. My sisters didn't die, but he drove Meg away and he drove our mom away, and *I have suffered my whole life because of him, too.*''

He stared at her like a wounded animal, baffled now as he tried to decide whether the approaching human was friend or hunter. Ben rounded the car and neared from the other side, gun steady. He didn't blink; couldn't take the chance of missing the moment when the intent to flick that lighter showed in Cronin's eyes. Ben would shoot to kill.

The bullet might ignite the gas vapors, anyway, but it also might not. Cronin's quick death might be Abby's only chance.

Sirens sounded in the background. Running feet slapped on the pavement. Ben's gaze never wavered from Jim Cronin's eyes.

Abby was saying, ''Think about what it would have been like to live with him.'' One step at a time, she advanced on her would-be murderer. ''I knew your sister. The night after I heard, I cried for Debbie. I was so scared the same thing would happen to me someday, when my father lost it completely. But you didn't know that, either, did you?''

He shook his head, agony and confusion twisting his face.

''You wanted to hate somebody, so you chose us. Well, let me tell you something. I am not Ed Patton.'' She stopped at the edge of the pool of spreading gasoline. "Do you still want to kill me?''

Jim Cronin began to cry. He stumbled back from her until he lurched up against the fender of his own pickup truck.

"Your mom and sister have been dead a long, long time.'' Abby's voice had become gentle. "Would they really have wanted you to ruin your life to avenge them?''

He made a raw sound of pain. The hand holding the cigarette lighter trembled.

Ben was swearing, a nonstop litany.

"If you light that—'' Abby took another step "—we'll both die. You know that, too, don't you?''

A sob tore out of his throat. "Stay away!''

"You set my place on fire, and then you couldn't leave me to die, could you? You're the one who phoned.''

Cords stood out on his neck; his hand shook so hard now it rattled his whole body.

"You're not a killer.'' Abby's hand closed over his—the one that held the lighter. "Don't be your father.''

She gently took it from him and passed it to Ben. And then she wrapped her arms around the man whose pain had driven him to try to kill her. She held him while he cried. At last she walked him to the ambulance, where the EMTs took over.

She stank of gasoline when she finally turned away. Tears streaked her face, too. But her eyes sought Ben immediately and she ignored Jack Murray as if he didn't exist when he tried to stop her to ask questions.

Ben waited until she was right in front of him. Then he gripped her upper arms, his fingers biting in. "You shouldn't have done that," he said, far more mildly than he felt.

"I felt sorry for him."

"Uh-huh." He swallowed. "You were one twitch of his thumb away from being incinerated."

She gazed at him as if they weren't surrounded by a crowd. "He's not a killer."

"Oh, God." He let her go and realized with a detached part of his brain that his hands were shaking. He shoved them into his pockets. "I can't live without you."

Her eyes widened. "Ben?"

He looked around at the interested stares. The county sheriff—Ben's boss—stood the closest and was the least successful in hiding his grin.

"Let's get the hell out of here," Ben growled. "You need to get cleaned up." He grabbed Abby's arm again. "Let's go home."

"No." She dug in her heels. "I want to see Renee sworn in."

He squeezed his eyes shut. "Oh, hell." *He* was the one who was going to lose it here soon. He hadn't known what fear was until he'd seen Abby walk into that pool of gasoline to take the hand of the maniac who was threatening to light them both on fire.

"There's a shower inside." Jack Murray nodded helpfully toward the jail wall half a block away. "Somebody can loan her something to wear."

Somehow Abby was hustled away. Speeches started outside; Ben recognized Murray's voice and realized he was droning on to kill time. Abby reappeared wearing oversize jeans and T-shirt, her wet hair pulled into a ponytail.

They stepped out the front doors and watched Renee Patton, cool as a cucumber, take the podium and, in a clear firm voice, swear to uphold the law and lead with integrity and mercy as well as an iron hand. Or something like that. It was a blur to Ben. All he wanted was to get Abby home.

They didn't make it that far. After hugging and congratulating Renee, they walked silently to his Bronco and got in. He drove two blocks and pulled over to the curb, setting the emergency brake.

"Everything you were saying earlier. About trying to please me." His voice was ragged. "Did that mean you love me?"

She flung herself into his arms, which closed with bruising force around her. "Yes. Oh, Ben! I'm so sorry!"

"Sorry?" His heart hammered in his ears.

"That I ruined things. I'm not very good at—"

He shut her up with a kiss. When he lifted his mouth from hers, he said with quiet ferocity, "You are very good at everything you do, Abby Patton. You are the sexiest, smartest, most loving woman I've ever met."

She stared at him.

"You are going to marry me, and I'm going to show you how wrong your father was about you. Get it?"

Puckers formed on her brow. "I don't usually take orders very well, you know."

"You love me. I love you. A wedding ring on your finger would make me very happy."

"My goal in life, of course." Her eyes narrowed. "Naturally, you'll wear a ring, too."

He hated rings. "Yeah, yeah. Whatever."

Abby's smile was breathtaking. "Kiss me again."

He devoured her mouth and gloried in the fierce desire with which she kissed him back.

"Is that a yes?" he murmured as he nipped at her neck.

"Oh, yeah." A quiver ran through her. "Ben?"

He lifted his head.

"Old habits die hard." Her eyes held naked honesty. "Even with Renee and Meg, sometimes I have a hard time talking about what I feel."

He cupped her chin and ran his thumb over her mouth. "Contrary to my previous behavior, I am a patient man. Just…remember I love you. *You.*"

Her throat worked; she blinked hard. And then a wicked smile dawned on her face. "Patient?" She wriggled on his lap. "Really?"

"Most of the time." Ben lifted her onto her own seat. "But not now. You have no idea how tempted I am to make love to you right here and now."

"Good." She smiled happily. "Then how about we go home?"

THAT NIGHT, Ben left Abby sleeping in their bed. He pulled on pajama bottoms and went downstairs in the dark, his bare feet quiet on the stairs. The purple bottle still sat on the kitchen counter. When Abby awakened, he wanted her to see it on the bedroom windowsill, sunlight pouring through the purple glass.

He reached the foot of the stairs and flicked on the

light. Out of his peripheral vision, he caught movement. Ben turned his head sharply.

There, on the couch cushion, lay Cindy. Her head had shot up, her pupils dilated, and her ears were erect. But she didn't flow off the couch and dart for the dining room where she could escape through the window. Instead, she stayed still, alert but not panicked, her tail curled around her body.

"Good kitty," he murmured, and waited until the expression in her eyes was less alarmed.

So, she was sleeping on the couch every night. Smiling to himself, Ben went into the kitchen for the bottle. With it in his hand, he took one last look at the calico cat whose chin had relaxed onto her paws, and then he turned out the light.

It was only a matter of time. She'd be sleeping at the foot of his bed. His wife would be nestled in his arms, his cat in the crook of his knees.

And—who knew?—perhaps a baby in a crib down the hall. Life was rich with possibilities, for a man with some patience.

Smiling, he went back upstairs to his bed and to the woman who had promised to love and cherish him forever, till death do them part.

HARLEQUIN®
SUPERROMANCE®

Tate, Michael, Shea—
three very different brothers.
Three very different lives.
One great opportunity.

The Delancey Brothers

THE THIRD WISE MAN
by Muriel Jensen

It's Shea Delancey's turn to find love. Well, strictly speaking, he found it some time ago, with Samantha Haskell. But he put an end to the relationship when he found himself in financial trouble.

Now he learns that Samantha's in trouble. And he learns that she has a baby. *His.* The only solution is to persuade her to come to Oregon…with his son.

She agrees to come for Christmas—and Shea figures his large, loving family will do the rest!

On sale December 1999 at your favorite retail outlet.

HARLEQUIN®
Makes any time special ™

Visit us at www.romance.net

HSRDB2

HARLEQUIN®
Makes any time special™

WIN A DREAM

In celebration of Harlequin®'s golden anniversary

Enter to win a *dream!* You could win:

- A luxurious trip for two to
  The Renaissance Cottonwoods Resort
  in Scottsdale, Arizona, or

- A bouquet of flowers once a week for a year
  from **FTD**, or

- A $500 shopping spree, or

- A fabulous bath & body gift basket, including
  K-tel's *Candlelight and Romance* 5-CD set.

Look for **WIN A DREAM** flash on
specially marked Harlequin® titles by
Penny Jordan, Dallas Schulze,
Anne Stuart and Kristine Rolofson
in October 1999*.

FTD

RENAISSANCE.
COTTONWOODS RESORT
SCOTTSDALE, ARIZONA

K·TEL

 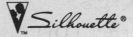

HARLEQUIN®
SUPERROMANCE®

Three childhood friends dreamed of becoming firefighters. Now they're members of the same team and every day they put their lives on the line.

They are

AMERICA'S BRAVEST

An exciting new trilogy by

Kathryn Shay

#871 FEEL THE HEAT
(November 1999)
#877 THE MAN WHO LOVED CHRISTMAS
(December 1999)
#882 CODE OF HONOR
(January 2000)

Available wherever Harlequin books are sold.

HARLEQUIN®
Makes any time special ™

HARLEQUIN®
SUPERROMANCE®

By the Year 2000: **BABY!**

What have *you* resolved to do by the year 2000?
These three women are having babies!

Susan Kennedy's plan is to have a baby by the time she's forty—in the year 2000. But the only man she can imagine as the father of her child is her ex-husband, Michael!
MY BABIES AND ME by **Tara Taylor Quinn**
Available in October 1999

Nora Holloway is determined to adopt the baby who suddenly appears in her life! And then the baby's uncle shows up....
DREAM BABY by **Ann Evans**
Available in November 1999

By the year 2000, the Irving Trust will end, unless Miranda has a baby. She doesn't think there's much likelihood of that—until she meets Joseph Wallace.
THE BABY TRUST by **Bobby Hutchinson**
Available in December 1999

Available at your favorite retail outlet.

HARLEQUIN®
Makes any time special ™

Visit us at www.romance.net

HSR2000B